THE ADVENTURES
OF KING PAUSOLE

THE ADVENTURES

of

KING PAUSOLE

by

PIERRE LOUŸS

Translated by
Charles Hope Lumley

Drawings by
Beresford Egan

Fredonia Books
Amsterdam, The Netherlands

The Adventures of King Pausole

by
Pierre Louÿs

ISBN: 1-58963-862-X

Reprinted from the 1933 edition

Fredonia Books
Amsterdam, The Netherlands
http://www.fredoniabooks.com

CONTENTS

BOOK I

BOOK II

BOOK III

BOOK IV

CHARACTERS

King Pausole.
The fair Aline, daughter of the King.
Mirabelle.
Queen Diane, called " Diane à la Houppe ".
Queen Françoise.
Queen Gisèle.
Queen Alberte.
Queen Denyse.
Little Queen Fannette.
The portrait of Queen Christiane
Macarie, the King's mule.
Mme. Perchuque, first lady in waiting.
Galatée, a young girl.
Philis, her little sister.
Mme. Lebirbe.
Nicole.
Thierrette, a young dairy-maid.
Rosine, guardian of the rasp-berries.
The King's lady-reader.
The sister of the little peasant.

A laundress.
A tradeswoman.
A young girl still a virgin.
A young girl no longer a virgin.
A hotel manageress.
The King's first chamber-maid.
The King's second chamber-maid.
M. Taxis, the Grand Eunuch.
Giglio, the King's page.
M. Lebirbe.
Kosmon.
Himère.
The head cook.
The Chief of Police.
The Director of the " Chil-dren's Rescue Home ".
Three orators.
A farmer.
A Catalonian sailor.
A little peasant.
A father confessor.
A camel.

366 Queens. — Equerries. — Ladies in waiting. — Pages. — Horticulturists. — Guardsmen. — Palace servants. — Dancing-girls. — Police. — Farm-girls. — Guests. — Hotel servants. — Countrymen. — Countrywomen. — The common people.

BOOK I

I

HOW KING PAUSOLE ENCOUNTERED THE VICISSITUDES
OF LIFE FOR THE FIRST TIME

> It is noticed that amongst the nations
> where the laws of decorum are most rare
> and lax, the primitive laws of common
> sense are the most observed.
>
> MONTAIGNE, III, 5

KING Pausole dispensed justice from under a cherry tree, for, he was wont to say, that tree gives just as much shade as any other, and has the advantage over the traditional oak that in the summer it bears delightful fruit.

While he himself was clothed in historic costume, the amplitude of whose draperies seemed to him to be admirably befitting the majesty of his royal personage, he was by no means the enemy of reasonable advancement. One must move with the times. King Pausole bore a crown which hid beneath its thin but glittering film of gold an aluminium setting. He enjoyed mentioning discreetly how much lighter was this headdress than the top hat worn by his cousin the King of Greece. Certain passers by were not at all deceived as to the true metal of the article. But, said the King again, if one is sufficiently cunning to discern from a distance the quality of a piece of jewellery, one would experience no serious impression on seeing the crown were it made of solid and weighty gold. Therefore it was unnecessary to burden his head.

King Pausole was absolute sovereign of Tryphemia, admirable country whose omission from the political atlases, I could, if required, explain by putting forward the hypothesis that since happy peoples have no history, prosperous peoples have no geography. On maps recently published several unknown lands have been left blank : Tryphemia has been left in the blue, in the Mediterranean. This seems most natural. But no ! This is not the reason for such a vexing omission. If Tryphemia is a name erased from all encyclopædias, if the map of Europe has been falsified, if this green peninsular has been cut from the coasts of our country, it is because there has been organised against her a " conspiracy of silence. "

Everyone knows that such is the name of the immediate and clandestine understanding that is established amongst the literary critics on the birth of powerful works, and which stifles the young talent in the midst of its first smile. Explorers and cartographers showing a spirit no less base, follow the same procedure to keep tourists away from a country which they know to be delightful.

Let them be; I will have nothing to do with such miserable combines. Tryphemia is a peninsular prolonging the Pyrenees to the waters of the Balearic Islands. It borders on Catalonia and French Roussillon. I know because I've been there. It is important that the reader will not look upon this true and contemporary account, which I have been writing for him during the last few minutes, as fiction.

These preliminaries having been explained, let us enter into the cataclysm of events.

It was during the twentieth year of his reign that one day, after many a peaceful one, King Pausole experienced the trials of life and the burden of a perplexed soul. He rose, on this June morning, long after the sun, and gently rocked by his mule, was carried to the seat of justice.

Numerous servants accompanied him, one carrying his cigarettes, another his parasol, but the majority doing nothing.

None was armed. The King invariably went abroad without a guard, demonstrating the care he took to be loved rather than feared. " Fear " said he " cannot always endure nor be endured " — whereas the love of the populace is a perpetual sentiment which lives in memories, receives the least gesture as a fresh favour, and demands nothing in return than to be valued highly by the object of its love.

The court of justice which the King held daily under a cherry tree in his gardens was accepted by all as final without any appeal. No other tribunal had knowledge of what took place in this department of justice. In order to simplify the Book of Laws bequeathed by his ancestors, Pausole had produced a code consisting of two articles, and one which at least had the privilege of holding the ear of the people. Here it is in its entirety :

CODE OF TRYPHEMIA

I. *Thou shalt not harm thy neighbour.*
II. *This being understood, do as thou wouldst.*

It is superfluous to remind the reader that the second of these articles is not contained in the laws of any civilised country. It was precisely that one which was most obeyed by the people. I do not hide from myself the fact this shocks the minds of my fellow-citizens.

Pausole reserved himself the daily pleasure of granting certain individual liberties. It was not a tiring duty; and besides, this splendid man would not have accepted any other, for his own liberty consisted in not resisting any real interest, and he respected the whim which persuaded him to be lazy.

On this day, a dozen complainants and an impassive crowd were waiting on the shady lawns, when the King appeared under the branches, amidst a murmur of veneration, sympathy and curiosity. He replied by waving before his face, like a welcoming kerchief, a soft and friendly hand. Then he mounted the three steps to the tribune, which immediately placed him above the level of mankind.

A first complainant stepped forward.

He was a stranger, a Catalonian sailor. He stretched out his dark skinned arms from a shirt with rolled up sleeves.

" Sire, " he cried, " I plead for justice against my wife ! She has run off with another man. "   " Oh dear, " said the King, " What do you want me to do ? "

He plucked a cherry from the tree, tore the skin with his teeth and sucked the juicy fruit with evident refreshment.

" But, Sire, we were married before the alcaid and by a priest. She swore on the Gospel.... "

" And if she had sworn not to die for thirty years, would you send her to prison on the day she got the plague ? She has sworn, you say ? That is the one fault of hers that I recognise. Also, according to the laws of your singular country, it was the most fruitless of the compulsory oaths. You have justly received the proof. If she was still deceiving you, if she was feigning to love you to avoid being driven away, you could... But she does not deceive you because she has left you. Her frankness is irreproachable. And why has she gone ? Obviously because she has found someone who is your superior in personality, in youth, in beauty, in character or, who knows ? perhaps even in fortune. You admit that a young girl may weigh all these arguments on the day that she accepts a husband. All the more then, when she has become a woman and experience has taught her. "

" But it is written in the Code, *Thou shalt not harm thy neighbour* ! "

" That is the very reason why I forbid you to pursue your successor. Next case ! "

" Your Majesty, " exclaimed a deep voice, " a scoundrel of a goat-herd has violated my only child. "

" Oho ! " cried the King. " Let us never be hurried to assume resistance. I should be curious to see the victim. "

She was brought before him.

2

She wore the favourite costume of the young Try-phemian girls; on her hair a bright yellow kerchief; on her feet mules of *clair de lune* colour; and the rest of her body quite nude. Pausole was of the opinion that the sight of an ugly, old or infirm person is displeasing to some, and he had forbidden not only the members of institutions for the deformed, but also those with grotesque features to appear uncovered. But as the sight of a young girl or a man in his strength can only awake the most healthy ideas, those conforming most to true virtue, Pausole had made it clear to his people that with the exception of certain weeks when even the Mediterranean knows winter, one should hasten to reveal to all such a precious and also fugitive gift as human beauty.

" My friend, " said the King leaning towards the ear of a servant " the cherries still on the tree are too high for me to reach without trouble. And I won't change my tree. I am used to this one. Tomorrow, hang on the lower branches a dozen selected cherries. "

Then he turned towards the young girl who awaited his words with more hope than confusion.

" Well ! " he said, " Do you also complain ? For I will only hear your father if he pleads in your name. "

" Oh, Sire, speak to him yourself so that I shall not be beaten. I am too upset this week to be silent for two days in succession, and I shall not be ashamed of anything before you who are so just. Last evening I went into the mountains to see my sister, with a jug of milk for her little child. She talked a lot to me of those things which sweeten life, and which I sadly miss during the long nights. Then I was coming back through the woods, my cheeks perhaps a little flushed and my heart

aching, when I met beneath the willows a goat-herd
of about my age who also seemed sad at being all alone.
Sire, he was leaving the water where he had been bathing,
he was so beautiful, so clean, so smooth all over... he
muſt have seen in my eyes that truly I admired him.
Men believe always that it is they who attack us; and yet,
they never approach those who forget to look at them; if
they take us — even with violence — it is only after
having seen that it would not be disagreeable to us...
Oh ! for my part, I swear to you that I did not do it
purposely. I didn't want him to touch me. Or at
leaſt... I did not think I wanted it. But anyhow, I
looked at this young man at the moment when I admired
him moſt and at once he seized my hand... Then, my
father has told you the truth. Sire, I resiſted with all my
ſtrength. Not a cry, because not for worlds should I
have called anyone to my help in the position in which
I was — and besides, I hoped to be able to get out of it
of my own accord. — I fought with my four limbs as if to
defend my life, from sunset till the dark night. Then I
saw it was too late to go back to my home, and I became
discouraged. Until the next morning I loſt courage
several times, and I then determined not to put any more
energy into such an unequal conteſt. Your Majeſty was
asked juſt now to proteƈt my weakness againſt any renewed
violence. My father's is the only one I fear. I need
no one to calm that of others. "

Pausole had liſtened to this pleading without interrupting by a single word. When she had finished he spoke
at once.

" Here is a child vaſtly superior to her father in maturity
of spirit, initiative and common sense. Well, then, let us

free her. I do not know by what right I should exercise
any authority over a little head that reasons so well !
Go, little clever one, you are free. Do no harm, but
live your own life according to the Code of Tryphemia.
Call the third case. "

As it turned out, however, the third case was not
precisely what the King expected.

During the young girl's speech there was seen in the
avenue of magnolias leading to the royal palace the
comical and blundering career of an elderly lady lifting
high her skirts and fluttering like a grasshopper.

She approached by leaps from one foot to another.
Soon she could be heard groaning and panting in her
despair. She rushed towards the royal throne, crooked
her weak arm over a branch to save herself from falling
till the last moment and breathed " Sire ", but in such a
weak voice that one would have imagined that she had
already departed this life.

" It is an old lady from the palace " said a servant.

" Duenna of the private apartments " explained
another.

And as the etiquette of the Court underwent changes
before the good nature of the King, the whole retinue
expressed its joy by crying from the depths of its bored
soul.

" Something has happened ."

The King rose.

" What is the matter ? "

" Sire — the fair Aline... Ah ! Sire... The Princess,
your daughter.... "

" Well ? "

" Oh, dear ! "

And the old lady sank down in a lamentable swoon.

At this moment a second and calmer lady in waiting arrived carrying a little note. She folded her yellow sunshade before expressing herself in the following chosen words.

" I regret to announce to Your Majesty that Her Royal Highness the Princess Aline left the palace in mysterious circumstances which, however, cause no uneasiness as to her precious health. The lady in waiting whose duty it was to awake Her Highness and to reveal her dreams, respectfully presented herself at Her Highness's door and knocked for four hours without getting any reply. Justly uneasy at such an inexplicable silence, she took the liberty of entering, in spite of the boldness of such a step. Her Highness was no longer in her room. The Princess Aline had left her apartment without telling anyone of her intention and without taking any luggage except her little powder box, her rouge case, her purse and an article of feminine toilet whose object is doubtless of no interest to Your Majesty. No one knows the time of her departure nor the road it pleased her to take. One can only imagine that she left by the window. In the course of the investigations carried out by us, we found on the dressing table a note with these words " For Papa "; I place it in Your Majesty's hands ".

Pausole did not wish to understand. In vain had the lady in waiting made her story as clear as daylight. Pausole remained blind.

" My dear, " said he " you exaggerate. You are making inconsequent remarks... You are demented, that is obvious. Why on earth should my daughter have left ?   Where could she be better off than at the palace with her father ?   And how could one believe that she has gone off without bidding me goodbye ? You are dreaming, I tell you.   If she has not slept in her room it is because it is too hot.   She must be on the terrace in her hammock.   I'm sure no one has thought of that.   Go and find her instead of bringing this deplorable annoyance to my mind. "

As he finished speaking his glance fell on the note which he still held in his hand.   In the middle of a tinted envelope the words " *For Papa* " stood out unevenly, fantastically, and clearly.   And below was a line which tried to be horizontal, but wandered gambolling upwards.

The King tore open the envelope after a moment's silent hesitation.   He withdrew a letter which ran as follows :

" My dear Papa,

" If I thought that you would suffer I should never have the courage to be leaving in two minutes' time; but you cannot be sad, because I am happy and you have always said that you have my happiness at heart.

" I shall come back in seven months, for my coming of age, the day that I reach fifteen years.   Wait for me and don't worry.   I am going with... "

No, he hadn't misread it.

" ... I am going with somebody very nice who will look after me as you would.   I kiss you, if you are not angry.   LINE "

The crowd had gradually drawn nearer, not knowing what was happening, but curious and almost clamorous.

They saw the King's agitation, which was an exceptional phenomenon. Some of the complainants were getting impatient. The recently-emancipated young girl of the last case, fearing that her good cause might be wrecked, was bold enough to ask :

" Then I am free, Sire ? Will your Majesty deign to repeat that to my father ? "

The King made a violent gesture.

" Devil take the other cases ! Footmen ! fetch my mount. Oh ! this cannot be true. The silly child must be controlled. I must get her back as quickly as possible. There never has been such a catastrophe. Footmen ! Stupid rascals, run on ahead ! "

And on his mule Macarie, which galloped for the first time in a long and peaceful existence, King Pausole was seen to fly off in a cloud of white dust, whilst the rush of wind lifted his light crown and facetiously hung it on a supple branch of myrtle.

II

WHEREIN ONE IS INTRODUCED TO KING PAUSOLE,
HIS HAREM, HIS GRAND EUNUCH AND THE PALACE
OF THE GOVERNMENT

> But in my extreme inconstancy which
> ebbs and flows,
> No sooner do I say that I love than
> I love no longer.
>
> SAINT AMANT

THE day when Pausole had a fit of introspection (it was long before the year of the birth of the fair Ailne) he decided that he had three habits and one fault in his character.

His habits were, in descending order, laziness, pleasure and benevolence.

He courted, in the first place, inactivity.

Then satisfaction.

Lastly philanthropy.

His characteristic fault, which plays a large part in this story, was an exemplary and general irresolution of which he never complained because it, alone, by contrast conferred a sensuality superior to the peace of his idleness.

He felt his act was irretrievable when he closed a window. To choose a fruit, a woman or a cravat caused a perplexity which was almost agonising. He never tore up a piece of paper or even an envelope for fear of regretting at a later date such an ill-considered decision. Hardly had he expressed a wish or dictated an order than he immediately stopped those who hastened to obey, with " Wait, this is not the moment ", or " We shall see later " or " Leave it ", which maintained his existence in a provisional and circumspect state, so much did he dread anything definite.

He dreaded it, but for himself only. As a sort of revenge for his personal hesitation, he saw the duties of others with a peremptory clairvoyance and made his public decrees with remarkable determination. A curious result of this assurance in the face of chicanery was the unquestioned reputation which extolled his justice. — Self-confidence is easily attained ; and nothing is more dangerous for a superior than to hesitate before replying. — Pausole never hesitated under this tree of justice except when making a choice between two cherries rosy as maidens.

As soon as Pausole had found out his own habits and fault, he did not occupy himself by correcting them by means of the unattainable, but by indulging his weaknesses and by extracting from them the greatest possible benefits for himself and his familiars.

So it is that warned by long experience he found it wiser to give up all idea of choosing each evening a companion from those collected in the harem of the Palace. He caused pitiful delays at this daily election and almost always allowed himself to be swayed by the boldest instead of following peacefully his mysterious preferences.   Immediately afterwards he regretted having ignored the loveliest.

One day, establishing a permanent rule to spare himself the worry of these intimate decisions, he reduced the number of his wives to three hundred and sixty five, exactly.   One of those whom this fiat sent back to her home gave expression to her grief with so much amorousness that the King, always fatherly, consented to keep her, by supplementary deed, for leap year.

By this means, the employment of his nights was regulated in such a way as to avoid the necessity of his interference.   Each evening a face new and yet known, approved, and even perhaps regretted for a year, came and laid upon the pillows cheeks which long desire made very precious.   And Pausole, delivered of the cares of arranging for the following night, tasted the simple joys even more willingly than before.

The apartments set aside for the Queens naturally took up practically the whole of the Royal Palace.   They were divided according to the four seasons, in a long polychromatic building where the thousand sun blinds of the facade floated like the bunting of a fête.

Two Pavilions, one storey higher, flanked this enormous block.

In one lived the King himself.   In the other the ministerial Cabinet met.   Pausole had to pass through the harem to preside over the Government.

It is better to confess without any evasion, that leaving the South Pavilion, he never reached the North Pavilion. It was he himself who planned the buildings and foresaw the result.   For, said he, since the greatest monarchs have been luxurious queens who left the administration severely alone, I will dispel from my mind by sound stratagem all inspiration which might lead me to conduct public affairs.

And in fact everything was for the best. No one complained, neither the people nor the sovereign;— or at least, the few malcontents accused " the ministers ", who, cunning behind their collective anonymity, and further very satisfied to work " on their own " gave thanks to fate.

Pausole had brought his obsession for renunciation to such a pitch that he did not even rule his wives.

In charge of the harem, and combining with his duties of Grand Eunuch those of Lord High Steward of the Palace, a peculiar individual officiated in the King's name.

It was the Huguenot Taxis.

Tight-laced, fastidious, with a concave profile and a crafty eye, with an unapproachable and presumptuous nature, Taxis in the following story (shall we say it for the sake of clarity ?) will play the necessary part of the Repugnant Person. Pausole, however, had chosen him, and no one could doubt that the King accorded his functionary esteem, confidence and almost admiration.

This former tutor of algebra, professor of Protestant Theology, since employed with success on divers political missions and finally promoted Grand Eunuch, was possessed of a sense of order and a respect for principle greatly in excess of a mere passion therefor. One could perceive the universal aptitude for duties discharged by the State, and Taxis knew how to make himself indispensable, if not to his subordinates, at least to his superiors. One example stands out : the harem was pacified a week

after its chief had been nominated, whereas till then
Pausole had never even in his wildest dreams counted
on this remote chimera.

It would be embarrassing to lay stress on the qualifications which Taxis had put forward to assist his candida-
ture for the position of Grand Eunuch : embarrassing
and anyway of no interest.   Taxis benefited by a perfectly
natural gift for this privileged post.   Heaven had spared
him, and also, through an excess of pity, spared the
women who came in touch with him, the lusts of the
flesh.   Providence did not wish him, untouched by
desire, to be caused the pain of exciting it in those around
him.   He was neither the victim nor the instigator of
sin.

Nevertheless he had to resign himself not to make
proselytes of the young members of the harem.   That
would have been exceeding his duties.   He held himself
well in check.   The King, enemy of all wars, hated those
of religion : friend of liberty, he allowed all to think
freely whether Jesuit or freemason.   Inside his harem,
as throughout his kingdom, Pausole tolerated all religions,
and himself practised several, so as to experience the
consolations of the various paradises in turn.

The altar which the King preferred was a small temple
dedicated to Demeter and Persephone situated in one
of his parks.   The two goddesses having no longer any
worshippers on earth listened benevolently to him who
remembered them.

From the one he prayed for good harvests for the
people : from the other the favour of not being presented
to her till the last possible moment.

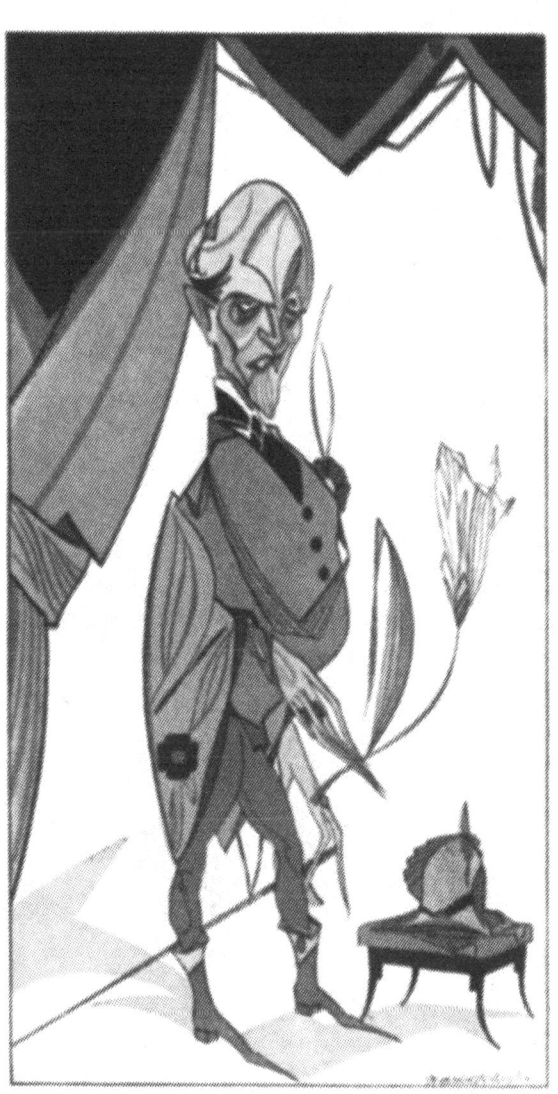

Such then were Pausole, his wives, his Grand Eunuch and his palace. When later on we have explained who the fair Aline was, we can stop the descriptive chapters, that is to say, we can make it no longer necessary for our fair readers to skip so many pages at a time.

III

WHEREIN THE FAIR ALINE IS DESCRIBED FROM HEAD TO
FOOT SO THAT THE READER MAY DEPLORE HER FLIGHT
WHILST PARDONING HER AT THE SAME TIME.

> If artists have painted the nude, their sin
> is very great because they could not well
> succeed without seeing the natural.
> General examination of conditions etc. 1676.

THE fair Aline was the daughter of a Dutchwoman
and also, in all probability of King Pausole.

At least, no one ever had any doubt about it.

Her hair was fair, her complexion clear, but subject
to violent blushes, her nostrils open and her lips gay.

I know that it is not usual to detail the portrait of young
ladies beyond the shoulders. What does it matter ? In
a few years, we are told, this world will have become
obsolete and, if only to occupy painters in such a commendable path, I shall pay no attention to established rules.

Fourteen years and five months after her birth, the
fair Aline took the most lively interest in following the
development of her graceful form. It is quite natural
that we should accompany her before her mirror where

one morning she was contemplating herself with such tender curiosity.

She ran there as soon as she awoke, leaving on her bed her long chemise, so that of her nocturnal attire there remained but her dancing plait of hair. The interview with her reflection was quite a touching scene.

It commenced with a smile of welcome. Then noisy kisses burst forth by the aid of two hands and ten fingers. During the first minute, affection for herself was all prevailing. Her glances said unforgettable things : it was a communion of souls whose beauty added nothing to a sympathy already absolutely devoted. But, gradually, this sentiment gave way step by step to one which finally developed into admiration.

She had become a woman since only a few weeks. Source of innumerable discoveries. Her breasts, formed in so short a time, maintained in her hands all the freshness of new playthings. Familiarly (and imprudently) the child that she had remained held the fragile roses like toy balloons : she tried to bring them together : she tickled the pale points : she teased them in a thousand different ways. Then suddenly changing her pastime, her left leg held out straight, her right leg bent, she measured with her eye the graceful sweep of a very young hip which, however, was becoming more rounded every day. — In fact, there was nothing she did not admire. Curiously enough, a matter which pleased her amongst the rest was the fact that she did not yet bear all the external signs of her adolescence : but, taking all in all, she found therein something Grecian which was not unbecoming.

And whom should she have admired if it was not her

own sweet reflection ? Her father had not given her any other friend.

One has already guessed it : Pausole so tolerant in the matter of the morals of his people was less tolerant as regards his daughter. Sweet as was the opportunity for him to meet young virgins without clothes in the streets, he had no desire to present the hereditary Princess to his faithful subjects in the same costume. Certainly not. He was restrained by I don't know what sense of routine : but the sun of the Midi scorches, and sunburn only suits brunettes. It gives the skins of blondes certain tints of the cooked lobster, and the fair Aline would soon have lost the Homeric epithet which distinguished her from all other girls, had she been allowed to run about in the open air without protection. Therefore she was made to clothe and even to carry a sunshade.

The same reasons — I mean, inspired by a paternal tenderness — had prevented Pausole from applying to his own daughter his well known theories on the education of children.

Moralists never fear to show themselves contradictory. They rightly think that they have done enough in preaching wisdom, and that personal example is not a necessary adjunct to influence their ideas. Without doubt, said the King to himself, "I understand that monkeys are brought up with extreme freedom, and are left to their own instincts, that is to say to the first joys of their poor little existence. But my daughter was born in very special conditions. Her interests call for a special treatment. No rule is made for the whole world. " In short, he imprisoned his unfortunate child.

She had of course heard it said that fortune had favoured her with three hundred and sixty six step-mothers, the majority of whom excelled in character or in beauty : but the harem was closed to her day and night. Her mother had been dead some time. She had no sisters and no companions. The ladies-in-waiting themselves had instructions not to speak to the Princess on any subject other than her literary education. However, not comprehending any better life the fair Aline kept her gay spirits.

In the morning, all the parks belonged to her. That was the time during which the Queens and the King slept. She played by herself but with the same heartiness and activity as though a crowd of children shared her joy. The trees were her friends, odd corners her confidants. She returned sometimes out of breath from a game of hide-and-seek with a green lizard or a contest of speed with a rabbit.

And then, all of a sudden, she found it more interesting to let her imagination run riot, and to dance a minuet with her reflection.

About six weeks later, Pausole learnt from her letter that she had left the palace " with some one very nice " who claimed to look after her.

So, even in the solitude in which her father had imprisoned her, the fair Aline had known how to find the companions she needed at the age of her transformations, without advice, and without any example, but helped happily by her young imagination.

IV

HOW KING PAUSOLE RETURNED TO HIS PALACE AND WHAT HE CONSIDERED SHOULD BE DONE ABOUT IT

> Seated on a log, pipe in hand, an elbow resting against the fireplace, eyes fixed on the ground and with mutinous soul, I reflect on the cruelties of my inhuman lot
> SAINT-AMANT.

THE mule Macarie pulled up on four quivering legs before the steps of the porch, deeply hurt to have been constrained to a mad race which was suitable neither to her age, her habits nor her character.

The King Pausole was seen to enter the arched portico, crownless, with hair dishevelled, his garments powdered with dust, and his hands raised on high.

He sneezed. He almost cried. He was indignant, pitiably perspiring, out of breath and crimson.

No one was anxious to explain matters to him. The passages, more deserted than the galleries of a museum, led to empty rooms.

The guards had left their halberds, and the ladies-in-waiting their knitting pierced by a hasty needle.

Pausole took a flying kick at a lonely gramophone which bleated into his ears the serenade of Mephistopheles.

He thought that everyone had gone off on the Princess's departure, and that the Court had left to please him by imitating her gracious precedent.

However, in the corner of a bay-window a laundress found it impossible to get away.

The King intended to ask her : " Is it true ? "

No sound came from his throat. In any case the bewildered attitude of the maid showed him the uselessness of putting such a question.

Pausole continued his way through the apartments.

He crossed fifteen salons, in all of which the chairs were in their usual positions. None was occupied.

He passed into the portrait gallery and stopped before a painting which still recalled to his confused memory the very docile Queen Christiane, mother of Princess Aline.

He addressed it :

" Unhappy woman. Is this then your blood ? Your race ? "

But the Queen Christiane, whom the painter had depicted as Danaë, continued to smile and to separate her knees without the slightest shame troubling her fair brow.

Then the King went into the silent harem.

It was the hour of the siesta.

The great hall exhaled the breath of three hundred dreams. All the women lay where sleep had overtaken them. They covered the cool rush matting, they embossed the cloth coverings, they swelled the large meshed hammocks with their buttocks. Pausole could not walk, seat himself nor even raise his head without touching a naked sleeper. A suspended net united two and pressed one against the other. Those who were troubled by the heat slept in the shallow pool, and with their heads on the marble border, stretched their legs under the water as far as the central mermaid's figure : pistil of an open tulip formed by their radiant bodies.

In the midst of this vast silence, Pausole calmed down gradually. Peace, like trouble, is contagious. The calm and the shade of the harem diffused his thoughts.

Glancing over his costume, he saw that it was deplorable and already his mind was sufficiently free to advise him to change his clothes.

This he did, but not without trouble.

For the laundress had had time to spread all over the palace the news that the King had returned without crown, voice or reason; that he had nearly strangled her; that it had caused her to become unwell two days sooner than usual.

Also the first valet who appeared in the division of a hanging curtain in reply to a call from the King, went there certainly as much from curiosity as from contempt of death : but he swooned with surprise when he heard Pausole in his well known voice ask for his " turkish dressing gown and his cigarette case ".

The sovereign of Tryphemia, in order to recover possession of himself so soon, had thought matters over.

It was not enough to declare that the fair Aline would be pursued. And that itself was not a decision to be taken lightly. Assuming that this extreme had been decided on, how to lay down a programme for such a delicate search ?

Who was to be put in charge ?

And — always supposing that these difficulties had been solved — what instructions should be given to the ambassador in the event, easily possible, of the Princess refusing to comply with the entreaties, the pressing appeals, the respectful demands which doubtless would be addressed to her? Obviously these problems could not be dealt with in five minutes.

And, besides, there was no hurry.

Why do anything in haste?

All pointed to the fact that it was already too late to protect the fair Aline against the most serious danger.

But it would always be soon enough to bring her back to the palace.

Since nothing could undo the past, since it was patent, scandalous and known by all, it would be better to occupy oneself only with the sequel and to seek the remedy quietly.

So, having decided to decide nothing immediately, Pausole had a bath, smoked two cigarettes and ate some biscuits dipped in old port.

One picture, however, obsessed him. He told himself that at that precise moment when he was resting and reflecting in his room, his daughter was doubtless taking the most important step of her first adolescence. In spite of himself, he saw her in a position, too easy, alas! to imagine, and all the phases of the well known scene were reproduced in his thoughts with a probability which was most disagreeable.

He was particularly shocked not to have any information as to the second of the two actors in this adventure. It troubled his life : it caused great prejudice to his tranquillity of mind and he didn't even know whom to rail at. Such an event could not have occurred without some advice having been taken. In all branches of education, there is some special professor whose aptitude and competence cannot but be appreciated by the pupil himself. Pausole could not understand how on the day that his daughter decided for the first time such a classic question as choosing an initiator she neglected all inquiry as to whether he was qualified to give her lessons.

Yes. It was certainly a mistake.

But it could not now be repaired.

It would therefore have to be accepted with good grace. To criticize the irremediable is a mere waste of time.

The King recalled to his memory this maxim and several others equally trite as consolation.

To waste time — to " pausole " as he liked to say to himself, — would have been agreed to on any other day without any qualms. This evening, however, his musings were unpleasant.

He returned to the harem.

V

DESCRIBING THE COUNCIL WHICH THE KING HELD WITH
THE LADIES OF HIS HAREM AND THE COURSE WHICH HE
KNEW HOW TO TAKE IN SPITE OF SEVERAL SUGGESTIONS

> Why are the ladies so pleased when one
> tells them that other ladies make love as
> they do ? Because that diminishes their
> defeats.
>
> DIVERS QUESTION & ANSWERS — 1617

WHILE Pausole meditated in this way, four o'clock
sounded from all the clocks, and before the last
stroke had finished vibrating, Taxis, a little bell in his
hand, strode through the large hall with methodical and
determined steps.

All the women awoke reluctantly. Most of them turned
over with a sullen sigh trying to recapture their interrupted
dreams, but with no hope of this being permitted.

" Ladies, " said the Grand Eunuch, " it is time to
awaken. The right to sleep is yours no longer. Up
you get ! "

" No... please ! " cried suppliant voices.

" It's no use fighting against the rules, " said Taxis.
" We are taught ' To everything there is a season, and

a time to every purpose under the heaven. A time to be born and a time to die : a time to plant and a time to pluck up that which is planted. A time to kill and a time to heal : a time to break down and a time to build up ' (¹). There is a time for dreaming and a time for living. Get up ! "

Stopping in his stride he examined a corner crowded with long and tired forms.

" Ah ! " he cried impatiently, " a scandalous disorder reigns here. From to-night I will assign a strict and unalterable place to each of Your Majesties and you will not be allowed to move from it during the hour of siesta. "

A loud murmur arose which was instantly subdued by a glance full of menace.

" Silence, " cried Taxis. " My fiat is inspired in the first place by considerations of hygiene, of policy and of decency. But even if it were not, it would be by wisdom, for it is written ' Ye shall therefore keep my statutes and my judgments '(²). That which is chosen by whim is execrable : that which is laid down by authority is right. Thus should be the expression of a voice sane, strict and correct. "

" Excuse me, Sir, " said a young girl, " why not let us choose ? I prefer to sleep on matting and my sister on a carpet. If your orders are to the contrary, it will please nobody and we shall be unhappy. "

" It does not matter. You do not know what is good for you. Authority knows for you and gives it you in

(¹) Ecclesiastes III. 1-3.
(²) Leviticus XVIII. 5.

your ignorance in spite of yourself. That is its duty. "

" But if no one asks it ?"

" Authority is exercised. It yields to no one. It alone can dispute its own right, limit its domain and decide its action. "

" In whose name ? "

" In the name of principle. "

Then cutting short this dispute, he went rapidly towards a hammock where two languid friends still lay.

" I see, " he said, " by this example that legislation is urgent because my advice is ignored. Did I not tell you all how such an attitude is both incorrect and pernicious ? You pay no attention to my words. Very well. I will establish the rule at once. "

But one of the two to whom he spoke extended a tired arm from the hammock which inclined towards him, and as she was a Jewess she knew how to reply :

" It is written, Sir, ' If two lie together, then they have heat : but how can one be warm alone ? ' (¹). You surely would not contradict what the Bible teaches us ? "

" Madame, " replied the offended Taxis, " since you know the Old Testament so well, you would do better to choose texts which are clearer and — "

" Oh, it is very clear. "

" — and less subject to controversy. Where you see only one concrete and bald phrase, the exegetist sees a mystic sense whose depth is beyond your understanding. But let us leave that alone. I have warned you never to sleep two together so that you may avoid being led

(¹) Ecclesiastes IV. 11.

astray to certain mad practices which I am not authorised by the King himself to forbid, but which I nevertheless, on my own responsibility, declare to be abominable. "

" That is not forbidden by the Pentateuch. "

" Because they did not dare to foresee such a great deviation from the normal. "

" Oh, they foresaw many more singular things than that. They foresaw all except that. Let us then believe that it was permitted. "

" It did not exist. "

" What do you say ! It did not exist ! Oh, dear Sir, you are inimitable. "

In the midst of shouts of laughter, Taxis was going to reply when another infringement of the rules caused him to rush off in another direction.

" Sweets ? " he cried, " You are eating sweets now ? Sweets at ten minutes past four ? Tea is not till five o'clock. That is printed in the Time-table. It is absolutely forbidden to take food of any kind except at meal times. I regret to inform Your Majesty that she will not be allowed to walk in the park for four days starting from to-morrow. "

He hurried off again still farther.

" The same punishment for you, Madame, who have taken a book. Reading is not allowed till half past five. From four to five awakening, toilet and conversation, as you should know. "

The young Queen so punished did not take her penalty in silence. Employing that license which the King was understood to allow to his wives in the matter of behaviour and speech, she approached smiling :

" Don't be frightened, " she said, " I will not tell you

what I think of you, because I should put myself in the
position of being punished afresh : but I know up to
what point your modesty is dear to you and I am going
to violate it with impunity before your very eyes,
Grand Eunuch, with the always fresh resources of my
imagination. "

" Madame. "

" Prepare. I have deigned to warn you. "

And, acting as she had said, she accentuated the pantomime with words so lyrically sensual that Taxis, haggard
and dishevelled, recoiled in horror towards the wall.

" Madame, for pity's sake. "

" All that I have said is very beautiful. Why do you
take it thus ? "

" You do not know, unhappy child, into what abyss
of hell and damnation you are casting your eternal soul. "

" Alas, no ", said the young woman.

And then she added, " I will continue. "

But Taxis, unarmed against this intrepid and serene
lewdness whose flame with each word licked the souls
of all the multitude, could stand it no longer. He fled
away from the scandalous talk.

A shout greeted his eclipse. At the same moment
Pausole appeared and believing himself to be the cause
of such a touching gladness, the good King bowed,
overwhelmed.

The same warm shade still filled the large, now noisy,
hall : but the soft light of the setting sun breathed
purple transparent clouds and long copper rays where
specks of dust arose. The women seemed to be clothed
in golden gauze. Some there were, who standing up

leant out into the night. Others lying on mats seemed painted from head to foot in enamel.

Pausole hardly stopped for contemplation which circumstances would not allow.

He stretched himself out on a divan, and the seven Queens allocated to his tenderness for the week surrounded him at once with an agitated sympathy which was not without its chattering.

" Well ? "

" Then how are you ? "

" What news ? "

" Who would have thought it ? "

" It isn't possible. "

" What has happened ? "

" We know nothing. "

" Are they sure ? "

" Do they say with whom ? "

" Are you on their track ? "

" Where have they hidden ? "

The King shrugged his shoulders.

" I know no more than you. "

" But what has been decided ? "

" Nothing can be decided to-day : it would be absurd ".

" Why ? "

" Because unconsidered plans bring about the worst catastrophes. "

" But time is passing and the Princess has fled. "

" Bosh. She will not leave Tryphemia, you can be sure.   If I decide to have her followed (and that view is odious to me) it will be possible to-morrow, and still possible on the following day. That is obvious. "

" And then ? "

" Well, I have come for your advice. I do not know if I shall take it. Perhaps one of you may find the course I want. "

The women were excited.

" Oh ! I — " said one.

" I — " interrupted a second.

But before they could speak the Queen Denyse insinuated with her small persuasive voice :

" Sire, you should write to St. Anthony. You see, if you have lost anyone or anything it is the only way to find them again. "

Those around her seemed to doubt this.

She blushed and said stubbornly " But yes ! "

And she told the whole story of a personal experience which, one must own, was incontestable.

Pausole, during this evidence, looked earnestly at a very young Queen, still quite pure, who up to then had said nothing.

He questioned her shrewdly.

" Where would you be at the present moment if a similar adventure had carried you off from me ? What means would you have taken to flee and which route ? Would you have run far away to outstrip, or would you have remained near to outwit suspicions ? Tell me, Gesèle, and think hard. It is interesting. "

Gesèle was silent, taken aback.

" Yes, " said the King, smiling, " I understand. You do not wish to give away your tricks. "

" Oh, " she cried, stung to reply, " I should never have to use any. If I hesitated it is because one can hardly reply to such a question. We entice men to our arms, but after that it is they who entice us. I have read that in novels, Sire, for I have no other experience. However, ignorant as I am, I think that is obvious. I have left my father and mother to come where you now see me, and I would follow you also if it so pleased you. Be sure that the Princess has more confidence than presumption. You who know men better than I do, think what her lover could have done. It is the best way of finding where she is. "

" Later, " said the King. " It is unnecessary for me to give myself a task which can quite worthily be done by those around me. When a case is presented which is difficult and the subject of much thought, the necessary commonplaces are only gone through after considerable trouble. It is an early task in which I never interfere. In a few days the question will be cleared up without it having cost me even a frown. I shall then see if it is essential for me to reflect, but most probably I shall content myself in making a choice from amongst the best views put forward so long as that task does not seem too delicate for me. "

" And then what will happen ? "

" We shall see. To-day, you must think for me. I am impatient to hear you. "

" May I speak ?" asked Queen Françoise.

" I beg of you, " said Pausole.

" Well, in the case of an abduction, the first day is one of indiscretions and the second one of spite. The Princess is only a few steps from here. I know it as if I could see her. The young fool who accompanies her believes himself hidden by a bush or the curtains of his bed. He has not taken her far, it is evident, there can be no doubt about it. To-morrow he will see that he has

committed an absurdity and the day after he will have
taken so many precautions that all the police of the
kingdom will not be able to trace him.   You must act
to-day and at once without losing a moment.   Don't
you feel you ought ? "

" Thanks, " said the King.   " Here is the first common-
place.   I am delighted that it has been said.   I need
worry no more about that one.   In any case that advice
does not please me in the slightest degree.   But, Françoise, your skin is so shaded around your waist and so
fine between your breasts that I will agree with you for
at least five minutes. "

" You are laughing at me. "

" You alone think so. "

" Sire, " said the Queen Diane, " I also would like
to speak. "

Diane, who was called in the harem Diane à la Houppe,
so as to distinguish her from several others of the same
name, Diane à la Houppe trembled a little.   It was
she, envied by three hundred and sixty five rivals, who
that night was to share the King's bed.   It was said,
it was known, in short it was clear, that the year of hopes
and memories which was about to be ended had lasted
longer than her patience.   She was therefore moved and
stammered blushingly :

" Sire, they are deceiving you.   The first day of an
abduction is one of mysteries and the second, one of
forgetfulness.   The unknown who is with Princess Aline
was able to get her to leave the palace surrounded by
five hundred people without attracting any attention.
He had a clever and well executed plan.   Be sure that he
is still following that plan.   To-night, he will be thinking

that everyone is on his heels and he will take care that
he is not caught. And if he is hiding behind a bush,
it will be the last bush in which one would imagine his
retreat to be. But he must come out. Wait till he
passes. Better that you should show him that he has
taken too many precautions, then he will be imprudent
afterwards. His capture depends only on your reserve.
If no one pursues him you will find him in a week in
the main streets or in a box at the opera. Thus not
only will you be able to await him, but it is most important
that you remain undisturbed to-night. "

" I am overwhelmed, " said the King. " This advice
is as trite, as wise and as necessary as the first. Further,
since it is in exact contradiction it balances it equally,
and I do not feel my spirit burdened with either of their
two equal weights. "

After a short silence he continued :

" It is, then, with a feeling of exquisite and subtle
freedom and without any anxiety that I shall adopt your
advice, Diane à la Houppe, as my own. Tell it to me
again, for it pleases me. So, my pretty one, you suggest..."

" That the best plan is to do nothing, and that you
can go to bed. "

Pausole approved at once.

The beautiful Diane sighed, and completing her advice,
her sentence and her thoughts, added smilingly :

" With me. "

VI

HOW DIANE A LA HOUPPE AND KING PAUSOLE SAW SOMEONE ENTER WHOM THEY WERE NOT EXPECTING

> Only her nakedness reveals her wealth.
> The more one sees of her body the more
> one sees of her beauty
> Her pomp is innate and like a goddess
> She owes her splendour to her transparency.
> MALLEVILLE 1634.

DIANE à la Houppe, watched by a servant, was copying a Bacchus by Velasquez in the square salon of the Pausole museum, when the King valuing the perfection of her taste and guessing that of her form, begged from her not without deference, all the favours which she could give.

The young girl accepted on the spot. Her maid herself when consulted raised no objection. Only her parents would have liked to have kept their child at home, but they knew with what sacred principles Pausole meant to protect their individual liberty and they did not try to express in public their inexcusable egoism.

Conducted into one of the ante-rooms of the harem, Diane with great relief threw on to a couch all the clothes which she had been forced to wear during her years of family servitude.

And Pausole standing by observed the successive revelation of a tinted body, firm and sprightly, whilst one by one she slipped off the rough chemisette, the monastic skirt and the ugly white knickers.

She was more beautiful than pretty : her adolescence was equal to maturity. Her rounded body, straight shoulders, breasts firm as water melons, long and well covered legs were shaking themselves free from a mass of troublesome linen. All her skin was visible, very dark, full, fertile, downy even in the hollows of her back and the fullness of her thighs whilst her black hair freed from its tortoise-shell comb spread down her back the plumes of its wings.

The other women of the harem, when this beauty was presented to them, found that she gave cause for laughter and could only give her a chaffing nickname. Women have their own theories as regards the beauty of their rivals. Diane à la Houppe did not mind. She had a fine character, and then her first conversation with the King had put her in the mood from night till morning to find the whole palace charming.

Alas ! the twelve months which followed this one and only interview were not thus. In vain did Pausole explain that if he did not see her again, if she had to follow the common rule, it was because he was frightened of falling in love with her, a catastrophe which would at one and the same time have compromised both his peace of mind and the interests of the State. Diane did not understand this reasoning at all. Neither did she share the indifference of her companions who looked upon the annual ceremony as an excellent opportunity of getting

silks from Manilla or shoes from Paris. Diane à la
Houppe, as Saint Augustin ordains at the time of youth,
loved to love and asked for nothing more. Deprived
of the King, she would not even learn the various
traditional games of which the other queens gave her
examples at all hours and which they praised in her
presence either as sufficient or as incomparable according
to the turn of their minds.

The poor child lived a year in a state of expectation.
A year of tears and thoughts. As one may imagine the
last day was the most distressing. The royal Princess
vanished that morning. Diane appalled saw for several
hours, with the imagination of despair, the King himself
leaving and searching for her...

" Ah, Sire, " she cried as soon as the curtain of the
bedchamber had fallen behind them both " do not look
too much at my eyes. I cried so much this morning. "

" Houppe, you are charming, " replied Pausole. "True,
your eyes are swollen and still wet, but that adds to their
appearance the expression of voluptuousness itself. You
should be exhausted by the after-effects of pleasure and
on the point of swooning : your eyes, my Houppe,
gleam with that same brightness. Do not undeceive
me; at one moment I could have believed that they
owed it me. "

Diane bowed her head and smiled against her will.

The night full of splendour entered the dark room
through a wide bay opening on to a terrace. Under a
blind raised to the lintel, between the doors pushed
back against the walls, Tryphemia appeared softly blue
and white. It was an undulating land dotted with woods

and regular houses with a main road planted with trees, a road which would have led the King to his capital were it not that he had a hundred reasons (and even three hundred and sixty six) why he should not leave the palace. An enormous fig tree let fall its flat leaves and its lilac coloured fruit like a carpet over the balustrade. On the left the park was massed with its magnolias which had already lost their flowers, its shuddering eucalyptus, its squat Japanese palms, its magnificent lunar sago trees. A hedge of aloes hemmed in the dark garden and the plain stretched beyond, to the stars.

" How like this night is to my wedding night, " murmured Diane. " There has not been another lovely night for a year. This one is absolutely the sister of the first. Are there not some strange nights where the countryside looks back at us with the air of holding all the happiness which we would like to confine to ourselves ? "

Pausole did not reply.

" Someone is knocking, " said the Queen.

" It must be for dinner, " replied Pausole. " I'm very hungry. " And he cried " Come in ! Come in ! "

But instead of the Grand Cup-bearer, it was the Grand Eunuch, who suddenly appeared between the curtains, with the ugly physiognomy of his antipathetic person.

" Ah ! What is it now ? " said the King in a sulky voice. " I don't want you, Taxis, I'm busy. "

" Get out, " said the beautiful Diane, " there is nothing for you to see here. "

" It is my meal time, " continued Pausole, " I want to read no documents other than the menu. "

" Have you the menu ? " repeated Diane à la Houppe.
" No ? Then get out. "

" My friend, " said the King, " if you encroach on the
duties of the other officers of the Court, we are rushing
headlong into anarchy. Go, tell the Grand Cup-bearer
that to-night I beg him once again to choose in my name
the wine which I ought to prefer. I am too upset to
decide anything on this point or to hear you. Go. "

" But go on, get out ! " cried Diane at the height of
irritation.

And as Taxis, respectful but stubborn, made no sign
of obedience, Diane took him by the two shoulders and
with her face to his said in a most serious tone :

" Vile infidel ! If you receive from the King's bounty
permission to speak here, I will compel you to leave without having said one word : if not by violence, by means
which you know well ! "

The King raised his arms.

" Now then, " he said. " A quarrel ! Houppe, be
quiet. Taxis is going. He is a sensible man. He must
have already seen that we do not welcome his company
at this moment. "

Taxis put on a honeyed smile full of importance.

" Certainly, " he said. " And if the inflexible voice
of my conscience, if the only care for a duty often thankless,
if the passion for truth did not call me here, believe
me, Sire, I should have already deferred to the desire
expressed by Your Majesty. But my duty is higher than
my personal interest and even though I suffer I will do
my duty to the end. I do not encroach, although your
Majesty cruelly reproached me with this just now, on the
duties of my colleagues. I am High Steward of the

Palace, and as such I have to concern myself with the serious incident which occurred this morning on the ground floor of the South Pavilion. My initiative was not found lacking. I have caused a further search to be made for the Princess Aline. "

" Alas ! " groaned Queen Diane.

But regaining possession of herself at once and standing up she asked :

" Who gave you the order ? "

" The King gave me the sacred mission of preventing, stopping and repressing as required, turbulence and excesses in the precincts of the royal residence. "

" Ah ! to prevent !... Well, it seems that you did not ' prevent ', since a stranger was able to get in as though in his own house. Nor did you ' stop ', since the Princess left under your nose and no one knew anything for six hours. Now you want to ' repress '. The King forbids, it, Sir Grand Eunuch ! "

" His Majesty... "

" The King disapproves. That's all. That's enough. About turn. The King has just made a decision which is admirable and upon which he certainly will not go back to listen to your whims. It is best to do nothing for a day at least : I shall not explain why, but that is the order. Obey it. Get out ! Call back your men. Hold your tongue about what has happened and disappear till to-morrow night. Do you hear me ? "

Taxis tremblingly held out the three papers which he had in his hand.

" But, Sire, here are the reports. The suborner has been discovered. The Princess hasn't left him. Their

hiding place is being watched without their knowing it.
I only await the word from you to act. "

" Sir, " replied Pausole, " I am not accustomed to
hurl myself heedlessly into the midst of divers events.
I don't like adventures and I don't mean to have them.
You talk and you decide with a deadly precipitation.
There is neither wisdom nor method in such petulance,
and I don't know whence I got the esteem which I used
to have for you. Taxis, you're mad. Stop the surveillance which you have so thoughtlessly placed on the
retreat where my daughter sleeps. And that is enough for
to-night. I have spoken. Will you be good enough
to retire ? "

Taxis recoiled three paces, pointed to the ceiling with
a bony finger and said " The Lord will appreciate. "

On these words he bowed and disappeared.

Diane, alone with the King, seized her opportunity.

" Ah, Sire, when will you deliver us from that odious
person ? He is our tyrant. You don't know the things
he invents to annoy us. He rules everything, distributes
everything, and administers even our thoughts. We
can neither sleep, dance, run in the park, read novels,
nor eat sweets except at certain hours fixed by his fancy.
The slightest lapse is punished with the cells. If
one is a little late it is sufficient. He is killing us. To
drive him away we have but one method : it is that
which I wished to employ just now. And again, if
you had not forbidden him to talk propriety to us, he
would have punished us dreadfully for this, because
nothing makes him more angry than certain sights that
he must at times witness. But those methods are
repugnant to me and I don't even like to see them

employed by others. Also what a funny idea it was to put a Protestant pastor at the head of a naked harem. You wished it and therefore it is right, and I put questions to you, Sire, without expecting answers. Why not give us real eunuchs as is done in the East? My companions long for them sometimes saying that these poor creatures can, even they, give complete pleasure to women without sharing it at all and which cannot cause jealousy to anyone. I, of course, don't think of such things. I have pleasure in my recollection of you only, but I wish I need not be stopped from dreaming at my leisure and that a hateful face were not always thrust between us. "

" Oh, well, " said Pausole, " Taxis has his good points. "

VII

WHICH IS CONSIDERABLY SHORTENED HAVING REGARD
TO THE EXISTING LAWS

> " If one can recover one's virginity
> after not having slept with one's husband
> for nineteen years then I surely have
> regained my virginity. "
> DUCHESSE D'ORLEANS — Letter to
> the Duchess of Hanover, 2nd
> September, 1696.

I will not describe the feast which followed.

I have been told, in fact, that the laws of our country allow novelists to set out all the crimes committed by their characters, but no details of their sensualities, since in the eyes of our legislators murder is less of a sin than pleasure.

And as I no longer know exactly if they ban from our books the voluptuousness of the bed or of the table. and as, after consulting my conscience and my sincerity, it is impossible for me to conjecture as to which is the more abominable to eat a piece of bread-and-butter or to create a child, I prefer to take full precautions and not speak here of breasts or of pomegranates.

It shall be related then in a few words that the dinner of King Pausole and the beautiful Diane à la Houppe consisted of :

Hors d'Œuvre
A first entrée.
A relevé,
A second entrée.
A joint,
A salad.
A vegetable,
A sweet.
Fruit and little cakes.
Wines : X... Y... Z...

It was a small dinner. Let us say no more about it. In the same way we will draw a veil over what took place afterwards.

Diane, separated from the King for a year, and shut up in the harem after only one evening of love, had become once more a young girl. Let those who can, understand.

I explain nothing. In short the King also found that this second meeting resembled in many ways the first.

A little before sunrise, they both went to take the fresh air on the carpeted terrace. And to pluck the highest figs, Diane à la Houppe raising her arms, sorrowfully stretched herself, supple as a flower and three times splashed with black.

VIII

WHEREIN PAUSOLE CONSIDERS THE DISCLOSURES OF A LETTER THE IMPORTANCE OF WHICH WILL NOT ESCAPE THE READER

> " One can guess what a young man
> fairly conceited and used to easy success
> will say to a young girl when he has mounted
> seven flights of stairs to reach her and
> believes himself to be awaited. "
>
> Mme. ANCELOT — 1839.

TOWARDS mid-day Pausole awakened, simply and as usual. There was no 'petit lever Useless ceremonies never complicated his life.

His bell brought a chambermaid who that morning was making her first appearance in this duty. This young girl with trembling hands, stumbled, knocked a chair over and blushed violently when she saw Diane immodest and asleep next to the King.

" Ssh ! " said the King. " Speak softly. What time is it ? "

" Yes, Sire... No, no... I don't know, " stammered the poor girl.

" Give me my dressing gown and prepare my bath. Warn my reader and Master of the Kitchens. And now close the curtains so that the Queen may sleep as long as possible. "

Then with a thousand precautions, he silently put one foot after the other to ground. The prospect of saying good-bye a second year to the redoutable Diane did not trouble him in the least.

He stole away.

A short time afterwards, lying in perfumed water, he admitted to within six paces of his bath, the lady Reader-in-Ordinary who came each morning to give him a survey of the latest news by telegram and a summary of the principal articles. In pursuance of the first article of the Code enforced in Tryphemia (Thou shalt not harm thy neighbour) it was forbidden for the papers to insert any scandalous or slanderous items. Not one paper published the news of the flight of the fair Aline; and if here and there, some had allowed themselves a few hints, the reader had the tact not to understand them.

Meanwhile Pausole remained inattentive. When his toilet was complete, when the Master of the Kitchens had caused a steaming breakfast to be served in the rest room, and when Pausole had taken some nourishment — and finally, after he had smoked two cigarettes of fresh tobacco, he went alone into the room where his daughter had grown up.

Nothing had been put in order. The room still kept its animated appearance of a completed toilet and a hasty departure. In addition the schoolroom, the dressing room, the boudoir and the bath showed a peculiar jumble of button-hooks, atlases, black stockings and racquets. A volume of Telemachus floated on the calm water of the bath. Pausole wandered sadly from one room to the other for a quarter of an hour. He opened copy books, picked up a bodice, unrolled a leather belt and put three hairpins back in their box.

Then he pressed the middle finger of his right hand on the bell button and said to the valet who arrived :

" Inform the Lord High Steward of the Palace that I await him here and wish to speak to him. "

Taxis entered.

" Sir, " said Pausole, " I value your zeal and your methods, in that they save me daily from twenty worries with which I have nothing to do. But your inquiry yesterday was most untimely, especially if one considers the hour and the place in which it pleased you to offer me an account of your actions. I had moreover told you that between the hours of five in the evening and two in the afternoon I did not wish to discuss any undertaking whatsoever. You have exceeded your instructions in taking the initiative in a case where your competence was most questionable and in asking my orders without my having expressed the intention of giving you any. "

Here sedately he lit a cigarette, seated himself, placed the right elbow on the arm of the sofa, leaned his head in the same direction, crossed his legs, waved his hand and said :

" Now, read your report. "

Taxis had not faltered. The counsel which night brings having had a pacifying influence on his eagerness, he had stopped crying that the interests of his career yielded to those of his duty. Further, consulting his Bible, he had stopped at the following explicit passage

" And ye shall cry out in that day because of your king which ye shall have chosen you, and the Lord will not hear you in that day. " *

This removed all his scruples. He became once more the courtier.

" Sire, in a few words the matter is thus. The details and rough draught of my reports are in this portfolio, but I think it better to give you a summary of them. "

He approached the open window,

" Yesterday morning, probably about four o'clock, Her Royal Highness the Princess Aline seated herself fully dressed on the marble sill of this window. Having raised her legs and carried out a rotary motion from right to left traces of which remain in the dust, she jumped from a height of about seventy five centimetres into the middle of the flower bed. Her two feet have marked there parallel imprints which then become alternate — and there are no other prints. Therefore Her Highness left alone. "

Upon making this revelation, Taxis crossed his hands over his thin stomach and paused.

" Yesterday evening, " he continued, " the Princess made ready to pass the night at an inn called " Hotel du Coq " situated 3.2 kilometres on the main road to the capital. She arrived there at 3.40 coming from a little wood near by, accompanied by a young man of whom I possess a description, but who is unknown in this neighbourhood. "

" What is his age ? " asked Pausole.

" Very young. Seventeen, at the most. "

* I Samuel VIII. 18.

" Ah ! That's fine, " said the King.

" Had Your Majesty wished it, the suborner could have been arrested yesterday and the Princess brought back to the Palace. "

" I suppose by the police. "

" Or by special emissaries. "

" By whom ? You never see the delicacy of the situation, Taxis, nor the complexity resulting from duties imposed by scruples of affection. "

" I do not insist. Your Majesty is right — I am wrong. I deferred to your orders and surveillance was stopped last evening at eight o'clock. Since when I have kept myself strictly in expectation. "

" It is, however, most important that we should know with whom we are dealing, and to find out first of all if it is expedient that we should pursue or abstain from pursuit. Who is this scoundrel whom nobody has seen, who does not belong to the palace, who doesn't live in the neighbourhood and who suddenly obtains such an ascendancy over my daughter as to abduct her from under our noses without even taking the trouble to come and fetch her ? He makes her join him. He waits and she comes to him. She who has never left the lawns of the park. Here she is on the main roads in a cyclists' inn with a sixteen year old student whom she can never have met before throwing herself into his arms. Confess, Taxis, it's mad. I despair of ever understanding... But haven't you any clue ? "

After a short smile, Taxis replied in his precise voice :

" The day before yesterday and the preceding day, a troupe of French dancers gave two performances before Their Majesties of the harem. Princess Aline, permitted for the first time to enter the theatre, was present at the back of a box. During all the ballet she showed the most lively interest and it was noticeable that her emotion was most evident each time that she saw a... an idiot named Mirabelle dance. "

Taxis took his time and then went on :

" After the performance, the Princess caused a gift of money to be sent to this woman, in the form of a bank-note contained in a sealed envelope. I beg Your Majesty to weigh carefully all I am saying. In my opinion there is a connection between this little fact and the public misfortune which so quickly followed it. "

There was a disturbing silence.

The King continued to smoke.

Taxis deemed it necessary to go into further detail.

" In short, I accuse, " he continued, " I accuse the ballerina named Mirabelle of having contrived a diabolical plot whose aim it was to drag down a spirit which so much care and paternal piety had kept in a state of ingenuousness. I accuse this hussy of having been the procurer in the crime which has been committed. We shall know the name of the seducer later; it does not matter; but that he knew Mirabelle and that she let him gain his ends is what I wish to make it my business to demonstrate if Your Majesty does not place obstacles in my way. "

Pausole raised both hands.

" We shall never solve this ! " he said, discouraged. " It gets more and more complicated. And what became of the dancers ? "

" Left the same day for Narbonne. "

" You see ! We shall *never* solve it ! It is inextricable. "

" I beg your pardon. Two culprits; two inquiries. One is in France; we will telegraph to the Place Vendôme and after the necessary formalities we shall get him extradited. The abduction of a minor is most heavily punishable according to international treaty. There is nothing troublesome in this direction. As for the other culprit, we can hold him, he is there. Say the word and I will have him arrested. "

The King looked at Taxis, who was still standing up.

" You are a dangerous man, Sir Grand Eunuch. Useful but dangerous. If fate had placed you in my position, I would not have given a red cent for the happiness of my poor people. You're a crocodile, Taxis. You have the ferocious eye of a French senator. And anyhow you don't understand me. "

He knocked off the ash of his cigarette with a tired gesture.

" I will think over all this. Your report is instructive and if it even points to certainties, it does not exempt me from meditating over the hypotheses it suggests. I will consider it at leisure; and to-morrow I will make a decision. Wait. Keep calm. "

He rose and more readily he sighed :

" From now on I want to think of other matters. This preoccupation overpowers me. If it goes on much longer I shall be ill. Talk to me, my friend. Change my line of thought. "

Taxis puffed out his chest and with lowered eyes gave vent to an affected sigh. The King's good-natured tone encouraged him. He thought the moment opportune to broach a subject which he had very much at heart.

" Dare I, then, " he said, " draw your Majesty's attention to my own modest self ?   And if my services, or at least my efforts, are rewarded by the august approbation of him who alone can judge their importance, would I be allowed here to express the hope with which I sometimes soothe my solitude ? "

" What is all this rigmarole about ? " said Pausole.

" Explain yourself. Come to the point. "

" I am only Commander in the Order of Doves. Certainly and I hasten to say it, my humble personal ambitions are complete; but my old mother, from her Juramic hamlet, would experience a touching joy and perhaps a new lease of life were she to know me to be a Grand Officer...   I add that to my mind the high office with which Your Majesty has deigned to invest me merits an honorary distinction of which I had never dared dream had not the King's pleasure raised me to the head of the palatial hierarchy. I speak now, not for Taxis, but for the chief of the civic house and for the cause of authority...   My request is entirely disinterested."

Pausole temporised :

" We shall see. A little later. To-day you have a delicate matter to carry through. If you conclude it satisfactorily, you shall have the medal; it is a favour promised. Go on with your reports. "

" The Princess... "

" Again ? Has nothing occurred since last evening that you tire my brain with an event which is already thirty six hours old ? "

" Oh, yes ! But I did not dare... "

" Speak ! I ask you to. "

" Sire, it is about a dreadful and injurious outrage

which is also grotesque. A wave of madness is passing through the palace. It is not meet that Your Majesty bothers himself with such pranks, an unworthy subject for his consideration in the actual circumstances. I attended to it, and inflicted punishment. The author of this escapade can wait to be judged. "

" What trouble I have to get a statement of fact ! I am listening, Taxis. Who is the delinquent ? "

" It is a page, the last one appointed, the one of whom I have complained so many times to Your Majesty. He has put the crowning touch to his tricks by an act for which no name is too bad. I have more shame in repeating it than he had in doing it. "

" Come on, what did he do ? "

" This ! The honourable M. Palestre, Minister of Public Games, preserves in spite of his age a determined leaning towards making love with his inferiors. Your Majesty probably does not know it. As for me I cannot excuse it. Be that as it may this weakness of an old man otherwise so respectable amused the pages. The most mischievous of these rascals decided to surprise M. Palestre at the moment when it suited M. Palestre least to be surprised. He posted himself under the bed of the chambermaid with whom the minister was misconducting himself — your own chambermaid, Sire — and when by certain signs which I could not, nor would I, describe, he estimated that his two victims would be in a state of distraction suitable to his designs, he came out of his retreat and threw a tennis net over the couple... "

" Ha ! Ha ! Ha ! " laughed the King.

" ... He tied it to the end of the bed, thus forcing

M. Palestre and the chambermaid to keep, although they already had it, the most licentious of attitudes. "

" Ha !   Ha ! "

" And not content with having been the causer and witness of this sad scene, he called all the rest of the pages to the scene of scandal, thus making matters much worse on account of the number of spectators. The incidents which followed were of such a character that the unhappy servant kept her bed for a week through fatigue and emotion. That is why this morning when you awoke you saw a fresh face... Sire, I am astounded that you receive with this sympathetic gaiety a villainy which I should have thought worthy of every disgrace whilst awaiting punishment. "

Pausole protested :

" No, no ! You have a method of generalisation, Taxis, which very easily leads you astray. You classify gestures and acts by I don't know what table of moral mathematics, where they do not recognize their natural order. I hate obscenity even more than you do. There is no such thing as humorous voluptuousness. Pleasure is nearer grief than gaiety. This stated in principle does not make the anecdote you have just told me any the less excellent. "

" Your Majesty is joking. "

" I am doing nothing of the sort. The story is admirable and almost divine in that it is first of all revived from the Greeks. Thus was the guilty Aphrodite surprised and enclosed in a steel net with the god of battles. This classic memory inspiring one of my pages must satisfy me. "

" Classic ?   Sire, say rather pagan. "

" And then, notice how this young man, instead of following the Olympian tradition, took a tennis net aptly to envelop the Minister of Public Games. This shows personality and independent ideas... "

" Granted. They seem to me to be two defects. "

" Finally, I praise to the very highest degree the edifying intention which inspired the whole scene. It is ridiculous and disgusting for an old man of seventy eight years to share the bed of a servant who maybe is his great-granddaughter. One never knows. If M. Palestre complains he can only blame himself for the pitiful position in which these young men saw him. As for my chambermaid she only got what she deserved; shame is the result of her act, not punishment. "

" Then what shall I do with the culprit ? "

" Release him at once and invite him to come here where I await him. It will be from him that I shall seek advice in my present difficulty. "

IX

WHEREIN PAUSOLE MAKES A DECISION

> I think that Epicurus must have been
> a very wise philosopher who according to
> the opportunity and occasion enjoyed
> voluptuousness whether it was in repose
> or in movement.
> SAINT-EVREMOND.

THE costumes of the pages at the Court of Tryphemia dated from the Renaissance. They comprised yellow silk tights with a small flap relieved by two shoulder-knots, a cap with a guinea-fowl's feather in it and a royal blue doublet.

It was in this frivolous uniform that the victimizer of M. Palestre presented himself, saluting with his cap and bowing with his feet together.

" What is your name, you young rascal ? " asked Pausole.

" What you please, Sire. "

" That's good to start with, " said the King. " I know of nothing more stupid than the wish to force people to repeat a name which may not please them. You have won me with your first word. Tell me, all the same, what your name is, and be ready to change it if I ask you. "

" Sire, my name is spelt G, i, g, l, i, o. Pronounce it as you will, in the Italian or the French way. Djilio or Giguelillot. "

" Djilio, " said Pausole, " is a poet, and Giguelillot is a fool. I would that you were one or the other. "

" I wish it also, " said the page seriously. " And I wish it so ardently that possibly I may end by gaining my desire. "

" Why do you want to be a poet ? "

" To see nothing, even a fly, with the eye of my neighbour. "

" You do not love your neighbour. "

" I don't wish him any harm. I would rather not be he, that's all. "

" And why do you wish to be a fool ? "

" If my neighbour calls me a fool, I shall know at once that I am not like him. "

" But you might be worse. "

" That would be difficult. "

" How would you know ? "

" By his attitude. If he leaves me alone, then I shall have lost. If he attacks me, then I shall be happy ."

Pausole made an impulsive gesture.

" Take a cigarette, " he said.

And he offered one in a friendly way.

" Would you decide in the same way if your neighbour were feminine ? "

" Oh ! Not at all ! "

" Why ? "

" Women are not human. "

" I hope you don't tell them so. "

" I only speak well of them to their faces and I always think the same. "

" How do you look upon them ? "

" As the best of all creatures, the only ones who know how to return good for good or even for evil, if necessary. I have only gratitude for them, and yet I have done nothing for them, except to flatter many and to love one. "

Pausole looked at him carefully.

" Are you happy ? " he asked.

" No.   Nor are you, Sire, that is obvious. "

" Well, why are you gay ? "

" To persuade myself that I am happy. "

" And what is it you want ? "

" Like you, Sire, I miss the unexpected, the marvellous and also events. "

" Events !   I have too many. "

" But you don't profit by them. "

" Of which one are you speaking ? "

" That one of which you are thinking. "

" I do not see how that one can make me happy, since I am not happy, " said the King in a surprised voice.

The page was going to reply, but not knowing exactly whether the King was consulting him or asking him to explain himself, he waited to be enlightened on this interesting variation.

" Well, sit down, " continued Pausole.   " You have spoken of a difficult subject which engrosses my thoughts and you did not consider that it was better to appear to be ignorant of it. There you showed that you place the laws of conversation before those of etiquette, and I approve, my boy. Listen, I do not think that old men give the best advice. Experience is of no use : a fact never reproduces itself in the same circumstances. On the contrary : it must be admitted that spontaneity serves a purpose, for at twenty years of age one is making one's life and there is nothing more important than to make it as it comes. That is why, in spite of custom, I prefer to take your advice than to consult, shall we say, the venerable M. Palestre. "

Giglio remained unmoved.

Pausole becoming more and more expansive, went on as though addressing a familiar confidant :

" I will never, " he said, " cause this child to be pursued by the police of my kingdom. Nor is it meet that she should be brought back to the palace by a special emissary : for if I separate her from the unknown whom she has docilely followed, it is certainly not to give her over to the charge of a delegate just as compromising, and less sympathetic in her eyes. As for sending a woman for her that would be a dreadful idea. I would never think of it. "

" Why not go and fetch her yourself ? "

" I ? "

" You. "

" I, myself ? "

" Why not ? "

" I, to face adventures searching for a little girl who ran away with an actor whom nobody knows ? "

" Yes. "

" My friend, you are taking advantage of your vocation as a fool. "

" Pardon, Sire, may I ask you a question ? "

" What is it ? "

" Do you really wish Her Highness to return to the Palace ? "

Pausole laid his chin in his right hand.

" That is a question which I hadn't thought of, " he said.

But after short reflection :

" Yes. I truly wish it. This escapade will do her no good. "

" Are you sure ? "

" Certain. "

" Good.   Since on the one hand you have just decided that you could not send in pursuit of the Princess either a man, a woman, nor a beast of the police (that is to say in short — anyone) and as on the other you have resolved to beg her to return here, I can see no other means of letting her know than by going and telling her so yourself."

" You are logical. "

" That is a fool's characteristic. "

The King rose and paced the floor with long and measured steps, then opening his arms in a sigh of acquiescence, said :

" It is incontestable.   And I should have arrived at the same conclusions had I had the time to think of all this. "

" Then... "

" Then, " interrupted the King who was becoming visibly animated under the influence of his page, " everything is straightening itself out at once, and I have but one more resolution to make — Either I shall let the child take her journey of seven months of which she speaks in her letter — or I shall go and speak to her myself and bring her back to the palace which she ought never to have left ! "

The page saw at once that if he left Pausole to reflect in silence, all this beautiful ardour would burn itself out in ashes of inertia.

" Sire, you must go, " he stated, " That is better not only for Her Highness, but for you also. If, as can be seen, you are not happy, it is because a man has destroyed the peaceful future that you with so much wisdom are storing up for yourself. In order to deliver yourself from the cares of determining each of your deeds, you are placing your existence in the hands of one who understands nothing and is influencing them in the wrong direction. It is he who is deceiving you. It is he who is separating you from a happiness always possible and new each morning. You are perishing on account of his routine : you are dying of monotony. To-morrow his calendar imposes on you Queen Denyse. Do you love her ? No. You do not love her at all. And yet you suffer her. You continue to live in the same rooms, on the same sofa, to see the same horizon framed by the same window. Escape from all that ! There are so few days in one's life : make it that none of them resembles the next. "

" But who will advise me if I launch out on this escapade ? "

" Who ? Fortune, fate. Let yourself be tempted by fortune daily and walk under her star. Her advice is easy to follow. "

" Could it not be, " said Pausole, shaking his head, " that the same thing would happen to me as to Melchior or Balthazar before a white cradle and a little child ? "

" If that happened you would like it. "

" You're right. And anyway, we should be there earlier. The fugitives are sleeping only a few steps away. There is no question of a journey. To-morrow we shall certainly join them. "

" You will go ? You will really go ? "

" I go. Come with me. I take pleasure in seeing you live. "

They went out side by side. Pausole put his hand on the page's shoulder and walked with an energetic step.

On turning out of the corridor they met Taxis.

The King stopped, with his head held high.

" Grand Eunuch, " said he, " I have made a decision. I myself will go in search of Princess Aline. Announce my departure for to-morrow morning and have my mule saddled by half past ten. This young man will accompany me. "

Taxis was clever enough to say nothing.

Pausole looked at him for some time as though weighing his own daring and then in a suddenly milder voice he concluded : " In fact, you shall come with us. "

BOOK II

I

HOW THE FAIR ALINE SAW A BALLET BEING DANCED

AND WHAT FOLLOWED

> " She smiled and said, ' Know, O Captain
> Moïn, that I am a woman eternally taken
> with a little girl. And between us has
> happened what has happened. And there
> is a mystery of love. "
>
> (*A Thousand & One Nights*, XV 198.)

THE inquiry carried out by the Grand Eunuch
succeeded in its results but erred in its conclusions.
The fair Aline, when escaping, did not need the two
accomplices as Taxis imagined.

One alone was sufficient.

In fact one woman alone.

This is how it happened.

One knows already that the day before the Princess
left the palace a troupe of French dancers arrived to give
an exhibition of pink legs and flowered wigs to the
harem.

For the first time since her birth the fair Aline was
allowed to witness the performance. Pausole thought
to commence the theatrical education of his daughter
by a ballet deeming that a plot in pantomime is less

easy to unravel and therefore less dangerous to think about than a comedy in action. Also the dances took place in improbable surroundings. One does not meet in real life the characters presented and without ridicule one could not imitate the graceful gestures with which evil passions are mimed.

All this was well thought out. Unhappily the fair Aline had no need to understand in order to admire.

In the midst of *jetés-battus*, of *battements*, of *branles* and of *entretailles*, the little girl saw one thing only, and that a very beautiful young man (who might quite possibly have been a lady dressed as Prince Charming) receiving at each curtain the inflamed homage of forty other women, and truly meriting it.

She found him well proportioned, elegant, bewitching. She compared his gestures with those of the officials she met at the palace and she awarded him the prize for grace. He also won the prize for beauty, for intellect and for disposition. She watched him open-mouthed with her head resting on her shoulder, with such an intense look of tenderness that the ladies-in-waiting around her would have been most disquieted had they themselves not been following the sequence of the ballet with such absorbing passion.

After the performance she asked the name of this dazzling person. She was told that the part was played by a dancer called Mirabelle.

Where did this lovely person live ? " At the end of the park, " they replied, " in the common dwellings and for two nights more, till she leaves. "

How to express to her how much she pleased her ? " By a present " suggested an ill-inspired lady-in-waiting.

The fair Aline pondered.

When she reached her apartments and even before commencing her careful evening toilet, she asked for a bank-note to put in an envelope.

A little later she shut herself in her violet boudoir as if to carry out an intimate toilet which the lady-in-waiting could not witness; then, seated at her table and certain of not being surprised, she wrote the simple words :

" Mademoiselle,

You are very beautiful. Will you speak to me? To-night at two o'clock I shall be in the park under the big almond tree by the fountain.

Do not tell anyone that I have written. Everyone thinks that this envelope contains only a bank note. Please accept it so as not to give me away.

Princess Aline. "

Then she slipped the note between the leaves and wrote as an address " To Mademoiselle Mirabelle, " sealed the envelope with wax so that no one could open it undetected.

The same lady-in-waiting who had, in the innocence of her old age, advised this present, added to her responsibility by agreeing to carry the note to its destination. Let us think that she was inspired, in the first place, by the laudable desire of doing a charitable act : then by the temptation, none the less eager, of mixing with the ballet girls at the hour of their nocturnal toilets. Since, for an old maid to watch over the safety of her soul

6

whilst studying entrancing underclothes, is the height of happiness.

Alone and stretched at full length in her little neat bed, the fair Aline was overcome by an unbearable emotion. She tried at first to calm it by lying on her right side, then on her left, then on her back, then on her chest, sitting up, crouching, stretched out, expanded, closed : but in every position she was feverish and instinctively she moved to the edge of the mattress as if to leave room for a mysterious visitor.

Much too early she rose, put on her slippers, opened the curtains and looked at the moon shining into the furthest corner of her room.

It was a brilliant night, warm and soft. Through the open window, Aline could distinguish afar, beyond the hazy lawns and motionless trees, the white terrace of the compound where Mirabelle was reading her letter.

" What will she think of me ? " the girl said to herself dreamily. " Will she come ? Perhaps not... Perhaps she is tired... Perhaps she is frightened of the dark "...

In order to occupy her time, she drew on her blotting-pad odd diagrams obviously geometric — circles, crosses, lozenges, notches which developed into spirals. She shaded them conscientiously and perfectly. And then, still by the light of the moon, she commenced the portrait of a beautiful unknown who had three hairs, forty eyelashes and an eye much larger than his mouth.

But Art did not suffice to calm her impatience.

She returned to her mirror, let fall her long white chemise, and took up her self-examination at the point where she left off before opening the door to the lady-in-waiting. Young and ignorant as she was, she had read fairy stories, and since the stories of the good Perrault are only on the subject of love, she had quickly learnt at which point of a meeting love becomes what it should be. She knew that the Sleeping Beauty received the Prince in her bed, that " the curtain was drawn " and that " they did not sleep much " without any blame being attached to them by the author. Also, Line having the instinct for caresses at the same time as the desire to be the happy object of them, did not for one moment doubt that a lover's favours should gradually reach all parts of the body, where it would be sweet to await them and delicious to retain them.

That is why she wished to be worthy of the attentions which she hoped for without exactly knowing them. She powdered her skin. She looked at herself. From her perfume cupboard she selected verbena, citron and new-mown hay, because vegetable essences were peculiarly suitable to a meeting under trees, and she sprinkled the little naked body she loved so much, perhaps a little more than was required.

A pair of thread stockings were quickly drawn on, as also a day chemise : the corsets still more quickly flung to the bottom of a cupboard. Then she put on a very thin Empire dress, fastening the high belt with a safety pin which was hidden beneath the little bow and noticed that the stratagem separated whilst accentuating the 'two fruits of her young bosom which daily became more precious.

Eventually there chimed the quarter before the hour so eagerly awaited.

The fair Aline put on her hat which also was Empire and drew on a pair of dark gloves which left the tops of her arms bare.

She was ready.

Then, just as the Grand Eunuch guessed, she sat on the ledge of the open window, raised both legs at once, swung round and jumped.

There was nothing perilous in the jump, the window being on the ground floor.

Feet together, she fell in a soft flower bed. The guards were watching the boundaries of the park but not the interior. No one saw her pass.

So as to make no noise, and to remain in the shadow she proceeded along the paths but by the grassy border in the wood. Eager as she was to reach her objective, she walked slowly as though a certain pride counselled her not to arrive the first. But, apparently, the other had taken the same view for there was no one to be found under the big almond tree.

Annoyed, she continued her walk, lost her way and took a roundabout course; and then, vaguely troubled and beginning to wonder whether the other would come at all, she hid herself quite close to the tree and gazed fixedly towards the big white building.

Suddenly she saw a vision.

Mirabelle, realising that all prestige would be lost, were she to appear to this child who adored her, in the character of Prince Charming, dressed in everyday costume, had retained her disguise to keep this appointment, which pleased her on more grounds than one.

And the fair Aline, entranced, saw coming towards her from the end of the lawn the same young man beloved by the forty ladies of the ballet, but even more beautiful than ever, his spangled costume swaying in the light of an enchanted moon, his eyes fixed on hers.

II

WHEREIN PAUSOLE, NOT SATISFIED WITH HAVING FORMED

A RESOLUTION, GOES SO FAR AS TO CARRY IT OUT

> You will have the envious and the
> hostile; and your beauty will not tarry in
> causing love to Soliman than in causing
> hate to all the Sultanas.
>
> SCUDÉRY. *Ibrahim or the*
> *Illustrious Bassa* — 1641.

LEAVING Taxis and Giglio face to face, King Pausole went to the private apartments where he found the Queen Denyse waiting for him, the same who had advised him to write a letter to Saint Anthony to find the fair Aline.

The poor Queen, in spite of every endeavour to hide four parallel gashes which disfigured her left breast, had only been partially successful, by means of creams and powders.

She recited her misfortunes.

Diane à la Houppe, brought back to the harem after her lonely awakening, had been seized with an attack of despair and sobs on a divan. Surrounded by bad friends, exasperated by sneers, chaffed at the same time about her physical peculiarities, and her ill-bred passions, she had suddenly leapt up, still crying, a bitter taste in her mouth, her hands like claws. And instead of attacking those who were dancing round her tears, she had searched throughout the hall for the sweet and innocent Denyse to scar her breast and take vengeance on her for having to give up ner place to her.

Pausole listened to this story with an ear which was often inattentive. He had taken Queen Denyse in a lot of a dozen adolescent girls offered by a loyal city, and if he had not sent her back to her mother, it was through a feeling of pity which prevented him from insulting the girl before her fellow citizens; but he did not love her; he found her insignificant and prudish with a certain amount of awkwardness. To reconcile on her body the rules of the harem with the principles of propriety, Denyse used to wear a little lace loin-cloth which made her look like an elegant savage, and which, further, being unstable, airy and badly put on, produced just the opposite result to its real purpose. Pausole, who also had principles, preferred nudity, but disapproved of the transparent. The costume of Queen Denyse shocked him to a point of offence.

He dined very late, and went on the terrace to meditate on the grave event on which he had taken a resolution; further, when midnight chimed, he told his pious companion that the Saturday of Whitsun had arrived and that he thought she would not like to abuse a day of vigil and abstinence by voluptuousness.

Having said this he sent her back to sleep in the harem and Diane à la Houppe was thus satisfied.

Dawn broke on a day three times solemn. Pausole

looked at the walls of his room, his carpets, his trinkets, his familiar pictures; he thought shudderingly that he would not see them again that night... Under the emotion of his first awakening, which is first cousin to nightmare, he had a presentiment of all the calamities which await at each corner the seeker after adventure.

His natural inclination was towards peace, repose, quiet content and regular hours. What aberration was causing him to leave such sweet riches? — In a pastoral recollection, some verses of a sad idyll written by La Fontaine floated before his dreaming memory, and in the symbolic form of a plucked pigeon King Pausole saw himself perish in a lamentable destiny.

This impression did not last long.

A radiant morning filled his room. The new chambermaid, having become bolder, spoke in a fresh and zealous voice, gave information that wasn't asked for and dared even to ask questions. His Majesty would have fine weather. The wind was in the north. It had rained a little. The other chambermaid was very ill; the doctors spoke of inflammation of the womb. Last evening there was a noisy dispute between the Grand Eunuch and the young page Giglio. Did His Majesty know?

Pausole, beside himself, thought of threatening her with having to undergo from the whole corps of pages the same treatment as her friend, but not knowing whether this would strike terror or the reverse, he asked her quite quietly to fetch the Grand Eunuch, thus following the hierarchical path.

Whereupon he stepped from his bed and put on his dressing gown.

Well, Giguelillot was right, Pausole doubted it no longer. Peace was approaching boredom, repose was close to oppression, regular hours to melancholy. This room, on close examination, was simply fastidious. That view, whose minute changes he thought he followed with interest, had for a long time exhausted its circumscribed scale of lights. Only a small spirit could limit its curiosity to the fifteen figures on the terrace and the thirty aloes in the hedge. There were other fig trees, other flowers, in Tryphemia. The excursion would be fertile in unexpected pleasures.

Pausole knew how to escape from all regrets by changing the definition of happiness according to circumstances.

The dramatic entry of Taxis interrupted his reflections. The Huguenot placed himself close to the door as if to be ready to leave should his request be refused, and joined the end of his index finger to the thumb of his right hand, not with the signification which this little gesture had for the Athenian courtesans, but to demonstrate that he was presenting an ultimatum.

" Sire, " he said, " one question, one only. Am I or am I not the Palace Marshal ? "

" I don't understand, " replied Pausole.

" In short, am I the superior, the equal or the subordinate of the page named Giglio ? "

Pausole shrugged his shoulders.

" What the deuce is the matter with you, Taxis ? The question doesn't arise. We are about to leave in a few minutes. I am taking only him and you. I do not see why I should establish the supremacy of one of my counsellors over another, when both are at my side and each obeys only my command. "

" Sire, we are about to leave, but we have not yet left. However much Your Majesty may hate pomp and ceremony, his departure calls for preparation and his absence for precautions. And the young page whom I mentioned, animated by a useless zeal, claims to know your secret preferences in condemning all my actions and proposing others. Is he authorized to adopt this attitude which paralyzes my actions and injures my dignity ? "

" Oh, dear ! Another quarrel ! " cried Pausole. " I am not going to be mixed up with it. This young man has spoken to me about it. He is full of sense. He has a just and wise mind. I will not deprive myself of his advice. You, Taxis, you also have your qualities which none would scorn. You are unpleasant but indispensable, and I would not allow you to be rendered powerless. Settle your differences amicably, and try to agree without my having to take sides. "

" It's impossible ! "

" And why ? "

" Between this stripling's principles and my own, which Your Majesty seems to reckon as equal, there is absolute incompatibility. One of us must give way or break. I await from your lips, Sire, the name of the one to be sacrificed. "

The King impatiently struck a match which flared up like an outward sign of his bad temper. He smoked in silence for a few minutes.

" Then, " said he, " it is quite simple. You will command in turn. "

" Ah ! " said Taxis drily.

" You will divide the day. From midnight till mid-day, you, Taxis, will take the upper hand. Those are precisely the hours when I shall not see you, my friend. You will guard my sleep and attend to my pleasures. Later, from mid-day to midnight, your successor will direct my steps and inspire my wishes. I believe thus I have found a solution which eliminates all chance of friction. "

With a bitter look Taxis concluded with these words : " It is written 'I will receive the same lot as the foolish, wherefore have I been wise ?' "

He bowed and retired.

Three hours later, King Pausole between his page and his Huguenot, preceded by forty lances and followed by much luggage rode out for the first time on the road to his capital.

III

HOW THE MIRROR OF THE NYMPHS BECAME THAT OF THE
YOUNG GIRLS

> " Salvete aeternum, miserae moderamina flammae
> Humida de gelidis basia nata rosis. "
> JOANNES SECUNDUS.

THE spring and the great almond tree were situated
in the furthest part of the park. Alone, the fair
Aline loved well enough to take the long walk to enjoy
occasionally the quietude of this lost refuge.

From the mouth of a satyr with extravagant ears, the
water fell into a natural basin of red earth and green
vegetation where oleanders had taken root in compact
masses. It was by no means the musty and slimy basin
of our gardens where the useless spring soaks an earth
already soft with rain. It was a birth of flowers in the
purple soil of the Midi, a fountain of strength, a creative
urn whence life streamed in verdant motion, and the
old satyr, son of Pan, watched the youth of the woods
fall eternally from his lips.

Above the grotesque horned head which the fair Aline
took to be the devil, two marble nymphs embraced,

leaning towards the dark basin. At the end of each winter, the almond tree covered them with its little eglantines. In the summer they took on all the flesh tints under the sun. At night they became goddesses.

By this fertile and dark water which was called the Mirror of the Nymphs, the little Princess in her Empire frock saw, coming towards her, her Prince Charming whose spangled doublet glistened in the light of an enchanted moon.

She saw him in the distance shining through the trees like a slender white star. Then he grew larger and became more distinct. He walked with a quiet step, at times plucking a leaf from the branches and inhaling the scent as of a flower. He appeared and vanished according to the patches of shadow or light through which he passed. Line had never felt so moved. Eager as she was to embrace him at once, she stepped back to the fountain and with her hand before her lips, dared not utter a word.

" You called me and here I am, " said Mirabelle tenderly.

Line opened her large eyes. She looked at her Prince from head to foot, but especially at his eyes.

He was bare-headed, with his dark and short hair curling round his ears. His look was deep and fixed but with a soft expression which was not quite a smile. She saw the dear face bend towards hers and, as she closed her eyes, two warm lips were pressed to them.

The dark shadow of the embracing nymphs hid the two girls. Line trembled. The two lips slowly extended their caress down her cheek and only stopped at her mouth.

" Ah ! " she said at last.

Mirabelle drew away. This time a faint but tender smile played round her eyes bordered in black.

She raised her lids and looked round her.

" No, we are alone, " replied Line. " Stay. "

Then continuing : " Come with me. "

A few steps behind the spring there was a little Greek temple; five corinthian columns supported a round cupola. The columns were hidden up to half their height. A large circular seat in the centre of the edifice, in its dark shadows, was supplied with sea-green cushions, and the place was so intimate that hardly had she seated herself next to the dancer than Line plucked up courage to speak to her.

" They gave you my letter ? "

" As you can see. "

" Do you know why I asked you to come ? "

Mirabelle was very prudent.

" To talk to me, " she replied.

" Yes ! And here you are and I have nothing more to say to you. "

Mirabelle took her hand. Line believed that now she was trembling.

" I wanted also to see you quite close, " she went on. " How beautiful you are ... as beautiful as a young man ... During the whole ballet I looked only at your eyes. If only you knew it, I envy you ! I'm so sorry that I am blonde. I would rather be dark like you; but really just like you; I'd like to be your sister. "

Mirabelle decided that it would be useless to protest.

Line herself offered her lips.

" Kiss me as you did just now, will you ? "

And when their lips separated, she said :

" How delicious. Who could have taught you that ? "

" I invented it, " said the dancer.

" Oh ! but how wonderful. How old are you ? "

" Eighteen. And you ? "

" Fourteen ! Will you do that again ? "

The game was a dangerous one for Mirabelle. Mistress as she was of her own attitude of mind, decided as she was not to precipitate matters, to prepare the way discreetly, slowly and insinuatingly, there was in her mind a troublous moment when she could contain herself no longer. She fumbled firstly in the region of the dress where the little breasts swelled the thin and warm material; then, taking advantage of the exceptional facilities offered to sympathetic gestures by the costume of the fair Aline, she risked certain investigations which gave evidence, if not of affection, at least of curiosity.

Line, docile and instinctive, lent herself willingly to it all. Mirabelle lost heart. Encouraged by the shadows, certain that the voluptuous flush which flooded her cheeks would not be seen, she gave herself up mysteriously to the thrill which she felt approaching, and could moderate neither the surge nor the sigh nor the sudden start. She was coming to her senses when Line, troubled but encouraging, asked her :

" Are you cold, dear ? You're shivering. "

" A slight weakness, " said Mirabelle. " It's nothing... I am used to it. "

" Would you like to walk about a bit ? "

" Yes. "

" Come along. The park is deserted. We will go where you like. "

Line let her frock fall and got up to go out.

Both reappeared in the moonlight.

The green dress and the spangled doublet wandered thus for some time round the bubbling spring. The one was of emerald and the other of silver, but when they wished to mirror their entwined bodies in the basin in the manner of the marble nymphs, they found that the night had assimilated their colours with those of the water and the woods.

Mirabelle did not speak. Her uneasiness and her desire hardly interrupted were renewed. She knew that she had fallen in love.

From that time she thought only of the means of satisfying her desire. Assuredly, there remained still a few hours, but to employ them according to her present temptations was to waste them. A romantic idea occurred to her. She examined it in silence, found it practical and before expressing it wished to suggest it, such was her cunning.

" Good-bye, " she said, suddenly. " I shall never see you again. "

The fair Aline paled.

" Oh ! not yet, " she begged.

" I must. "

" But I haven't seen you, I haven't said anything to you... You come, and then immediately you want to go. Perhaps I bore you ; you don't understand why I asked you to come. Even I am not quite sure, but I am perfectly happy when I take your hand. "

Mirabelle took her in her arms.

" Stop, I beg of you, " continued the girl.   " Stop, or else come back to-morrow at the same time.   I will wait for you. "

" To-morrow ?   But we leave at dawn. "

Line became even paler and slowly started to cry.

" Is it true ?   Are you really leaving ?   And when will you return ? "

" Never ! "

" But I have only you to love : don't you know that ? Yesterday in the theatre I knew that there was something between you and me, and that we had to meet and that you were to be my friend.   I send for you, I await you, our lips meet and then it's all over for ever ?   If you go away, I shall go with you. "

Mirabelle's embrace ceased.

" Very well !   Let us go.   I will take you. "

" Truly ?   You really will ? "

" Come on. "

" Alone with you ? "

" Yes.   I will leave my companions.   We shall live one for the other and always alone. "

" Oh !   And where are we going to ? "

" To my country. "

" No, no !   Let 's stop in Tryphemia. "

" That's not possible.   You would be found to-morrow. "

" How ? "

" By the King's orders. "

" Papa ?   You don't know him.   To send to fetch me would be a serious step.   By the time he has taken it, we shall be far away. "

IV

WHEREIN PAUSOLE AND HIS COUNSELLORS DEMONSTRATE

THEIR CONTRASTS

> Thou sayest I have been sometimes scholar
> Sometimes courtier, sometimes warrior
> And that several trades have hardened my life.
> Thou sayest true, preacher; but I have no desire
> To become a minister or a hypocrite like thee.
>
> RONSARD

PAUSOLE his page and his Huguenot riding together between the escort and the baggage, were mounted on three animals which fairly symbolised the difference in their characters.

The King, who had put on under his light crown a white cambric veil as a shield for his neck, was seated in a saddle which resembled an arm chair, for it had a back, pillows, cushions, soft arms and a sunshade. Two wire rods, invisible from a distance, supported at the level of his hands the sceptre and orb; but the orb enclosed a flask of port, and the sceptre a fan.

The mule Macarie, an imperturbable person, bore this frail edifice with a distracted and resigned air, the

7

same air, in fact, which Pausole bore under the load of
the cares of State.   Her coat was white and the tip of
her tail and her mane were mouse coloured.   Her
carriage was erect but sedate.   She never slept less than
sixteen hours a day.

Taxis rode the black Kosmon, a gelding without vice,
without virtue and as stupid as only a horse can be.
Kosmon had neither pedigree nor form.   His master
prized him all the same because he always stepped off
with the same foot, scorned the immodest scent diffused
by the tails of fillies and was so imbued with a sense
of duty that he would have gone straight into a ditch,
had one forgotten to guide the rein in time.

Giglio had selected from the King's stables a young
zebra the colour of fire with four white hoofs, black
stripes on his back and a starred forehead. This animal
was called Himère; he was petulant and capricious.   His
coat matched the page's costume, and from the feather
in the cap down to the little shoes of the third pair of
feet seemed to form a coleopterous centaur with flame
coloured wings and blue corselet.

" See, Sire, " said Taxis, pointing to the lancers.
" See how well ordered and exact is the advance guard.
The horses and the men are all sized; the lances are
standardised and the helmets come from the same
mould.   I know the lives of those forty men.   There
are amongst them neither veterans nor rakes.   Each
carries in his wallet the Osterwald Bible, expurgated
edition.   I have so trained them that if at any moment I
were to ask them to recite to me the verse which streng-
thens them in the midst of their duty and which is
applicable to the circumstances, they would recite in

unison the same passage : ' *Let me vanquish my enemies, but preserve me from the violent man* ', according to Psalm XVIII. "

Giglio raised himself in his stirrups.

" That square escort with its lances in the air is as stupid as a hearse upset in the road. It is neither strong nor martial. Those fellows don't know how to sit a horse; they are upright, but as a footman on a chair or a girl in a cash desk of a restaurant. They carry their lances like candles and their reins like table napkins. It is quite enough to see their backs to know what they are, and at the first rifle-shot they would flee as would my zebra. Possibly not so daintily. "

" Poor fellows, " said King Pausole, " how hot their helmets must be and how heavy their lances to carry ! Why don't they take off their tunics in this terrible heat ? I hope, at least, that they have their rum flasks and some peaches in their haversacks. Taxis, you shall never be forgiven if you haven't thought of that. "

Taxis threw out his dried-up hand.

" I am giving them the pleasure of privation, " said he. " It is one of the greater joys. They know that in the fields there are brooks where one can drink, and at the roadside, inns gorged with wine casks, whilst they have parched throats, dry tongues and empty stomachs. They are tasting the bitter joy of thirst. I, who, alas, have just quenched my thirst, I envy their fortune of which I have deprived myself by a double mortification. "

Half turned round in his saddle, the King stared at

his minister. He examined him in detail from his flat, dull shoes to his squalid, brushed felt hat. He noticed his narrow waistcoat, the braid of the buttonholes and the worn appearance of the eight buttons. He looked at the square fingernails, the flat nostrils, the long greasy hair and the vertical lips.

Then stopping his mule to let it make water, and settling himself back into a comfortable position, he said carelessly :

" Taxis, it is lucky for you that you are indispensable, for you are an awful ass. "

The morning developed in a dazzling light. The shadows of the old plane trees which lined the road grew shorter and shorter. The dust of the white track powdered the grassy banks. Before the feet of the three animals some lizards nimbly traced their zig-zags of green lightning.

Beyond the ditches to right and left, the Royal Flower Gardens offered their bulging clusters and their greenhouses freshly sprayed with water, Here were cultivated thousands of rare species and new varieties which the ingenious minds of the horticulturists created from day to day. Each morning armfuls of damp flowers, light foliage and palms were brought to the harem. The gardeners had written down on an easily cleaned slate the variable whims of each of the Queens, and each received on awakening her favourite flower in a small long-necked vase.

Pausole and his two counsellors were passing the last greenhouse when the clock, fitted in its mosaic pediment, sounded the four quarters and the twelve strokes of noon.

Immediately the page, with a sharp kick, brought his zebra face to face with Taxis's horse.

" Grand Eunuch, " said he, " You know His Majesty's wish. The time has arrived when I succeed you. Kindly hand over command. "

" Receive it from the King, " replied Taxis crossly.

" I grant it you, my boy, " said Pausole.

Giglio saluted, turned his animal round and called to the escort " Left turn ! Gather round me. "

The forty guards hurried to him.

Then, sitting easily in his saddle, his legs hanging straight down and the feather of his cap standing erect, the page spoke these words.

" Comrades, this gentleman who was in command this morning, placed instruments in your hands which you will never have to use. The roads are safe, Tryphemia is at peace, the King is loved by his people. You will never have cause to plung your lances into the broad back of a barbarian, from omoplate to epigastrium. Is that clear ? Further, in art everything must have an object. That which has no purpose is idiotic. You will therefore put the steel part of your lances in the niches of this wall and bend the wood until it is broken at the socket. Carry out the movement ! "

" Sire ! But Sire ! " begged Taxis.

" Leave him alone, " said Pausole. " This is very well conceived. "

The forty guards broke with a will.

" Keep the shafts, " said Giglio. " And now follow me. "

They entered the Flower Garden.

The page hurried down the paths, inspected the clusters, and went into the greenhouses. He told the gardeners to show him flowers with long stems, iris, anthuriums, lilies, tiger lilies, Pomponne lilies and finally stopped in front of some giant tulips.

" This is what we want, " said he. " Each one of you tie one of these tulips to the end of your shaft with a rush and carry it in the road with the same respect as though it were a flag. "

Then he offered the King a rose, and Taxis a spider. He took for himself an arum lily.

The whole cavalcade then took up its march once more on the dazzling road.

" Admirable, " said Pausole. " But these fellows were thirsty and I don't think they have had a drink. "

V

WHEREIN MIRABELLE REVEALS HER LITTLE MALICIOUS AND SENTIMENTAL SPIRIT

> " Regarding la Sallé the critic is perplexed;
> The one says she has made many happy
> The other claims that she prefers her own
> sex. A third that she approves both… "
>
> Song on Mlle. Sallé, dancer at the Opera.
>
> Collection of MAUREPAS — 1755.

HAVING decided to fly that very night, the two girls went back each to her room to make preparations for their little journey on foot.

The Empire frock ran over the dark lawns, climbed the steps of the perron, went along the terrace to the gallery, was raised to climb into the open window of a room and disappeared into the sleeping palace.

The spangled costume went along the edge of the stream, then across the glade, and the two marble nymphs from the height of their pedestal saw it extinguished in a house in the distance like a little star which has gone to bed.

It did in fact go to bed, and somewhat roughly on a couch. On it were thrown little buckled shoes, white

Stockings and even the chemise. And then the young Mirabelle, lighted by a candle, and naked as a girl alone, plunged both hands in a dress trunk where as a matter of fact there were more tunics than bodices.

She took from it a wide collared shirt, such as is still worn by the sons of some beautiful women when it suits them better for their sons not to be sixteen years old. She put on some striped pants and dark blue breeches, a large white bow tie, a white waistcoat, a short vest and a woman's straw hat.

Clothed thus, with hands in her pockets and looking over her shoulder, she gave herself a glance in the mirror, which glance became a wink and then an ogle. Mirabelle's eyes were merry.

She even murmured a phrase which was both metaphoric and familiar in the sibylline language called ' slang ', a phrase which meant that her fancy dress reconciled her slightly to an artless and ugly sex which was not at all hers.

It would be useless to hide it. Mirabelle felt no inclination towards men. The strength of the male, the bull neck, the bottle-like muscles and the chest like a table... no ! evidently it was not for her that the gods had created their masterpiece. She did not like either the beard, the moustache, nor the blue chin. Oh ! that didn't prevent her from accepting a friend, and even an unknown friend when she was asked politely. She gave herself up, outside every performance, to the most choice exercises, and there, as when acting, her artistic mind caused her to feign an exaltation to which even in those moments she did not reach. Those special little ballets where she mimed a tender role affected

her not at all, except that each day she detested more
those who asked this effect of her. The poor child
resigned herself to it because the visits of the spectators
to the dancers are preceded and followed by invariable
formalities to which it suits one to find a strong persuasive
force. But her conception of love imagined more delicate
methods and her conception of Art was based on symmetry.
For, man as she had known him up till then had generally
shown himself as sentimental as a puppet (one cannot
express oneself better than Gavarni) and, moreover, it
is regrettable but necessary to say that a lady and her
cavalier at the moment when they settle down form a
whimsical, or rather, a badly matched couple.

These ideas, supported by the warmth of natural
leaning, had led the little dancing girl to seek voluptuousness amongst a small circle of girl friends. Prudent,
she had commenced with her young companions first
at school and then in the *corps de ballet*. The answer
had always been ' yes ' either by voice, gesture or look
according to individual modesty. Some accepted without
any idea of cultivating a soulful passion, but none knew
how to resist the attraction of an inoffensive and clandestine experience.

Six months after her first appearance on the stage her
reputation was great as was that of her theatre. She
invited people to call on her. She even had a ' day
at home ' when she assembled at her house, in a very
nude intimacy, ten or twelve friends who thought it
useless to hide from each other their common tastes.
And these parties became sufficiently scandalous to
tempt honest women.

These declared themselves by emissaries, letters or

collisions. They offered valuables, solid gifts and asked only two promises : voluptuousness which they called vice, and lies which they called mystery.

Mirabelle, extremely flattered, threw herself into the adventure. Soon tired of her early and modest partners who, however, should have deserved a less cavalier treatment, she left the stage for the auditorium with the wings of a butterfly. Innumerable revelations still awaited her, and she wanted them all. She had them. She knew the joys of adultery, the narrowness of a cab, the scent of a furnished room, the all too short hour, the invented name and the *poste restante*. A husband once entered a private room where, in spite of there being no man — and no bed — he declared himself supplanted. Mirabelle could hardly contain herself with joy : so great is the unconsciousness of crime.

But enough of generalities regarding this ambiguous person. We will not go into details; anyway, they would not be decent.

Here we will limit ourselves to explain why Mirabelle on the stage had, with an infallible eye, picked out the fair Aline enraptured with the charm of her dance : why her perspicacious glance had become attractive : why she had not been surprised to receive a note two hours after arranging a meeting : and finally how even she, being caught in the trap of a temptation stronger than her prudence, abandoned her troupe like the Prince Charming of the ballet to run away with the daughter of the King.

During this time, young Aline had gone back to her room. She picked up a pot of rouge, a box of powder, a purse which happened to be full and certain toilet

articles, in short all that the lady-in-waiting had enumerated
before King Pausole in fulfilling the sad duty of handing
him the note which had been found.

This note Line wrote in two minutes. She did not
hope to be forgiven, but she did not want anybody to
be uneasy regarding a health as precious as hers.

Her inner feelings disappeared in her joy as the stars
in the light of the moon. In her joy she was restrained
from shouting only by the silence.

If the ladies-in-waiting did not hear her jump, run,
clap her hands and throw her Telemachus into the bath
as a sign of emancipation, it was perhaps (and I hardly
dare mention the supposition) because the guilty guardians
had left their neighbouring rooms to seek elsewhere
the soft lassitudes which cure insomnia.

However it may be, the fair Aline fled in an almost
clamorous haste, encouraged by the mystery in which
her first departure was wrapped.

She ran through the woods to the Mirror of the
Nymphs and at first saw nobody.

The water still flowed and gurgled. The diabolic
mask and the two nymphs pale against the darkness of
the trees were the sole occupants of this corner which
had become deserted again.

Line went up to the little temple, made sounds and
called softly.

Slowly and wearily Mirabelle emerged from the
shadows between the columns.

She had changed her silver spangled costume for
another : there was a momentary deception : but almost
at once one saw that she was even more beautiful dressed

thus in modern clothes and that above her white collar her hair seemed even darker.

She did not smile. She sighed deeply. Playing the part of a lover of fifteen she took up before her friend the plaintive and unhappy pose which suits this virile age. It was not, however, that she wanted to play a part. The weight of her emotion had clouded her brow with a fringe of sorrow. A deep feeling of the gravity of the circumstances and of the recollection which she would always have of this moment in her youth caused her little heart to stop beating. She had a vision of herself at some later time, doubtless poor, selling oranges in the Rue Saint-Denis or pencils in the Canebière, at an age when one or the other of the sexes after having come to an arrangement to find her worthy of desire, would continue to agree to leave her to die of hunger. She already guessed that women sum up in a few luminous moments a past full of shadows, and she knew that beyond youth she would see till the end, above all forgetfulness, the moonlit and shadowy scenery of this exalted night.

So she took the hand of the little Princess Aline and made her, in her turn, enter the dark circle enclosed by the five Grecian columns.

She relived a little more sadly the hour already dead for ever, where she felt with so many tremors that she was pledging her freedom.

As a remembrance she took from the cushion a little white and green ribbon.

Nearer to the spring she gathered a scented leaf and a flower without perfume which she put in her handkerchief. Finally, under the blessing of the two nymphs alike and naked, who with two hands stretched over the water were united by the others, Mirabelle slowly kissed the eyes of the fair Aline. This kiss seemed to her to be deliciously fraternal.

" You want to follow me ? "

" Oh, yes ! "

Their lips met. Line closed her eyes.

Mirabelle stiffened and murmured :

" Do you love me ? "

" Oh yes, ! Oh, yes ! "

" Repeat it... Say it alone... Say 'I love you, Mirabelle !' "

" I love you, Mirabelle. "

" You will regret nothing ? "

" Nothing. "

" You will follow me everywhere ? "

" Not too far, please. But I will go wherever you are. You are my friend. "

Mirabelle looked at her gravely and caught her two arms.

" Do you know what a ' friend ' is ? No ? It doesn't matter. You will know soon. Don't leave me. Swear that you will stay with me... a week... a whole week with Mirabelle. "

" A week ? But much longer ! What are you saying ? "

" Swear to me one week. I don't ask more. If you stop eight days, I shall keep you eight years. "

" Why do you seem so sad ? "

" Kiss me. "

" There ! "

" You have sworn ? "

" Anything you want. "

Mirabelle, however, tenderly shook her head.

She stopped speaking, raised her eyes once more towards the pale and young breasts of the marble nymphs and finally :

" Let us go quickly, " she said. " Which is the way ? Where is the gate ? "

" Oh ! the gate is guarded. Come this way. I know a path out of the park. "

They went with quick steps. Taller than her companion, by a head, Mirabelle clasped her friend just above the waist. Her hand held the little swollen breast, enveloped it with five fingers, pressed it with a caressing palm and ran the tip of a finger over it till it had found the point. Line smiled and raised her eyes.

They left the park between two aloes, but across fields away from the road. Here the bank of hard dry earth bore their footprints. Mirabelle could no longer see, for the moon had set; Line slowly guided her by the hand and soon they were in the sunken road.

Where were they to go ? They did not know.

They followed a field of maize, then came to some market gardens where grew red pimentoes, water melons and batatas.

Gradually day was breaking.

Under hedges of prickly pear hung a mist curved like a snowy bank.

" I'm sleepy, " said Line, laying her cheek on her companion's shoulder. " How late it is ! Where shall we rest ? I haven't slept for hours. "

They discussed the matter as they walked. It is true that on their way there was a hamlet with an inn;

but how could they ask for a room before sunrise ?
They had neither a carriage, cloaks nor luggage.   Suppose
the innkeeper were to ask questions ?   How could they
explain in a few words that at this late hour they had
not yet been to bed ?

" Let's follow the road, " said Mirabelle.   " Over
there I can see an olive wood where we can sleep in the
shade until mid-day. "

After a walk which seemed long to Line who was
almost asleep, but which in reality lasted no longer
than about twenty five minutes, they came to the entrance
of the wood.   It is true that some olive trees raised their
flat and dark mass in front of other trees, but behind
them clustered red pines and cypress trees united by wild
brambles and soft grassy slopes.

Line threw both arms round Mirabelle, gave her a
sleepy kiss in the corner of her left nostril, and stretched
herself out without seeking a better place.   Immediately,
the sandman sowed sleep in her eyes.

VI

WHEREIN PAUSOLE AND HIS COMPANIONS CHAT FITFULLY
AND STOP AT A PIN'S POINT

Βάλλει καὶ μάλοισι τὸν αἰπόλον ά κλεαρίστα.
THEOCRITUS V 88.

IT pleases me, " said Pausole, beaming, " It pleases me greatly to be preceded by forty tulips on the road to my capital.   That armed escort was dead against my wishes and you were ill inspired, Taxis, to take advantage of my worries to make use of it today.   Might it not have been said, on discovering me behind this warlike display, that I was going to give battle to my neighbour, M. Loubet ?   I am by no means a bellicose chief, certainly not.   Extermination is not my business. And I allow no blood to be shed in my kingdom other than that of virgins or of little chickens. "

" Poor little chickens, " said Giglio.   " I would rather harm fifty young girls than cut the throat of a chicken.   And, moreover, the cries of a young girl are much worse. "

" Yes, " said Pausole, " one becomes used to it. "

As the heat was increasing, he opened his sceptre and withdrew his fan which was Japanese.

The Eastern artist had drawn thereon, with, an exact and well balanced reed and a realism which overlooked nothing, a young girl, nude, sitting on her heels with her hair dressed very elaborately and her breasts very pointed, holding in her hand a fan with which she veiled her left shoulder.

" The privilege of courtesans, " continued the King, " is somewhat shocking. Their type has become, in the art of almost all nations, that of feminine beauty, and it is as well that it is so, since all women abstain from competing. For a century or more, one cannot mention more than four or five European ladies of quality who have taken off their chemises before a sculptor, or a painter, allowing him to reveal to others the beautiful things which they hide. One has never known why. Everywhere, except in Tryphemia — and Japan so the papers say — a naked woman is a prostitute. But I grant you that sometimes the courtesans have more genius and more talent than their painters, that they reach refinements of an admirable delicacy, and that at the supreme moment at the height of their performance, one might sometimes be equally tempted to applaud as to embrace them : they are always, however, working girls, since their job is mechanical and there is no manual labour which will not soon be disastrous to the harmony of the body. They are even working servants since they regulate themselves according to our whims : and there is no obedience which is not fatal to the beauty of the spirit. Their aesthetic monopoly in Europe is then an encroachment, and I congratulate myself on having raised the mental level of my subjects by permitting them peacefully to prove the beauty of virgins whilst our neighbours blend all their art on the paunch of certain hussies. "

" You are an artist, Sire, " said Giglio.

" No, " replied Pausole. " I like nature as the gods made it, and I enjoy seeing it so much, that I have not the time to look at it through the eyes of others, as do collectors of pictures. I am by no means an artist. "

On this, he looked at his page as though awaiting from him fresh approbation.

" My friend, " he said to him, " what shall I call you ? You told me that one could pronounce your name in the Italian or the French way, ' Djilio ' or ' Giguelillot '. But I feel that in saying ' Djilio ' I do not use the tonic accent with the force necessary. A Milanese would laugh at me were he to hear me now. On the other hand ' Giguelillot ' is as ridiculous a pronunciation as ' Shakespeare' or ' Lohangrin ' : I can't get used to it. Since French is the language of my people, let me gallicize your name and call you simply ' Gilles '. "

" Sire, my name is Gilles, " exclaimed the page. " Since you wish it, I am always called Gilles : I have never borne any other name. Gilles ! Just Gilles : or Gilles Gilles : or Gilles — as you like. "

" Just Gilles is more brisk, more playful, more in keeping with your appearance. "

" But you, Sire, what name will you bear ? "

" I ? "

" I mean in history. "

" What do you mean ? "

" Sire, what one calls History is a sort of peasant woman in a badly draped red dress, seated on a Grecian throne, and bearing on her head a laurel wreath like a little girl who has won prizes. She has the breasts of a nursing mother, the shoulders of a navvy, and the nose of Pallas herself. One also recognises the curious way she has of writing the names of celebrated men on a brass tablet which she carries on her left knee : it must be due to this that she is called History (rather ask your artists), for the same peasant woman in a badly draped dress, with the same double sized breasts, and the same equine nose can just as well be Science or the Argentine Republic or the Omnibus Company : this depends on the articles which she balances on the extremity of her thigh — Well, when one is a great king ' one appears before History ' followed by several male foetus bearing coats of arms and symbolising Finance no less than Art and Letters. You will never persuade an engraver of medals to the contrary. For this solemn ceremony the name of the king is not sufficient. There is tacked on to it a famous surname which is generally attributed subsequently to popular invention. What surname would you like ? "

" I will think it over, " said Pausole.

" When I lived in Paris, I knew there a great poet and playwright who amused himself by giving historic epithets to the presidents of his country. He found Thiers the Brief, Grévy the Conqueror, Carnot the Just, Faure the Beautiful, and lots more. "

" Saint Pausole will do for me, " said the King, modestly. " Saint Pausole the Areopagite, or Saint Pausole of Tryphemia. After my death, if the Treasury is not in too bad a condition, I should like my successors to pay the expenses necessary for my canonisation. I have heard that it costs a great deal to become a saint. It is cheaper to become a count. But I believe there is a reduction in favour of crowned heads and that they are spared delays. I hope that the Holy Congregation of Rites will not find too many impediments to my entry to the seventh heaven. True, I have followed many creeds and I absolutely refuse to treat the numerous divinities as vain idols when the opposite has not been proved to me. But I have also followed the catholic religion; I have even practised its virtues; I am meek and humble of heart. I have tried all my life to make people happy, to pacify foolish quarrels, to reunite hostile hands, to spread peace and love. These are estimable qualifications, and without having a mind obsessed with paradisaic ambitions, I think that I should make an ideal saint."

Taxis jumped, but it was not a sign of opposition as one might expect. He had not been listening to the last words of the King. His glance had been held for a minute by a little brilliant object stretched in the middle of the road.

" Sire ! " he cried. " A clue ! "

And, having dismounted, he picked up the object, doubly precious owing to its nature and origin. He examined it and said seriously :

" Here we have a small gold trinket which is a safety pin. This safety pin bears engraved on its catch a capital ' A ' with a crown of cornflowers, that is to say, the cipher of the Princess Aline. I observe further that the pin is open; therefore it fell directly from the garment to which it was attached and not from a handbag. I deduce therefrom... "

" Taxis, you are fastidious, " interrupted Pausole.
" We are searching for neither Captain Grant, nor ' Long
Carbine ' and you will kindly not smell out the traces of
this little girl in the dust, nor count the broken branches
like a hunter of scalps. I, for my part, will certainly
not give myself up to the contortions of a hooligan on
the main road of my State. "

" Nevertheless, it is important... "

" To know that my daughter passed this way ? You
didn't doubt it, did you ? We know the starting place
and the first stopping place of her little journey. Between
these two points there is only one road. She must have
travelled over it. Even had she gone the most roundabout way between her home and the inn, that would
not prevent us from finding her if she is still there, neither
would it enlighten us as to the direction taken to-day
if she has continued her walk. "

The tone in which Pausole made this reply was full
of instruction. Giglio made no mistake : the King was
in no hurry to reach his goal. And unless one was
careful, he would be disappointed by finishing too soon
an excursion whose beginning had cost him great effort.

Giguelillot (I hope the reader is not inconvenienced
by the names alternately given to this individual Giglio,
Giguelillot, Djilio or Gilles), Giguelillot, then, thought
rapidly. Taxis had to be got out of the way.

" Excuse me, " said he, seriously, " You say the pin
had fallen open to the ground ? Which way was the
point turning ? "

He did not persist any further. Taxis took pride in

discovering all alone the results of such a question. They appeared to be most important.

"One moment," he growled, "I am coming to that. It is a capital point that I am about to establish."

Pausole looked at Gilles who did not flinch.

Kneeling on the macadam, Taxis was looking for the exact place where he had picked up the pin.

"Here it is! I've found it," said he. "The imprint is quite clear. The half in which the clasp is, is perpendicular to the axis of the road, but the point is open towards the palace in the opposite direction to the inn."

He got up.

"This," he declared, still frowning, "leads us to unexpected conclusions. The gold pin which I hold in my hand is such as women (I believe) are accustomed to fix at the top of the base (if I may so put it) of their back. It has as its use to close the immodest gaping of the skirt and to fix to the belt a garment which must not fall. It is always placed (I suppose, it is logical) point inwards. So, if such a pin loosens itself slowly and finally slips to the ground, as, apparently, it does not execute pirouettes in its obedience to gravity, as, on the contrary one may presume that it travels without turning round, its point probably indicates on the ground the direction taken by the lady who has lost it. But in the present case the point turns towards the Palace : therefore the Princess Aline must have retraced her steps on leaving the Hotel du Coq and is actually going in the exact opposite direction to that which we are following."

He raised two fingers and went on :

"But... that is not certain."

" Oh, but yes ! " protested Gilles.   " You've solved it. "

" I truly believe so, but presumption is not proof. And since here is the Hotel du Coq (it is the sixth house on the right in the village before you) the most simple thing to do would be to commence our inquiries and decide immediately afterwards in which direction we should proceed.

" Not at all, " said Giguelillot.   " We must run as hard as we can.   We will part here.   The King and I will carry out our inquiries in the village.   You, Sir will be good enough to turn back, search the roads and woods, inhale the wind, scan the horizon, and scratch in the sand : that interests us no longer.   Remember only that the King dines at eight o'clock.   Eight o'clock for eight fifteen, Grand Eunuch. "

" I take orders only from my Sovereign. "

" Who am I, " said the page humbly, " if not his will, his Walküre, Seigneur Taxis ?   It is he who is speaking by my lips. "

" I am not going to be mixed up in this, " said Pausole. " I approve on principle.   Go away, Taxis, since it is the advice given by my day counsellor.   It will be legal for you to express your feelings as soon as midnight has struck.   Till then, no discussions.   The system has no other aim but to avoid friction.   Prove to me that it is well conceived. "

Taxis cast a furious glance at the zebra and its rider. Then he seized the reins of the chaste Kosmon with an agitated hand, led the beast to the embankment, climbed to the highest point, executed not without difficulty what Mirabelle would have called in her choreographic jargon

' battements in the fourth position ' and finally fell into the saddle.

He was already trotting towards the Flower Gardens, when Pausole begging the good Macarie to be good enough to start walking, said in a melancholy tone of voice :

" Well, my boy, here is the inn. "

He was going to plunge into tragic events and question strangers; to learn what truly he did not wish to know; to conduct the most scandalous inquiries, and at the end of all this be faced by having to make a necessary decision. His voice manifested a lively displeasure at the approach to the fatal threshold. Giguelillot with one word averted this painful fear.

" The Inn ? " said he. " It is rather far. The first house in the village is a farm and if you wish, Sire, we could drink some milk before commencing our labours. "

" Ah ! That's a good idea ! " said the King. " Let us go in, I would like it. We have a Sicilian sun on this road. I feel absolutely pastoral and blowing like a bull. Let us go and see the woolly sheep, the beautiful eyes of the cows, the lambs whose wool is soft as sleep, says the Sicilian. Let us see the goat herd who tends his bearded goats... "

" And Klearista who throws him apples ! "

" And Klearista who throws him apples ! " repeated Pausole with enthusiasm.

VII

HOW GIGUELILLOT AFTER SEVERAL ABOMINABLE ADVEN-
TURES DEVISED A STRATAGEM AND DISCOVERED THE
FAIR ALINE.

> The downfall of honest women is often
> of an astonishing rapidity.
>
> OCTAVE FEUILLET.

THE farm which Pausole and his page entered, whilst
the forty tulips mounted guard at the porch,
had been built by an architect who possibly knew
Theocritus by heart but did not allow himself to be
entirely absorbed by his writings.

The buildings and the floor of the courtyard, covered
and paved with ceramic, met at the base of the walls in
rounded corners where the smallest germ, the last of
the thallophytes, the most microscopic microcosm, the
humble bacteria could not lead a peaceful life, love or
create young, as was the case in the days of Klearista,
who dared to draw across her lips a syringe infected with
pathogenic germs.

The rural smell of carbolic acid and the odour of
copper sulphate escaped from the cattle sheds along
with the fragrancy of new mown hay. At the end of

the courtyard under a metal pentroof about thirty special watering troughs were supplied, each with its own filter, and awaited the muzzle of an ox which also had its own bath, prophylactic against everything.

" Ah, Sire ! What is this place we are come to ? " asked Djilio in despair.

" A factory for milk, butter and fat chickens, " replied Pausole. " I think it looks very good, and I am reassured straight away as to the meal we are going to have. This is just the farm that the Greeks would have built, had they known as much as we do. It is clean and geometrical. "

The zebra pranced in the sunshine.

" Further, " continued Pausole, " the Greeks took a thousand precautions which we have invented in the last eighteen months. I have read in a treatise by a doctor of Ephesus that the water which they drank was boiled, cooled and re-boiled. They knew that river water was the worst of all, that wells are dangerous when in the neighbourhood of hot springs, and that accoucheurs should wash their hands immediately before work. My boy, what is called ' progress ' is never more than a return to the Hellenes or a development of their principles. The dairy farm which we have just entered is nearer to them than it looks. Hullo ! here's the farmer. "

An old man was running towards them, a straw hat in his hand, trembling, affected, proud, rejoicing... Let the reader have the trouble of finding all the epithets describing an old peasant receiving the King and his page.

Himère and Macarie, as royal animals, were led to special stalls. Pausole leant familiarly on the shoulder of his subject, for he never knew how to keep people at a distance; and Giguelillot, very much alive, interested himself in the girls about the farm.

There came towards him one, two, seven, ten, twelve, the ugly ones wearing a petticoat and a scarf, but the pretty ones unclothed according to the custom of Tryphemia.

Giguelillot noticed one amongst them who, naked from her wooden shoes to the silk handkerchief round her neck, seemed admirably suited to while away the hours of a day of rest.

And while the King Pausole was plainly questioning the farmer as to his views on the harvest and the movement of the corn market, the page approached the milk maid, who, incidentally, was regarding him with the sweetest of smiles.

" Do you know how to milk cows ? " he asked her.

" That 's all I do know, " replied the girl.

Her voice was lively and mellow.

" Well, " said Gilles, " show me the way. We will fill a bowl of milk for His Majesty who is thirsty and one for me who imitate him from a spirit of courtiery. "

She ran ahead, her breasts in her hands.

He followed her to a glittering stable which resembled that of a circus.

" What is your name ? "

" Thierrette, seigneur. "

" Thierrette, you have golden breasts like two little pats of fresh butter. Take to the King what milk you like; my lips want none but yours. "

" I have none, " said the dark haired girl laughing, " and I do nothing to make it come. "

" You have none ?   I'd like to know if that is true. "
" Try. "

He carried out the test, first the right and then the left, with an insistence which did not seem to displease. He sucked with hollow cheeks like a greedy child and the breasts swelled at the point between his lips, but he drew nothing but long shudders and satisfied blushes.

" Nothing so far, " he said at last.   " You make me wait.   Come nearer; you will give me some in a year. "

" That is a long time to wait if you are thirsty.   First of all drink this. "

She seated herself by a white cow, took the soft and trembling skin of the udder, and drawing the soft thick teat between a thumb and two fingers she shot forth obliquely the white stream of milk.

Giglio stayed at a distance, waiting till she came back to him; but she went off with a slow step carrying in front of her chest the china bowl in which quivered the thick cream.

" I will carry this to the King, " she said. " Wait, your turn will come. "

He did not wait a moment.

Hardly had she left the dark stable for the bright light in the doorway where her black hair took on blue values, when the page left by the other exit of the big hall.

He passed through light corridors, airy lobbies, stores which resembled an exhibition of agricultural machinery and which appeared to him to be laid out in the worst possible way.

Giguelillot who manifested no particular admiration for man's patient labour, and treated the most serious

subjects with a deplorable frivolity, was as indifferent
towards the arrangement of rooms where work was
carried out as to those where no work is done. Further
than that, his principles were all the more firm the more
recent they were, and if he found a grace of the unexpected
in certain disorderliness, nothing annoyed him more than
' arranging ', that is to say, placing in a regular succession.

With an energetic zeal, he disturbed everything he
could move. He threw rolling-pins into the reapers,
steel bolts and screws into the agricultural machines;
he put fine forks, thin spades, stout hoes into the boiler
and funnel of an unfortunate steam engine. Treating
the tiled floor as a simple working foundation, he broke
it open with a blow of a pickaxe.

The red earth appeared.

" Ah ! " he said, " What a pretty colour. "

He took a step back, half closed his eyes, looked to see
how the hall was lighted, whence came the day-light,
where the shadows massed; then, choosing, not without
design, another point in the central path and with yet
a further blow of the pickaxe, produced another " touch
of vermilion. "

He continued thus, wrapped up in his work, and for
over a quarter of an hour endeavoured to modify the
decoration of the hall without taking much notice of the
rules laid down by Owen Jones. Some scythe blades,
taken from their shafts and laid flat on the ground with
balance, precision and ornamental equilibrium, spread
their long blue blades and threw up the vermilion in a
scale of orange tones. The arborescent lines of the
shafts laid end to end gave a sort of solidity to the
composition. Two reaping hooks joined at the points

and the sockets around a mass of colour imposed upon the whole an artificial centre, a focus of reddish clay balanced at the other side by a second focus smaller but equally indispensable.

" Ah ! Ah ! " he cried again. " That is not so bad. Now anyone can come in. Things are in their places. "

Then enlivened by this twenty minutes' labour, he continued his walk across the farm.

A fruit garden, red with strawberries and raspberries, spread before him.

He entered.

" Good day, seigneur, " said a small voice.

And Giglio saw, behind a screen of purple flowers, the white lines of a woman's body set off by high lights.

Perhaps this one would show herself more tender or less artificial than the young Thierrette.

He wasted no time in asking her name, nor making decorative fancies with figs, bananas or tangerines.

Approaching her, he said :

" Rose, or Lilian, or Marguerite, or whatever may be the floral name by which you are known amongst your sisters, if I were lord of this place, I should require no other fruits than those of your body, velvety as a plum. Give me your oranges, your strawberries, and your sloes, and that heart of pomegranate so firmly closed. "

Kneeling before one of his readers, the young poet would doubtless have sought rarer comparisons, if there be any unpublished ones between the fruits of woman and those of the earth; but the Tryphemian girl to whom these compliments were addressed had never heard anything more beautiful.

She blushed, lowering her eyes with the smile of a

child, and since her first movement was to go and shut the door, Giglio perceived that he could continue his ballad up to and including the epilogue.

He clasped the girl between his left arm and his blue doublet. With one hand which seemed to point out to an invisible audience a horticultural collection, he first of all touched the lips which became the flower of a peach tree, then the breasts which, following the same simile, became two peaches bearing their stones; then he used metaphors which may have come from Chenier, but certainly not from Lamartine.

The guardian of the raspberries listened to this entirely oriental poetry with sensuality. Incapable of imposing her humble and weak discretion on the desire of a young man whom she found full of genius, she allowed herself to be led, without resistance, to a garden couch from which she swept off a lot of fruit and made it a point of honour to give generously what was expected from her.

" When will you come back ? " she sighed, after many another sigh.

Giglio replied unmoved.

" To-morrow. To-night. The day after to-morrow. Always. "

" But you have some girl friends ? "

" None. "

" You will have ? "

" Never. "

" Swear. "

" I swear. "

Reassured, she abandoned herself once more with all her heart, and then more confident she let him leave her.

The page crossed the courtyard.

Through the windows of the hall where they had conducted the King, he saw Pausole asleep close to the farmer, on a large leather couch. As he turned to one side, he saw Thierrette standing in the entrance with a threatening finger forbidding him to approach but forgetting not to laugh.

" Don't follow me ! " she cried, retreating.

He ran after her.

Rushing up the staircase, he ran along a corridor, entered a small room as bright and spotless as the rest.

She barricaded herself behind a towel-horse.

" You scoundrel ! Now you are in my room. Go out at once, or I shall call for help ! "

Giglio, comedian, putting on the voice of a lady visiting a bachelor's rooms, said :

" Oh ! How sweet your room is ! What lovely flowers ! "

He touched with his finger the painted paper where improbable yellowish pansies bent their cleft chins.

She pretended to dress herself. He stopped her with one hand and holding his feathered cap in the other, lowered, he said with a thousand graces :

" Beautiful Thierrette, I adore you. "

" Really ? "

" Too true. I'm mad about you. Don't you see it in my eyes ? "

She saw all she wanted to see and in spite of that asked :

" Will you still love me to-morrow ? "

" Always. "

" Always is a long time. Tell me a little shorter time shat I may believe you. "

" Eighty years. "

" Still less.

" Seventy nine and a half years. I speak from the bottom of my heart, Thierrette. If I am offering you a long love, it is because I hope to live to an old age and I shall love you all my life. "

Thierrette let herself be persuaded. Her unworthy and delightful lover had understood from the commencement why she had refused for almost one hour to hold out and open her arms. It was because previously she had not judged it decent to grant that to anyone.

Was she right to let Giguelillot be the first to take this vacant space next to her? Can the reader doubt it? Thierrette was, however, careful and if on this June afternoon she suddenly found herself accessible to a man's caresses, her body supple and her breasts firm, it was because in the secrecy of her room her senses conquered without fight all her energy.

In default of moral force, Thierrette showed courage; then passion; then zeal. The sum total of these qualities passed, and by a long way, the standard of modesty set by the young girl of the hall of fruits.

She began by accepting the proofs of this first occasion without a murmur, going in fact a step farther with a vigour which was auxiliary to the design; and gradually becoming enthusiastic over the revelation which had suddenly penetrated, Thierrette showed that she would frustrate it no longer under any pretext and that she would not allow one simple momentary peaceful contemplation. Giguelillot, polite prisoner, gave proof of his solidarity.

All the same, at the very moment when she searched his eyes and thought that she would certainly find there the flame of a love as violent as hers, the little absentminded page was thinking of other things.

He told himself, not without respect but also not without candour, that he was wasting his time with a regrettable ease : that he had become not only the favourite page but also the counsellor of King Pausole : that in this position he ought, above all, to counteract the influence of the ominous Taxis : that to do this it was not sufficient to send this solemn man back six kilometres making fun of his shadow, but that it was necessary to act whilst he was straying, make inquiries without him, direct affairs, and on his return present to him the irretrievable with a pained air.

These reflections had plenty of time to mature and even to bear fruit in the form of a happy idea, for the young ardours of Thierrette measured neither minutes nor the approach of dusk.

The happy idea which came to him was a kind of stratagem which at first sight appeared to him to be a little complex, a little weak and far fetched, but not too much so to succeed.

He baited it thus :

" My darling, " he said suddenly, " I loved you at first sight, but now I couldn't bear to leave you for a single morning. "

" Oh, no ! Don't leave me ! "

" You know that I am page to the King. My costume

causes me to be recognized everywhere. How shall I be able to go out and how hide myself? Listen to me. You dress yourself in the winter, don't you? Where are your clothes?"

"Why?"

"Give me a skirt and a shawl, a scarf to cover my short hair and the straw hat with a broad brim that you put on to go in the fields. Also give me two milk pails to carry and let me go out like that. I will wait outside whilst they search the farm and until the King has gone without me; then I will come back where you like and we won't leave each other all night."

"It's true," said Thierrette. "We cannot see each other here. During the day, the place is empty and to-day I have nothing to do because the King is here. But, what would happen if they found you here to-night?"

She rose.

"Dress yourself quickly. The sun has already set."

She helped him, passed the skirt over his head, fastened the linen sleeves over the blue doublet, knotted the shawl, bulging it in front, wrapped the silk kerchief over his head, fixed the big harvesting hat and said:

"Now go. The milk pails are in the first room on the ground floor. Take two. It is nearly dark. I am sure that no one will recognize you. To-night I will go alone to the little wood of olives on the right going towards the palace. And you?"

"I shall be there."

"Every night?"

"Every night."

"Oh! I think you're lovely."

She took him in her arms again, and Giglio found it

most difficult to put on an air sufficiently obtuse so as not to guess that this kiss of farewell would have consequences.

He went out, crept down the stairs which did not seem solid to him, and found the dairy where the evening's milking stood, still steaming and frothy.

Bending down he raised the handle of the first pail, pulled, straightened his shoulders, but never succeeded in lifting the pail with its entire load of milk and cream.

A syllogism of the most simple kind and the only one accessible to his tired mind demonstrated that since ' one ' goes into ' two ' , if he could not lift one pail, he would be all the more unable to walk with a pair.

Very calm and still resolved on decisive expedients he tilted the lip of the pail towards the doorway and created a milky way on the dark blue tiles.

In a similar way he emptied the next pail and adjusted the covers taking care to let the froth whiten the edge and run down the sides. Then he lifted the empty pails with the ease of an acrobat.

" For what I want to do, " said he, " a crown of froth suffices. "

Impudently he went right up to the curtainless window through which he had surprised the sleep of King Pausole. The King was still asleep, his nose a little lower and his beard crumpled.

It was night. In the Midi, in spite of what Voltaire says, the summer days are shorter than behind the trees of Auteuil. It was not eight o'clock when Giglio dressed as a peasant girl and carrying the pails in his hands passed between the forty guards beneath the porch, who still held their tulips, slightly withered.

When he reached the road, Taxis, dusty and proud, crossed his path.

" Hi ! " called Giglio.

Taxis did not recognise him, for the voice was disguised as also the clothes and gait.

" Well ? What do you want ? " cried he.

" Are you looking for the King ? "

" That's no business of yours. "

" Of course not. I said that... it's because if you were looking for him... as he has returned to the palace..."

" What ! "

" He was terribly angry that you weren't there. But that also is not my business. Good-night, sir. It is a beautiful night. We must pray that it rains a little. "

Taxis made a movement as if to say " How annoying. "

He pulled the rein of the patient Kosmon and for the second time turned back.

Meanwhile, Giglio, with an even and well balanced step followed the road to the little village. His arms were as rigid as if he were carrying twenty litres of heavy milk in each of his closed fists. He passed dark houses, he avoided passers-by, and, to add a definite reason for his new costume, he arched his back like a girl carrying her mistake.

The Hotel du Coq which he entered was only a little inn, surrounded by an old garden. One went in through the kitchen, and as it was dinner time, neither the innkeeper nor the servants had time to look at him.

After the first greetings to which they hardly had time to answer, he explained in a stupid voice :

" I am new to the farm.   I have brought milk for the gentleman and lady who are dining in their room. "

" Go up.   They're on the first floor.   The double door, " said a busy servant.

" It is the lady in green, isn't it ? " he repeated calmly.

" Yes, I tell you.   Go on. "

Giguelillot gave a sigh of contentment.   His thoughts in the arms of Thierrette had not been badly devised.

Amongst the various hypotheses which might have appeared in the midst of doubts, he had put his finger on the true one.   The fair Aline, confident of the apathy of the King, had not left the hotel on her first night of love.   This settled, it did not need much skill to guess that she would hide herself in her room all the same, that she would secretly take her meals there, and that in a wayside inn this peculiarity would be sufficient to point her out.

He was going towards the staircase when the cook stopped him and pointing to the two pails :

" You aren't going to take all that upstairs ? " she said.   " There is enough there for twenty people. "

" It's all right.   It isn't heavy.   The lady will take what she wants. "

" And then you're late.   They finished dinner ten minutes ago.   The table has been cleared. "

" All the better.   It will be for during the night. "

Without hurrying in any way, he went upstairs with the same swaying and heavy step, found the double door, knocked the two empty pails together as if by accident and called out whilst tapping on the door :

" Madame !   I've come to do the room. "

VIII

WHEREIN THE FAIR ALINE HAS HER BATH ABOUT FOUR O'CLOCK IN THE AFTERNOON

> " The chambermaids, mother, and some
> ladies I was allowed to see, such were the
> mistresses of iniquity who taught me evil
> practices at an age when I was incapable
> of doing wrong. "
>
> *The Triumph of the Celibate* by a Young
> Lady of Quality, 1744.

IN the wood of olives and red pines where slumber had overtaken her, the fair Aline slept for nearly ten hours, from dawn till vespers.

On awakening, if she did not murmur " Where am I ? " like the heroine of a fairy story, it was because next to her, silent, and raised on one elbow, Mirabelle was looking at her with a watchful tenderness, already almost conjugal.

" It is you, " she said, " And are we alone ? No one has found us ? Good-morning, Mirabelle. Did you sleep well ? "

No, the dancer had not closed her eyes. Used to sleepless nights she had passed this one in waiting and desire. During the first hour of day, she had knelt in front of Line's face to throw her shadow on her. But later, after the light had changed, a tall crypress, black and opaque, having taken over the same care, she had arisen to steal some figs and when eventually the fair Aline had abandoned her last dream, they both set to and ate them.

The meal was meagre and the shade hot. Over the myrtle bushes they saw the blue reapers in the golden crops and passers-by on the road.

" You see, " said Mirabelle, " We are by no means alone. We can't stop here. Will you walk as far as Tryphemia ? The town is two leagues from here, it is not far. We will hide ourselves better there than in the woods. "

Line clung to her shoulder and they crossed the fields. A little further on they came to the first village. The road was white and deserted. An inn stood on their right.

Its facade freshly painted the colour of straw, its shady arbours, its garden, its old trees suddenly tempted Mirabelle.

At this hour, the peasants were working in the fields. There was no one near the open door : if they slipped in quickly, there was no witness to give them away. Such was at least the reason or rather the feeble pretext which made her so quickly obey her whim.

" Let us go in there, " she said.

" Wherever you wish. "

They were given the best room. Immediately, Line wanted a bath and a new sponge and a basket of cherries

and some chocolate and a fan and some lemonade and some ice cream, a lot of ice cream, and some hot water a lot of hot water.

She got these very precious things and then fastened the two bolts. Mirabelle followed her to embrace her; but Line clasped her hands, smiled behind a little pout and put on a pleading voice explaining that it was hot, that they were alone, that no one would scold them, in short they could undress together and get quite naked.

Mirabelle shivered.

The simplicity of Line disconcerted her. Used to all the expedients of urban debauchery, to resistance which allows itself to be overcome, to bodices which yield to one hook, to many hot petticoats, to hospitable drawers, the dancer no longer understood the state of mind of this little girl who demanded nudity as the correct costume for a game, without any of the transitions customary on divans.

The women who successively, behind the scenes, in cabs, on the ground floors of houses, had taken it upon themselves to form, by means of intimate conversations, her young mind subjected to their influences alone, had done it in such a way that Mirabelle imagined their kind to be of two types, always opposite : chaste women and satanic women. In her idea there was no feminine character between extreme propriety and perversion. And as at a very early age a necessitous aunt had asked her to choose between virtue and vice, without unduly insisting on her embracing virtue, she had learnt every vice so as to distinguish herself as soon as possible in one of the two parallel paths which in her eyes represented the moral future of a pretty child.

Mirabelle, at the dawn of her eighteenth year, and as a good Frenchwoman and reader of novels, did not suspect that there was a third path, and that one could be naked without having in one's eyes the flame of ancestral lust (as our novelists express it). For her, the gesture of a woman was uniformly the mimic with double meaning of the Statue of Modesty or Blatancy : who did not hide herself, drew attention to herself : who did not protect herself, desired to incite.

Listening to the fair Aline and seeing her innocent eyes Mirabelle said simply :

" Are those the customs of Tryphemia ? What a curious country ! "

She was the first to take off her clothes with motions which alternately hesitated or hurried over the buttons. She did not dare to smile once, and even, surprised at her confusion, she did not know what to do with her arms when she had nothing more to take off.

Standing up, nervous, her hands clasped behind her head, one leg trembling and her body supple, she bit her lip, bent her supple neck and constantly looked in different directions.

Meanwhile, seated before her, her chin resting on her fingers, Line finished her examination carried out with prodigious interest.

Mirabelle impatiently cried out :

" Do I please you ? "

" You remind me... Do you want me to tell you of whom ? Of a statue of Narcissus which is at the end of the park. But Narcissus is a man... You are the first girl whom I have seen thus : I have never had a girl friend, you know and I see papa's wives only from a distance. I think you are much more beautiful than they. "

In fact, and except for a small detail which it was not necessary to examine all the time, one could strictly have taken Mirabelle for a young man. It was not without good reasons that she played parts in male disguise. Such was the ambiguity of her form and carriage that to mime the *jeunes premiers* with their true physique she had no need to don either doublet or breeches. The *tutu* alone sufficed.

She was tall but thin, with straight flanks and flat stomach. Her legs, the legs of an agile dancer proved their robustness by a fine and complex system of muscles, which came to the surface when she stood erect. The upper part of her body was more slim.

On the pale and delicate skin of her chest two little dark dots alone marked the place of her breasts. Her brown hair, short and curly, divided in a parting on the right and swelled out into a wave on her forehead.

This type of beauty is not exactly that which inspires lyricism in Hindu poets; but Mirabelle, who did not read many of the stanzas of Bhartrihari, willingly felt herself to be 'different' and even *piquante* according to the style of compliments which she received after midnight. She was therefore not offended to hear her new little friend declare, as many before her, that she resembled a boy. Brought back by this phrase to the line to which she was accustomed, she came briskly and sat herself on the knees of the fair Aline.

The latter had not taken off her green dress.   Mirabelle wanted to undo it herself, and this slow disrobing was interrupted by endearments which Line found most pleasing, without, however, daring to return them.

Gaily, she threw both arms in the air much as another threw his cap over the sails of a windmill, sat cross-legged in the flowing clear water of her bath and shivered with pleasure, her loins in motion.

But suddenly, returning to doubt and twice pressing with one hand on her sponge, she asked whilst raising her head :

" Is it really true, Mirabelle, that you are not a man ? "

IX

WHEREIN PAUSOLE, HAVING SHAKEN OFF THE MELANCHOLY
OF REGULARITY, EXPERIENCES THE AFTER-TASTE OF
IMAGINATION.

> She resembles those flooded waters
> which, far from all line of reasoning, last
> through the night and with muffled waves
> enter your house whilst you sleep.
>
> LOUYS DORLÉANS. — 1631.

SEEING that night was falling and that the King
Pausole still prolonged his refreshing siesta, the
farmer told his daughter to await the King's awakening
whilst he went up to his room to put on the dark suit
of his distant youth, and arranged the feast which he
had to improvise.

The little Nicole, youngest daughter of the farmer,
was a young lady consumed with hope. Her four
sisters over a period of twenty years had chosen husbands
of different class as the wealth of their father had grown
more solid and more vast. The first had obtained, or
rather seduced, a young trainer of monkeys who, after
having had the happiness of giving her a child, travelled

still further on the path of concessions in giving himself for ever. The second had married a bailiff. The third, more difficult, a society procurer. The fourth was the wife of a Prefect. After this continuous rise towards honours and divers fashionable circles, Nicole wanted no falling off.

When she saw the King enter the farm of her ancestors, Nicole believed that her fate was approaching in person, purple of raiment and crowned.

Hardly had Pausole fallen asleep, than she began intriguing to be left alone with him. At first it would not be permitted, then as the hours passed and the royal nose drooped more and more towards the beard, the sleep of the illustrious visitor took on an eternal aspect which obstructed all precautions. The farmer slipped off, leaving Nicole on guard.

The little girl felt her heart beating : it was the hour of her destiny.

Ah ! What was she to do and how was she to act the part which fortune was offering ?

All she knew of court etiquette was from the poems and dramas given her each New Year by her sister, the wife of the Prefect. That was something; even though one does not perhaps always speak to the Prince of Wales in the language of H. H. the Princess Maleine, of Blanche Triboulet, or of Herodias, one is not completely ignorant regarding the throne if one has studied literature, thought Nicole.

And she proved it.

Taking from a painted china vase a rose made of gilded

paper, she approached the King, kissed him on the forehead, stretched out her right hand and repeated in her best manner :

" Oh, King ! Come forth from your dreams ! Awake ! See ! "

" Hum, " yawned the King. " What is it ? What do you want ? "

" I am here, " stammered the girl. " I am here, I the Unknown, I the Artless, the Strange, slender and naked, I am here ! " *

" My child, " said Pausole, not yet quite awake, " one should never rhyme two adjectives together, much less four or five. Apart from that, all you tell me is very charming. But who are you ? "

She was slightly disconcerted, and then continued rather faster :

" I am the first star. I am the one believed to be in the tomb, but who rises. My breast is troubled, voluptousness oppresses it. I never weep, I never smile ! "

The King fell back in his couch and opened his mouth with terror.

Nicole went on, faster and faster :

" I plucked this flower for you on the hillside. Oh ! I feel that I am living in a supreme moment... Oh ! dream of my nights, dear desire of my days, whom I never expected but ever hoped for, I long to see you and to see you again, and here is my heart that beats... "

" Oh, that... "

---

* Je suis venue, moi l'Inconnue, moi l'Ingénue, la Biscornue, menue et nue, je suis venue.

"... only for you. My lord, I have never looked with fear on the august majesty imprinted on your brow, for a young man is beautiful, but an elderly man is grand. Since I have placed my lips to your cup still filled with the kisses of the Zephyr who will raise me anew, Pausole, take your lute, look. I am beautiful; the exalted dawn, as a flight of doves crosses a field carrying flowers. "

" What are you talking about ? " shouted the King in such a voice as to silence her at last.

But at the same moment, and as the terrified girl stood with gaping mouth, Pausole saw beyond the window many lights flitting, here and there; he saw torches approaching, people running, arms waving, a sort of gigantic sheep lower its shaking head from the level of the upper windows down to the ground. The door was flung open and Diane à la Houppe came in.

" Ah ! " she cried. " I knew it. "

Poor little Nicole hid behind the King.

Pausole giving a table a resounding knock with his large hand cried out :

" By Heavens ! What does all this mean ? Am I still asleep or have I gone mad ?... Taxis ! where is Taxis ?... Gilles, Gilles ! Djilio ! Giguelillot !... Where is my minister ? Where is my page ? Where am I, myself ? In what brigand's cave has this ambush been laid ? "

" Ah ! Sire, you are in my arms, " explained Diane à la Houppe.

" You are in my shadow and I in your radiance, " corrected Nicole.

" The deuce take all women and courtiers, " swore the King, now beyond himself. "Taxis ! but why doesn't he come? Taxis! Taxis! Giguelillot! I shall never get out of this by myself. Where are my guards, my soldiers? Why did they break their lances? This was indeed the right day to do it. This fellow Giguelillot is a scamp. Taxis was quite right in speaking ill of him. Taxis! But where is he hiding? They have all abandoned me, delivered me into the hands of madwomen, delivered me into the hands of madwomen."

Indeed, in the midst of a continually growing din, Diane, dragging Nicole by the arm, gave her a fine sounding box on the ears. Willing hands tried to separate them.

" Taxis! Taxis! " repeated Pausole.

And he in his turn struggled, unrecognised by the farm girls who had hurried in at the sound of the quarrel. People were gathering in the doorway, giving advice and shouting. Sharp cries were heard in the courtyard mingling with the whimpers of Nicole, the barking of all the chained dogs, the sepulchral bleating of the enormous mount which had borne the Sultana on her flight, when above all the clamour the plaintive voice of the farmer was heard wailing :

" A camel! A camel! A dromedary in my house! "

X

HOW GIGUELILLOT ARRIVED AT THE BED-SIDE OF THE FAIR ALINE, AND WHAT ENSUED

Mulier quaenam pudibunda ?
— Quae tegit faciem cum indusio suo.

Nugae, Venales, 1644.

BEFORE showing how the preceding scene was cleared up, we must find Gilles again at the point where we left him, according to the fundamental rules of romantic tradition.

He presented himself then dressed as a peasant girl at the door of the fair Aline's room, invoking a false reason borrowed from domestic customs.

" Come in, " cried a voice.

He entered most sedately and looked around him.

Neither in the bed, nor in the room was there anybody.

However on the wall there hung a green dress, a man's breeches and several underclothes which we will not detail, indicating the presence of at least two people.

Calmly raising his voice to the medium of soprani :

" Monsieur is not there ? " he said.

" Why ? " replied the voice.

" I have something to say to Monsieur. "

A mad laugh came from the bath room : the little door opened slightly.

" Well, go on.   What is it ?

" Couldn't Monsieur come here a moment ? "

The mad laugh became even louder.

Then there was silence, a sort of alarm, and after a lot of whispering :

" Are you alone ? " asked the voice.

" Yes, Madame. "

" Lock the door. I am coming. "

Giguelillot locked the door, and as an extra precaution put the key in his pocket.

Then calmly, not hiding from a chambermaid, the fair Aline came forward. She held a bunch of muscat grapes between her hands and her teeth, and that was her entire costume.

" Monsieur cannot come, " she smiled. " Speak with me. "

Although he believed himself to be gratified by the favours of Thierrette, the page, before this apparition, felt reborn in him all the fires with which Pyrrhus was inflamed : but showing an exceptional reserve on that evening, he thought it dangerous to prolong an examination which would have damaged other projects.

He resumed his masculine voice.

" Madame, I deeply regret having seen Your Highness... "

" A man ! A man ! " cried Mirabelle, running into the room with a most aggressive air.

" Ah ! we are discovered, " cried little Line.

And she lost consciousness in the arms of her friend.

Gilles, doubtless very astonished, but nevertheless prepared by his experience of the intimate side of life for this sort of surprise, opened the bathroom door, made sure that neither in the room nor in the adjoining apartment was there any other lover than this young girl with short hair. Everything was immediately explained.

He made two gestures.

The one said : " How clear it all is. "

And the second : " How charming. "

Then whilst Mirabelle carefully and with caresses revived her little accomplice whose pallor was heartbreaking, Giglio shut himself in the closet, took off his skirt and shawl as also the scarf and straw hat. He did his hair, put on his cap, brushed his blue doublet, pulled down the legs of his yellow trunks, adjusted the flap and washed his hands in warm water.

Then, presentable, he came out and bowed.

Line uttered another anguished cry.

" Good heavens ! One of papa's pages ! "

Mirabelle had risen with flashing eyes. Obviously she was repressing a desire to hurl at the intruder a quiverful of insults (she would probably have said " shovelful ") which the prolific language of the " wings " easily supplies to the dancers during moments of battle.

But she repressed it well, for instead of breaking out, she seized Giguelillot by the wrist with a trembling hand and forcibly drawing him into the bath room, she embraced him with a passion in which he saw at once an alien purpose.

She seized him in her arms, moulded her naked warm body to his thin tights and placed a kiss of a penetrating type on the page's lips. Then she showed him in concise terms that he could dispose of her beyond the limits of propriety and at any time he wished, if he would, in return, show himself charitable towards two unfortunate friends, not give away their hiding place, not assist at their games and taste the pleasures of the one sufficiently to forget the other.

"Well," said Giguelillot, "You have a nice opinion of me. It only remains for you to offer me your rings with a statue of painted bronze. Come! Calm yourself. And now ask my pardon. Better than that. Clasp your hands together. Lower your eyes. Say 'I beg your pardon, sir, I will never do it again.'"

Mirabelle kissed him once more, but this time on both cheeks.

"You won't say anything?"

"I had never dreamt of it."

"But you are the King's page? You come from him?"

"Pages are not dressed as farm girls when given official missions. I assure you it is not in the protocol. No, really."

"Then, why have you come here?"

"Because in half an hour, if you haven't left, you will be in prison."

"Ah! I knew it! I wasn't believed. But for whom are you doing this? Which of us two are you saving? It is not me because you don't know me. Is it her?"

"Obviously it is both of you. Otherwise, I would

have found a way of separating you. Have confidence
in me. Do as I tell you and hurry. There is not much
time for any of us. I am warning you at the last moment
and I am taking the risk of being surprised in this room
at any moment. That would prejudice my career."

Three little knocks on the door interrupted the
conversation.

"What can you be doing in there?" asked Line
anxiously.

Mirabelle opened the door and went back into the
room.

"He has come to warn us, darling, to save us. What
do you think? They are already pursuing us."

"Who?"

"The King," said Giguelillot. "He left this morning
with his Grand Marshal and me. I sent the seigneur
Taxis in an absurd direction and I left the King sleeping
in a local farmer's house. But Taxis will return, the
King will wake up and you will be caught as in a cage,
Highness, in less than a quarter of an hour."

"Quick, Mirabelle, let's get dressed. My dress!
My stockings! Where are my stockings?"

The page stopped her with a sign.

"Ah no! you are marked. Your costumes are
known. You must change them, that's obvious."

"But we haven't any others."

"Excuse me. I have brought one. In the country
in which we live, one dress is sufficient for two people."

He ran into the bathroom, came out with the milkmaid's
clothes and without further ado put the long skirt on
the bewildered Line.

" We are in a hurry, " he said. " It is I who am dressing you. "

The skirt trailed on the floor. He lifted the waistband as far as her chest and crossed strings round her waist : all this was soon hidden by the little pink Spanish shawl which he tied in a tight knot in the middle of her back. The broad brimmed straw hat completed the disguise.

" Your turn now, mademoiselle..... "

" Mirabelle. "

" Oh ! really... "

" Why do you smile ? "

But Giglio had not the time to explain his impertinences. He made Mirabelle sit down, lifted her short hair and put in four pins, fixed on top of her head a little round empty box which bore the trade mark of a scent maker and which was lying untidily on a table. Then he wound the orange silk scarf round it.

" There, " said he, " I have made you a *chignon*. You are ready. "

" Is that all ? "

Giguelillot put on the voice of a smart dressmaker : " You surely would not dress yourself to go out, Madame; you would be so noticeable. "

" Excuse me, " protested Mirabelle. " I am not a Tryphemian. I was born in Montpellier, in the rue du Petit-Saint-Jean... I'll put on my suit or a dress, if you have one to give me, but I'll not go out like this, my friend. "

" That doesn't seem to have worried you for the last quarter of an hour. "

" Now, a man in a room is quite natural... Had you been fifteen I would not have hidden... But outside in the street in front of no matter whom...

She leant her back against the wall and hid her face in her hands.

" Oh ! I'm so ashamed. "

Line went up to her.

" Would you like my dress ? I will go out quite naked; I don't mind. "

" No, no ! " said Giglio. " The Princess might be recognised. It is she who must be hidden; the peasant's hat and this short dress are not too much. Let her keep them. You, on the other hand, no one knows who you are. The police take you to be a young man. Put them off the track once more if they start the pursuit again. It has been abandoned by order but all may be changed to-morrow morning. I am responsible for nothing between midnight and noon. There is not too much time to save yourselves. Each of you will hold one of these buckets I have just brought. You will go out quietly, but openly and calmly. Those you meet can tell the police that at nine o'clock they saw two milk-maids pass carrying milk, one whose face they did not see, the other tall, dark and naked. I defy whoever it may be to guess from that description that it was the fair little Princess Aline with the unknown person they are pursuing. "

"How well thought out, " said Line clapping her hands. " And how kind you are, sir ! I'll kiss you if my friend will allow me. "

" No ! " said Mirabelle quickly. " We haven't time. Let's leave at once, since we must.

" One moment ! " said Giglio. " Where are you going ? To Tryphemia ? Where will you sleep to-night ? "

" At the hotel. "

" That's perfect. So that your descriptions may be given in six hours by the servants. "

" Anyway we can't go to private houses, nor sleep on a bench in the Royal Gardens ".

" That was never contemplated. You will take the second turning to the right, in the Avenue du Palais, then the first to the left, cross the square... Will you remember that ? "

" Yes, yes. "

"... and keep straight on till you reach the rue des Amandines. Ring the bell at number 22. It is the house of the Tryphemian Union for the Protection of Childhood, an excellent institution which gathers together minors of both sexes that are found to be brought up with too much severity. "

" And shall we be left in peace there ? "

" Obviously. That is the Society's object. "

" Are there boys there ? " asked Mirabelle.

" Three sections : one for girls, one for boys and one mixed. You may choose. You will be asked further if you want the dormitory or a private room. They are very kind in that house. "

" But supposing they want our names and addresses ? "

" You will refuse them. They are used to children not daring to say where they come from for fear of being returned to their families. I know these good old people. They will do all they can to protect you even

if they discover who you are.   Don't forget the number :
22, rue des Amandines.   And now quickly !   Be off ! "

They went out hurriedly, Mirabelle pressing the page's
hand, and Line giving him a long glance of farewell in
which there was nothing but gratitude,

Giguelillot was alone   The square marble clock
struck half past eight.

" I am late, " he said to himself.   " But it's not worth
while hurrying any more. "

He examined the room.

It was in great disorder.

A large divan which certainly looked suspicious was
still covered with a clean but tumbled sheet; it had two
pillows, one on top of the other about the centre.
Although the table had been cleared, a banana lay handy
on a china fruit dish.   Across the mirror of the wardrobe
a little phrase traced with the sharp point of a ring
testified to an extreme and repeated happiness.

In a corner, Giguelillot discovered the theme of the
clock, a group of ' Paul and Virginia ', probably removed
by Mirabelle as having a bad influence.

On picking up this curio, he found the white envelope
of a letter, addressed " To His Majesty King Pausole. "

" What ! " he murmured, " she was writing to him ? "

The envelope was not closed.   Giglio, having become
the confident and accomplice of the fugitives, unfolded
the letter without hesitation, read it, sealed it and placed
it in his purse.

Just as he was seeking the best way to escape, his eyes fell on the clothes hanging on three pegs.

He could not leave them.

In case of an inquiry, it would point too clearly to the fact that the fair Aline and the unknown person had changed their costumes.

On the other hand, should he destroy them?

How?

Hide them?

Where?

Have them taken away by others, that would be the best course. It was the Saturday of Whitsun. To-morrow, a great feast day, two little peasants would be delighted to air this blue suit and green dress in the neighbourhood. Thence a false trail, a precious false trail.

Giglio took off the sheet which covered the large divan, packed the clothes in it, went out on the balcony, and with a mighty throw hurled the bundle over the wall into the next courtyard.

Then he let himself down into the garden by means of a pillar and crept in the shadows till he came to the hedge at the end, looked for an opening, found none, made one and was outside.

It was certain that Thierrette was already waiting for him in the little olive wood, the same wood where Mira-belle had led the fair Aline some days earlier.

Giguelillot, distracted enough by the recollection of his two *protégées*, felt no desire to see poor Thierrette again, but he would be sorry to make her wait in vain during the long night hours as also to deprive her of the satisfactions for which she showed such warm longing.

He was meditating on this question when he found himself before the door of the farm house. And discovering the forty guards still standing beside the entrance, said to himself :

" Ah ha !   Taxis guarantees these men. ' There are amongst them neither veterans nor rakes. ' Well, it's easy to prove.   Halloo ! "

The guards gathered round him.

" Halloo ! " repeated Giguelillot, " Which of you would like to spend the night with the prettiest girl in the village ? "

" I !   I !   I ! " they cried in unison.

" Do you all accept ? "

" Yes, yes ! "

" Good.   Go to the olive wood on the right of the road.   There you will find a milk-maid called Thierrette if I remember rightly.   Tell her that duty calls me to-night, but that I send her forty lancers with a bouquet of tulips.   Go ! and if she resists, do her the honour in spite of herself. "

As they were already galloping off, Giguelillot called out into the night :

" But do it respectfully, and one after the other. "

BOOK III

I

HOW THE FORSAKEN HAREM HOISTED THE STANDARD

OF REVOLT

> Why should man blush to expose one
> part of his body more than another?
>
> WESTERMARCK.

THE Harem gave one wail only, but an uproarious one, when Mme. Perchuque, first Lady in Waiting, announced on the stroke of twelve that the King had gone on a journey.

" On a journey ?   He must be ill ! " said a disrespectful voice.

" The health of His Majesty is happily flourishing, " replied the old lady nodding her black bonnet.   " God grant that it may so remain for a long time. "

" But why has he gone ?   He must have altered. "

" Ah ! " cried Diane à la Houppe.   " He has gone off with a woman. "

Mme. Perchuque, her elbows close to her sides raised her hands and her eyes.

" An adulterer, Lord ! Do you believe that possible,

ladies ? The King is incapable of acting towards Your Majesties with this depravity. He has left this palace with a view to fetching Her Highness the Princess Aline who disappeared mysteriously the day before yesterday. Forty guards precede him. One page follows him. M. Taxis accompanies him. "

At these words the hubbub became general.

" Taxis has gone ! Taxis ! No more Taxis ! " repeated three hundred ecstatic voices.

" Then we are on our holidays ? " said Queen Gisèle who had just left a convent.

" To the gardens ! To the gardens ! " was the cry.

" No ! To the theatre ! We will act charades. "

" To the Banquet Hall ! "

" To the Pages ' quarters ! "

Aghast, Mme. Perchuque hurled herself towards the door and barred it with her gaunt body.

" Ladies ! Ladies ! What incontinence; truly, what ill conduct ! "

" Let us pass, good Perchuque... "

" I cannot allow it. "

" And why *not*, pray ? "

" Because Taxis deigned to hand over his duties to me at the same time as his responsibilities. I beg you, ladies, to understand my feelings. If I prove myself unworthy of the confidence reposed in me, there is for me not even the place which I occupy at your feet. I shall be hounded from the palace, degraded, perhaps exiled... "

" So much the better " was the answer. " Perchuque, we don't recognise you any more. Since you replace

Taxis you are the worst of rogues and you shall pay for him. "

From the centre of the hall there was a cry :

" Listen to me. "

" I demand the right of speech, " said a joyous little voice. And over the black, golden and red carpet formed by the crowded heads of the women, could be seen the childish form of the future Queen Fannette, who was treated by her companions like a little sister, and whom the King would not wed at the age when she herself would have allowed it.

Perched on the warm shoulders of her great friend Alberte and crossing her long legs over the breasts which she envied, she held up her right hand, clicking one finger against another.

" Speech !   I ask to be heard ! "

" Let Fannette speak, " they all cried.

She was surrounded.

" Friends, " she said, " they have treated us like children... "

" Shame ! "

" When they took us, poor innocents, from our schools, we believed that we were being freed.   But all we did was to change our gaol. "

" It's true. "

" Prison for prison, I prefer the first.   There they gave us tasks, I know, but as we did not do them, it was only more pleasant.   There we were forbidden to play at married couples in the dormitories — but we did it just the same. "

" Yes, yes.   It was delightful. "

" There, above all, we had days when we could go out, weeks of leave, and months of holidays. Whereas here we spend all our life crying for being ' kept in, ' but having done nothing. "

" It's unjust. She's right. "

" Well, this can't go on. If one of us asks by chance for twenty four hours of liberty, she is always offered the same choice : Repudiation or chains. Let us go on strike and we shall soon see if the King repudiates three hundred and sixty six women like us ! "

With one acclamation the strike was voted : but Fannette had not finished. Still upright on Queen Alberte, who took part in the applause, she continued with a pretty gesture :

" Perchuque, will you let us pass ? "

" I cannot... I cannot... " repeated the old lady, bristling with apprehension.

" Then we shall force our way, but first of all you will have to undergo a severe punishment, you old broomstick. We shall hang you by one foot on the statue over the pool, your skirts turned over your face to hide your confusion, and we shall take possession of your white knickers as our standard of revolution. "

Mme. Perchuque was heroic.

" Victim of my duty ? Right ! " she said, " Here I am. I shall die of shame, but M. Taxis will not have placed his confidence on my aged head in vain. "

Some of the women would have liked to spare the poor old lady such a treatment devoid of the respect due to aged persons : but mobs and children are implacable.

In the midst of an increasing uproar, Mme. Perchuque was actually suspended by her left foot to the central

Statue : her black dress was hastily drawn over her apoplectic face and her venerable knickers descended the grand staircase at the point of a halberd, whilst in their wake a rosy crowd tapped the hundred resounding steps with slippered heels.

But when this still shouting crowd reached the Gate of Honour, Taxis stood on the threshold, and at his appearance a sudden silence fell on the multitude.

" What does this mean ? " he screamed.

It was enough. At once, scattering through the halls in flight down the corridors, swarming to the top of the stairs, the army was swept away by the storm of defeat. About seven or eight young women, those who in grave circumstances coped with the Grand Eunuch, stood their ground nervously : and bad fortune overtook them as, let it be said, was to be expected.

Taxis, drawing out a dirty note book, said :

" I will take a few names. You, madame. And you. And you. Those shall be punished for the rest. I flatter myself that I shall present to the King an unsparing report on which action will swiftly follow. "

During this time, Diane à la Houppe, instead of taking the trouble to argue with this man, had profited by the general disturbance to reach a neighbouring room, interrogate a servant and learn that Taxis had returned alone, that the King had not left the first house in the hamlet. Immediately running to the unguarded stables, she jumped on the back of the camel she used for riding, in order to escape.

Taxis had barely started his inquiries in the harem before the young Queen was speeding the main road on her long striding mount.

II

WHEREIN M. LEBIRBE COMES UPON THE SCENE AND WHEREIN PHILIS UTTERS A SHORT CRY

One with beautiful green eyes
Smiles, raises herself and looks at me.
SAINT-AMANT.

GIGUELILLOT was following with a critical eye the charge of the forty guards on the little grove of olive trees when a slim and polite old man appeared, took off his hat in an old world manner before the royal doublet.

" Milord, " he asked, " are you the King's page ? "

" Sir, I have that signal honour. "

" Good. I am M. Lebirbe, president of the League against Domestic License, officially recognised by a Royal Decree dated July 1st, 1899. I live in a house close by, spontaneously called the Chateau, not so much on account of its size, as by comparison with the modesty of the surrounding buildings. This house is certainly not worthy to give shelter to my sovereign, but I have learnt that His Majesty has halted not far from here on his way to the capital. Seeing that it is getting late, I doubt if the King wishes to start his march again, at this advanced hour of the evening, and without having the temerity to give him an invitation, I would nevertheless have it made known to him that all is ready under my roof to receive him and his suite in case he should deign to pass a night there. The apartments that I would dare to offer him have since their origin borne the name of " The King's Chambers, " awaiting the eventual visit which I delighted to foresee, knowing that King Pausole disliked long marches and that my house was midway between his palace and Tryphemia... "

" Have you any daughters, sir ? " interrupted Giguelil-lot.

" Yes, milord. May I ask why this question ? "

" It is the mark, the guarantee of a highly respectable and decent house, Monsieur Lebirbe. Without that I would not listen. "

Then with a familiarity accepted as benevolence he took the left arm of the old man and drew him forward.

" Lead me, " he said. " You have arrived at the exact moment when I am charged by the King to prepare a resting place for him. Whilst being certain that you have arranged everything in the very best manner possible, I will however accompany you so that I may on my return present the personal report expected from my vigilance. "

They entered the iron gate of the courtyard at the moment when Giguelillot was finishing the phrase which made an excellent impression on M. Lebirbe.

On the entrance steps Mme. Lebirbe and her two daughters stood anxiously awaiting news.

" Well ? "

" I have hopes ! This young lord is the King's page and has come to view our efforts. "

Having thus presented his companion, the old man introduced in turn his wife, then his elder daughter Galatée and his younger daughter Philis who modestly turned away her head, but looked with curiosity out of the corner of her eye.

Galatée was big and tall. She appeared to be a little over twenty. Her hair, of a dove-coloured fairness, was tightly drawn back but not without taste, and she held herself upright in her grey linen dress finished with a large white collar.

Timidly clinging to her arm Philis in contrast to her sister was naked, at least if one were not to take into account as articles of clothing, her large garden hat, her floating tresses and her scarlet moiré belt tied at the side in a large bow. Her large eyes could not be more than fifteen years old. Her chest, only recently blossomed, bore two young divergent breasts, all rosy with anxiety and pleasure. She did not take her eyes off Giglio.

" Allow me to precede you, " said M. Lebirbe bowing again.

" Certainly, sir ! " said Giguelillot.

Turning from a narrow passage, the page who was the last, passed his two hands under the arms of Mlle. Philis and drawing her to him by her chest planted a silent but exquisite kiss behind her ear.

" Ah ! " she cried.

" Have you hurt yourself ? " asked her father.

" I pricked myself. It is nothing. Don't stop. "

Giguelillot at this moment formed the most favourable opinion of all that had been done to receive King Pausole. He decided that the room was sumptuous, the bed truly royal, the frieze in the best style and the pictures worthy of a museum. Doubtless, further to give testimony to a more direct sympathy with the family of his host, he extended his investigations to the private apartments and succeeded in establishing the fact that the rooms of the two girls were separated and provided with double doors, which was even more than he had dared to hope.

Thenceforth his opinion was unshakable.

" I will tell the King ", he said, " that he would be unable to find anywhere a more worthy reception than at your fireside, Monsieur Lebirbe. "

Speaking thus, he retired, followed by a radiance of smiles.

III

WHEREIN A HORRIBLE CRIME IS DISCOVERED

> I lay on the grass, deprived of all my
> faculties and burning with a thousand
> desires.
>
> Comtesse de Choiseul-Meuse — 1807

THE little left breast of Philis was so poetically moulded that Giglio, alone on the road, felt himself to be as lyrical as an Alexandrine.

" I have just five minutes, " he said to himself, " just time to compose a sonnet. "

And not wasting a moment seeking a subject for his poem — a trouble which he was not used to taking — he rapidly raised his eyes to the friendly stars.

To the west, Venus, pearl of the sea, shone brilliant as a fragment of the moon and as she can be seen in the clear Southern nights. Before her in an arc of a circle of which she formed a distant centre, Sirius, Pollux, Castor, Capella, and the triple Perseus appeared to gravitate to her flame. And Giglio, imagining mysterious lines from the planet to the stars, decided that first of all he would make with this celestial chandelier a fan studded with nine gems (this for the first tiercet), then the eight doves which draw the chariot of Aphrodite Oranus (this for the fourteenth line).

" Now, " he thought " for the rhymes of the quatrains... lux... Pollux... Nux... No ! were I to add ' dux ' it would sound like a Latin exercise. Let's take Capella in the second stanza ; it is a good word ; ' par delà '... followed by a *rejet*; — a past definite — that's it. For feminine rhymes... ' Pollux, la double Chèvre et le triple Persée ' With that rhyme it will soon be done. "

But suddenly he cried :

" Ah ! What is it ? What do you want ? "

Two little bare arms were raised in front of him.

" It is I — Rosine — Don't go into the farm. I believe that they want to kill you. "

He recognised the young girl to whom he had sung of flowers and fruits on a garden seat in an arbour red with strawberries.

" They want to kill me ? Who does ? " asked Giglio with pardonable curiosity.

" Everyone ! " replied Rosine. " Terrible things have happened and they have blamed you for them all. Come here behind the palm trees and I will tell you. Sit close to me. "

The page was careful of his yellow silk tights and the earthy bank offered did not allure him. He first of all waited till Rosine had seated herself, then he sat comfortably on the girl's lap and passed an arm round her neck under the most tender of pretexts but also the most untrue.

" Well, tell me. What happened ? "

She told him all, but all at once, without special attention to that beautiful clarity of language which doubtless had no place in her literary theories.

A camel had been stolen, the machine store plundered, the reapers broken, the pitchforks damaged, the tiled floor cracked — it was a catastrophe... The dairy, too, was in a most lamentable condition — the milk spilt and the buckets taken away. On the camel there was a beautiful lady, a very beautiful lady in a large basket like a bower with carpets.

" She found Nicole on the King's lap. Nicole swears that she had behaved herself, but the lady said that she saw... Anyway, it isn't certain, but Nicole is quite capable of it. She knows a lot, that child, she is always reading and she tells you love-stories as though they had happened to her. As soon as the lady entered she flew into the devil's own temper, the King too and everyone shouted. You ought to have seen it. Never has anything been heard like it... And the worst of it is there is a victim. The dairymaid has been murdered. "

" Murdered ? " repeated Giglio becoming pale.

" Murdered. "

Then in the manner of a suburban dweller who reads a paper every morning she added :

" Theft was the motive for the crime. "

" What are you talking about ? "

" Ah ! There are wicked people, all the same. It was in order to take her four garments that they killed this poor girl. Just a kerchief, blouse, winter skirt and hat. She had been heard crying out in the late afternoon but nobody dared to go up to her. It was the gentleman from the palace who went in first, the same one who locked the lady up... "

" Oh ! my brain ! " groaned Giguelillot. " What lady ? What gentleman from the palace ? "

" A gentleman all in black with a flat hat. "

" When did he arrive ? "

" In the middle of the battle. He calmed it all in five minutes. Apparently, he is a Minister, a man who looks very serious. Without him they would never have reached the end. "

" The end of what ? "

" Of the lady. He shut her up in a bread storeroom with a candle and a large book like a breviary to console her, he said. Then, when all was over, he was told that the dairy was all upside down. He asked for the dairy-maid. She could not be found, and they dared not go up to her room on account of the groanings that had been heard. But he, he was not afraid. He went up right away. And what did he see ? It appears that she must have been killed on her bed. Half the sheets were on the floor and the rest soaked in blood. The crime was flagrant, as he said. And the body can't be found. Probably the murderer has thrown it somewhere. The gentleman from the palace is going to have the wells emptied. "

" And it is I who am accused of this crime ? " interrupted Giglio who at last was beginning to understand.

" Yes, of the murder and everything else. The King is waiting for you to send you to prison. The gentleman from the palace even said that for you they ought to re-establish tortures and burn you alive at the stake. "

" A modern Servetus to pass the time. "

Giguelillot rose and struck a dramatic attitude.

" Now, Rosine, you do not know what courage is ?
The hero of old, the gallant knight, the indomitable
paladin, the bellicose marauder, the lion ! The lion !
Don't you know what a lion is ? "

He ruffled his hair, struck his chest and gave forth
a roar that hurt his throat.

" What are you going to do ? " asked Rosine fondly.

" Defend myself in person.   I am going to the farm ! "

" But they'll annihilate you.   I won't let you go. "

Giguelillot clasped her to him with a fictitious thrill,
then freeing himself by a step backwards said in pulsating
tones :

" Remember always that you have embraced a man for
whom death is but a word...   Farewell ! "

As she fell fainting on the ground, Giguelillot went
away with a light step, lit a cigarette and commenced a
second sonnet on that celestial sector which interested
him.

It was no longer about the chariot or the fan : the
central star became the eye of a peacock and the eight
others the ends of the plume : the plume then set itself
on the brow of a woman : her tresses increased, became
the sky and millions of pearls floated in it.

IV

HOW GIGUELILLOT PRESENTED HIMSELF TO THE KING

AND WHAT WAS SAID BOTH FOR AND AGAINST

HIS GOOD CAUSE

> Ipsa tulit camisia :
> Die Beyn die waren weiss.
> Fecerunt mirabilia
> Da niemand nicht umb weiss;
> Und da das Spiel gespielet war
> Ambo surrexerunt :
> Da ging ein jeglichs seinen Weg
> Et nunquam revenerunt.
>
> Popular German Song— 16 th century.

GIGUELILLOT did not go straight to the King.
He slipped into the stables by a window for fear
that his advent might be awaited at the main gate, and in
passing he patted the nose of the little zebra Himère,
who snorted with satisfaction.

As the poor animal was standing disturbed before an
empty manger, Giguelillot took the good and fresh
straw with which the rack of Kosmon had just been filled
and passed it on with a simple left to right motion.

This Kosmon exasperated him : he was paying dear
that evening for the honour of belonging to a huguenot

rider. The page was not satisfied with removing his nourishment; he took from a peg the big clippers and cut all the hair off his tail which then showed as a miserable and badly shaven stump. He cut almost all the hair off, leaving here and there a few sad looking bristles; then with the utensils used on the farm for branding cattle, he composed and branded on the lustreless coat of the old horse the figures 1572, hoping that the Huguenot would read therein defiance, insult and threat.

Satisfied with the marks of infamy with which he had decorated the living pedestal of Taxis, Giglio followed the long corridor that led to the bread store.

As Rosine had told him, the unfortunate Diane à la Houppe wept almost over the humid dough of this farinaceous prison. He did not know her because the pages, for reasons which it is useless to discuss, were not as a rule allowed to take tea with the Queens. But as soon as he saw her by the light of the candle set on a little table, he deplored not having been introduced to her before she entered the harem. Diane, ignorant of the fact that she was being spied upon by a pair of eyes from behind the shutters, had taken up a homely attitude which carelessly displayed her very particular beauties. She lay in an oriental manner, her hands behind her head, her back against some cushions and, doubtless to get fresh air after a torrid day, she had spread open her knees with the soles of her feet together. She was in the habit of sleeping thus. Giglio, although surfeited with recollections of fairly recent events, suddenly felt his spirit led astray towards new presumptions, and he retired not so much in order temporarily to keep them in subjection as to meditate on the chances of immediate and secret success.

Gracefully and with a face as calm as though all the bombardments of the royal power had not been directed on him for the last hour, he entered the throne room without knocking, where Pausole still perturbed was eating a badly cooked dinner.

" What ! You here ? " cried the King. " You dare to return ? "

Taxis who was gnawing his food at the far end of the table threw himself towards the door to barricade it, but Giguelillot saw his intention. He locked the door himself and handed the key to the Minister, saying :

" Here you are, Sir. "

Pausole, standing up, placed one hand on the tablecloth and raised the other accusingly.

" You have come back ! " he said. " Truly your coolness is even greater than your crimes ! You make me undertake a senseless journey, you take me from my palace to throw me into this farmyard, and you leave me for six hours without guard, without support, without advice in the midst of a revolution. You post an idiot at my bedside, you cut the throat of a peasant woman, you plunder the farm, you disband my troops so as to leave me at the mercy of the anger of the crowd, to the madness of I know not what woman escaped from the harem, through your fault once again. And at the end of this abominable day of pillage, murder and lèse-majesté you present yourself hat in hand with a sinister smile. You did not think to meet me again alive. "

" Sire, " replied Giguelillot, " I do not wish at first

to hurry to prove my innocence, because I am not
concerned about myself, but you and your well being,
a hundred times more sacred to me than my own safety. "

Pausole fell back in his chair.

In a respectful and quiet voice the page continued in
these honeyed words :

" Your Majesty's most ardent wish at this moment is
to rest in bed.   This gentleman here does not seem to
have occupied himself with this important question.   I,
in his place, have had the honour to have caused to be
prepared today in a neighbouring castle some vast apartments provided with thick curtains and spacious beds
which are worthy in every way to receive the King."

Pausole diminished his frown by one crease and then
by two.

" Secondly, Your Majesty cannot have forgotten that
you took this journey with the end in view of finding
Her Highness the Princess Aline and bringing her back
to the palace.   We have but two clues to this august
affair.   Her Highness " coming from a little wood of
olive trees " was recognised at the Hotel du Coq.   I
have sent the forty guards to this little wood of olive
trees to gather, if possible, further proofs.   And I myself
have made inquiries inside the hotel in absolute secrecy.
The Princess has already left but I have brought away
most precious information : no more nor less than a letter
in her own handwriting.   Here it is. "

Opening his purse he drew from it a letter and placed
it before the King whose state of mind was gradually
becoming transformed.

" I thought I might withdraw the guards, " he continued.   " Your Majesty never asks for them and never

needs them, so beloved are you by the people. If any scandal or trouble has occurred today it is through Monsieur the Grand Eunuch whose sole duty it is to preserve order in the Harem and who no doubt arranged matters badly since one of the Queens was able to escape in the least secretive of costumes and come here to excite not only the mob, but comment. "

" Sir, " cried Taxis, " I call on you to prove... "

" Come, Come ! Let him speak, " said Pausole. " This little page is defending himself from a grave accusation. He does not make a bad case of it. I wish to hear him. You will reply : it is the right of a public minister. But our duty is to listen to arguments in favour of the defence, especially when they are expressed moderately and frankly as in this case. "

" I have nothing more to say, " replied Giguelillot, unless Your Majesty interrogates me as to the details of my inquiries. "

" No, " said Pausole, " we will go into that to-morrow. "

" And the murder, " insisted Taxis violently. " He doesn't mention that, I notice. A dairymaid named Thierrette had her throat cut whilst in bed, at sunset, by the hand of this page. "

" That is hardly probable, " said Giguelillot " since she was very well at nine o'clock at night.   She is at this moment in the wood, and the guards (your guards, Taxis) are having their lusts calmed by her in the intervals of their search. "

" My guards. What a suggestion ! "

" Go and see. You will be edified. "

" This is not possible. "

" It is. "

" My guards are married. "

" Doubly, to-night. "

" They are above the flesh. "

" I would never have dared say so. "

" This pleasantry falls flat. "

" Like their attitudes. "

" But the blood ? The blood that is scattered everywhere ? The blood which still stains the victim's couch ?"

" The King told you this morning, Sir, that in Tryphemia no blood is shed except the voluptuous blood of virgins or that of little chickens. "

And as the King gave in with a short, clear laugh, Giguelillot with lowered eyes pronounced this conclusion :

" Are we not on a farm ? It must have been a chicken."

V

WHEREIN EACH ONE IS TREATED ACCORDING TO HIS VIRTUES

HÉLÈNE. — " Fata-lité ! Fata-lité ! Fata... '
PARIS. — " ...lité ! "

MEILHAC et HALÉVY.

" OF your pleading, " said Pausole, " I remember the first point. You have had prepared for me a comfortable resting place and you are watching over my well-being : you are a far-seeing man. During this terrible journey, I begin to see that you alone have made an effort in every direction where action was necessary and that evil has come from another. Shut up ! Taxis, you are hideous and stupid. As an Algebraist, your spirit is wrong : as a Protestant, it is narrow : as a Eunuch, it is envious. You're nothing but a numbskull. Go and indemnify the farmer for all the damage done here of which nothing will persuade me that this young Gilles is the author. It is a question which will be dealt with in the right time and place, to-morrow or later, and which does not interest me in the least. Busy yourself with the charges which I leave behind me : take the Queen who escaped back to the Harem. "

" Oh, Sire ! " said Giguelillot " Could you be so cruel ? "

" Eh ! What should I do with a woman during a secret journey ? "

" Don't humiliate her. She loves you. Let her follow you in silence. "

" Just now you were deploring the fact that she had joined me. "

" I regret that she was able to escape and upset your hours of repose — but the thing is done. It must be accepted, if only to silence the mockers. "

" It is not Queen Diane's day, " interrupted Taxis. " I am opposed to all favouritism which detracts from system. "

" What does Your Majesty decide ? " asked Giguelillot without too much irony.

" I don't know, " replied Pausole. " Please get out of the habit of asking me for decisions every minute. It fatigues me. Who is my counsellor at ten o'clock at night ? You, Gilles ? Do as you like and be sure that I will approve, my friend, for possibly there are just as good reasons for pardoning as for punishing. I prefer to leave myself to your judgment than to draw lots. Go, speak in my name for I have confidence in you. "

The page bowed, fetched the key, went out and freed the unhappy Diane, not without letting her know in a whisper that he had had the honour to plead for her.

His projects were extremely simple. Within two hours, in all probability, Taxis taking power on the stroke of midnight would reverse all the decisions of his predecessor : but the Queen would have had time to instal herself at the chateau.   Giglio would go to her and Diane would imagine that she was giving as reward all that she was offering through desire and immediate thirst for vengeance.

Returning to the King, she kept a wounded and silent bearing.   As she seemed to be waiting for words of regret, the King held out his hand, but he did it affectionately, and obviously feared being received with rapture.

" Houppe, you will not go back to the Harem to-night, as I threatened you earlier.   I am passing the night in this village, and so are you, but it is none the less true that I am most annoyed with your escapade as also for the worry it has caused me.   Come : we will go out on foot.   Taxis will look after the horses and my page will take your hand.   In the meantime, give me my crown ."

Giglio took from the peg the purple mantle and the light crown.   Pausole robed himself, and gave the order to depart.

Four young girls, with only their night veils and carrying torches, slowly walked before the King, for the twenty five paces which separated the farm from the neighbouring castle.

Behind, followed Diane à la Houppe led by the page, her hand held high and at a respectful distance.

She looked long at the King : then as he did not turn round, she cast her eyes at the page.   After a thoughtful examination which lasted several minutes and which covered the young man from head to heels :

" What is your name ? " she said.

" Djilio, Madame, " he replied.

And he thought fit to give vent to a melancholy sigh.

" Djilio ? " said the Queen.   " That is a pretty name. "

VI

WHEREIN M. LEBIRBE AND KING PAUSOLE FIND WITH SURPRISE
THAT THEY ARE NOT IN AGREEMENT ON EVERY POINT

> " It seems to me that the conjunction
> of Venus will cause men and women to go
> together to the bath quite nude. "
> Prognostication of Maître Albert — 1527.

PAUSOLE was received at the gate by the courteous
M. Lebirbe.

At the same instant, at the window, Philis turned round
angrily.

" You see, mamma, you've blundered. You have
made us put on dresses and the King arrives with a lady
who has none.   We shall be made to look ridiculous. "

" I asked your father, my child.   It was he who told
me to dress you. "

" You are young, Philis, how young you are, " Galatée
said simply.

" What have I said that's so childish ? "

" It is best to *start* with a dress, " explained the elder
girl.

But Philis did not understand at all, and as the King

introduced himself, all three, their dresses in their hands, dropped low curtseys before the gate.

After the first sentences, full of respect, the mistress of the house was led away by Diana à la Houppe. They had relatives in common and sitting close to one another they exchanged reminiscences.

Giguelillot, in another corner on a divan apart chatted to the two girls. His voice, loud to start with, became more discreet, then dropped almost to a whisper, and soon not a sound could be heard except occasionally, a stifled laugh.

In a window M. Lebirbe was holding forth.

" Sire, the League against Domestic Licence, a League of which I have the honour to be President, is a work of moralization and of public salubrity. I know that it has your approbation... "

" Oh, yes, of course, " said Pausole. " Of course. But remind me once more of its aims. I cannot recall them for the moment."

" Its aim, its sole ambition, is to merit its great motto, which is expressed in three words " Example — Frankness — Solidarity. "

" Those are fine words, " said Pausole. " But how do you interpret them ? "

" Your Majesty knows that the Opposition in Tryphemia wishes to hold to the old principles especially as regards home life and costume. In that society all the women, even the prettiest, are clothed up to the chin when they go out of doors and only consent to justify masculine admiration in the secrecy of a closed room and before the lover of their choice. This shows an egotistic, avaricious and depraved soul. "

" Agreed, " said Pausole.

" The men of this same society fight desperately against the propaganda of our influence and for what they call the decency of the streets, but as they have the instincts of the flesh in no less degree than their adversaries, they go and hide their lives in low houses where love is debased, is transformed and becomes a form of vice. "

" They're wrong, " said Pausole. " But what has that to do with you ? "

" Sire, we are of the opinion that acting in this way they are not only hypocrites and false, but, if I may say so, monopolists. In our century, it is no longer admitted that an amateur may acquire a gallery of pictures and keep the enjoyment to himself. Any man who possesses three Rembrandts must let everyone in to see them or lay himself open to attacks the correctness of which no one will doubt. Well, the same reason whence this custom springs should produce in every right-thinking man a superior and benevolent conscience which would prevent him from shutting up behind the walls of his house all that ancestral idleness has added to the beauty of woman and all whose art, luxury and space adorn the love in his arms. "

" Those more or less, are my sentiments. "

" This society which calls itself benevolent and which passes for such in many places, gives an evil example whose debauchery I would wish that Your Majesty might fathom. To place a dress on a young girl is to awake at once in the young people unhealthy curiosities which they are forbidden to satisfy : it is prompting vice. I recognise that this type of perversity is becoming rarer

and rarer in Tryphemia. In nearly all families the women
order their first dress at the time of their first pregnancy.

" But, I repeat that it is in certain houses where they
dress even the little girls that the harm is at its worst.
The example given bears fruit; often it is discussed;
sometimes followed; a deplorable hesitation leaves the
national customs floating between two extremes. One
no longer knows what fashion demands and I myself,
(shall I confess it ?) I do not always dare to present my
children in the strictly pure costume which I set myself
to extol. The aim of our society is to put an end to this
uncertainty by unifying the customs at the same time as
the consciences. "

" And how will you bring that about ? "

" By two means. Firstly propaganda. The resources
of the League are considerable. We have secured the
twenty years' lease of a large piece of ground which is
part of the Royal Garden at Tryphemia : there we have
built an open air theatre under the trees and we give ballets
and new plays which attract an enormous crowd and are
played according to our doctrines. "

" That is to say ? "

" That is to say, according to life itself, in its reality
as in its beauty. Should the scene represent an interesting
discussion in a lawyer's office, the actors are dressed in
black, according to the customs of the place; but when
in the middle of a love duet the prima donna cries : " Oh !
Voluptuousness ! Ecstasy ! Rapture ! ", she is naked,
logically, for the contrary would be unsuitable. And
when the ballet presents to the audience a Venus, the
three Graces, twelve Captives or sixty Bacchantes, it is
evident without any mystery that the same people should

be seen as within the frame of a picture, for it would be inconsistent to have two artistic representations of the same subject — one in painting and one for the theatre. "

" So far, I agree with you. "

" Further, by means of the cheap book, the newspaper and pictures, we are spreading untiringly amongst the people the taste for human nudity with the double sentiment which it inspires, in the spirit on the one hand and in the flesh on the other, if one can separate into these two free and distinct elements the one being urged by love. These books refrain from teaching that which most of the popular novels describe, that is to say, the best way of picking a lock or murdering an old woman, and if one must go into details, we prefer to suggest to the workgirl a little-known sensuality than to teach her in six columns how to make counterfeit money. "

" And if this sensuality is sterile ? " said Pausole.

" If a transitory joy is sterile, what does it matter ? A woman's body holds eighty thousand ovules and cannot conceive more than eighteen times without danger. So (taking this figure of eighty thousand as strictly precise) it follows that nature itself and the design of the Creator confer on a young girl in the middle of her twelfth year a reserve of seventy nine thousand nine hundred and eighty two pleasures both sterile and lawful, in no way frustrated since they *could* not bear fruit. The important thing is to keep the woman in the natural inclination which makes her lean towards voluptuousness. Let her have the simple or multiple desire, she will conceive sooner or later and bequeath existences which will justify her own. But it is clear that matters will be entirely different if it is suggested that virgins who do not find a husband will have I do not know what ideal of solitary life and one of negation which is fatally sterile, abominable and unnatural. "

" Continue, " said Pausole, " I am most anxious to see where you will ultimately arrive. "

" I hasten to add that were we to propose constant but discreetly balanced research into all the delights with which lovers are rewarded, we should find that those which have conception as their result if not as their aim are by far the most frequently described in our popular pamphlets. These are also the ones which are still in general favour, whatever the doctors may say. Proof is easily furnished. At the time of the foundation of our League, the excess of births over deaths in the city of Tryphemia was no more than four per cent. To-day, in the third year of our teachings, it is nine per cent. In order to promote and to subsidize, if I may so put it, a fruitful emulation in the lower classes of society, we have instituted competitions from which courtesans are excluded as professionals, and in the spring of each year we crown those young girls who by special care have raised their physical beauty to the highest point of perfection and who by their intimate talents and the warmth of their embraces are acclaimed by general vote as having provided each evening the most commendable example in their districts. "

" All this, " said Pausole, " is propaganda. But you employ two different means, if I have understood you aright. What is the second ? "

" I am coming to that," replied M. Lebirbe. "Our propaganda by public performances, books, journals, pictures and prizes at annual competitions is chiefly directed, need I say, towards the young girl. She has to play high stakes to follow us; the trials of pregnancy and confinement scare her, and there is no need to seek further for the reason of her reserve in regard to the opposite sex. At fifteen years of age, a child of the people is apprenticed and learns her lessons. If she becomes enceinte she loses her place and in most cases her lover, and if she is attached to one or the other there is nothing left to her in the seventh month but misery, despair and physical pain. Well, we want her to brave all this, to to lay herself open to this and triumph ! The country demands it : she wants sons. Naturally, this is not the way we speak to the pupil; she would have the right to reply that the country would be no richer were she to present it with a child but she herself would be poorer. And we should never be able to make her see what was wrong with her reasoning. We flatter her with a totally different hope. What we do tell her and what she understands at once, is that the supreme pleasures of the rich belong to the poorest; love, for which fortunes are hoarded and which dissipates them, does not become more perfect the higher it gets in the scale. As soon as a workgirl knows how to be a lover, she can tell herself that she may ignore all the joys of life excepting the most intense, for she embraces and holds that one. "

" That certainly is correct. "

" That is why our ambition is satisfied when we know that after having read our brochures, the dressmaker or the mender after leaving the shop of an evening, goes into a neighbouring room and lives — thanks to us. For besides we know that her working hours are full of memories and lightened by hope. We know that her day will not he entirely weighed down under a task without recompense; that her bed will seem less disagreeable and her room less cold in winter if she closes her bare legs over a being she loves.   May she arrive at this point as soon as nature invites her; but whatever may be the sensuality which tempts her and which she chooses, we consider ourselves happy if she learns it at our school, for the leisured classes must share with the poorer not only their surplus riches but the too well guarded secret of their mysterious pleasures of which the people claim their share. "

" I would like to know, " said Pausole, " what your second method is. "

" I resume, " said M. Lebirbe. " In fighting the domestic licence, in bringing discredit on secret meeting places and on vile old men who disparage nudity only to find it less tame between the corset and the black stocking, we are making great efforts towards the antique and pure nude, we favour life in daylight, freedom of morals, example and direct teaching of restraint — in a word, the expansion of public voluptuousness in the country of Tryphemia. "

" Nothing would please me more, " said Pausole, " but your means ? "

" Our means ?   We have two.   The first I have told you, Sire, is propaganda.   The second would be a sanction. "

" A sanction ! " exclaimed Pausole.

" A penal sanction.   Our energies are being hurled against irreducible opposition.   On our side we have youth and the people; but we can do nothing or alomst nothing against a certain caste which is exercising an incontestable moral authority which we are fighting foot by foot. It is against this that I ask for arms, Sire, against this and for you, for the immediate victory of those ideals which are dearest to you. And first of all let me mention a law which we await anxiously and which you could sign to-night; the law of compulsory nudity for youth."

" Oh, no ! " said Pausole. " My dear Sir, Tryphemia is not a topsy-turvy world; it is a better world, at least I hope so, but I have not spared my people certain bonds in order to cause them to suffer other chains. To compel nudity in the public streets ! But really, Monsieur Lebirbe, it would be as ridiculous as to forbid it ! "

Then accentuating his first words by striking the air with his fist, Pausole said slowly :

" Sir, man demands to be left alone. Each is master of himself, of his opinions, of his behaviour and of his actions, within the limits of inoffensiveness. The citizens of Europe are tired of feeling at every moment the hand of authority on their shoulder, an authority which is made unbearable by being omnipresent. They still tolerate the fact that the law speaks to them in the name of public interest, but when it begins to interfere with the individual in spite of or against his wishes, when it directs his private life, his marriage, divorce, last wishes, reading, performances, games and costume, the individual has the right to ask the law why it has poked its nose into his affairs without having been invited. "

" Sire... "

" Never will I place my subjects in the position of being able to level such a reproach against me. I give

them advice, it is my duty.   Some do not follow it, it
is their right.   And so long as one of them does not put
out his hand to steal a purse, or to give a rap on the nose,
I do not have to interfere in the life of a free citizen.
Your work is good, Monsieur Lebirbe; let it spread and
be imposed, but don't expect me to lend you police to
throw into irons those who do not think as we. "

VII

WHEREIN AN ACCOUNT IS GIVEN OF A JOURNEY INTO A MOST REMARKABLE COUNTRY

> " I will recite some sonnets and believe
> that you will be able to guess their subject. "
> " Yes, " replied the Shepherdesses, "they
> will be about Love. "
>
> REMY BELLEAU.

AT this moment a small joyous and almost affected voice dared to call out from the end of the room : " Mamma, mamma ! What good fortune ! Monsieur is a poet. "

" A poet, Philis, really ? "

" A poet ! " repeated Diane à la Houppe. " Oh ! do recite some verses. "

Giglio approached, bowed and replied deferentially :
" Madame, it is sufficient that you have expressed this desire, to cause me to break all my vows, for I had sworn never to recite my own verses : but I know that you would never order anything that is not according to the King's pleasure, and I would like to be sure that I would not displease him by interrupting his conversation. "

" You would interrupt nothing, Monsieur Djilio : see, the King is listening to you. "

" Recite your verses, my boy, " said Pausole. " It would suitably break into my conference on interior politics, for M. Lebirbe and I were commencing not to agree, in spite of the utmost courtesy to each other. But choose a short poem which you know well because lapses of memory make a very bad impression on me. "

" Sire, " said Giglio modestly, " I have my complete works with me. "

He put his hand to his belt, undid the button of a short leather pouch like a cartridge holder, and withdrew three little volumes of 32 mo. super royal size.

One was published by the *Mercure de France*, limited to 183 copies, of which four were on flame-coloured satin, eight on dust-grey silk, nine on wrapping paper of a colour approaching goose manure, seven on lobster-pink old blotting paper and the rest on Indian laid paper. It was called *Mannequin d'Opale*.

The second was published by the Librairie Fischbacher. The author's portrait, reproduced by a curious process of photogravure, ornamented the title page and the title was *Larmes d'une Ame*.

The third was published by a Jew. On the cover a young and very gay widow, her veil over one ear, was lifting her black dress to her waist probably to show that she had nothing on underneath, and the title was so scandalous that perhaps it would be as well to say nothing about it.

(For after all, this novel is only being read by ladies).

Giguelillot seemed to hesitate, he looked at his hosts,

the King, Philis, Galatée and Diane à la Houppe...
Then he replaced the first two volumes and opened the
third at page 59.

" What a pretty book ! " said Diane à la Houppe.
" What is it called ? "

" *Yes.* "

" Charming ! "

" Just *Yes* ? " asked Philis.

" What more do you want ? " cried Galatée.

" Oh ! that says everything ! " sighed Diane.
And casting a veiled glance she added :

" It is a word that you have heard, sir ? "

" Never, Madame. It is only used in poetry. "

" How is it said in prose ? "

" One says ' No ! ' "

" It comes to the same thing ? "

" Happily. "

" Then it is merely convention. "

" A nicety ! "

" Why ? "

" Indeed, Madame, you cannot know... A very old
custom amongst Christian peoples requires that a man
cannot meet a woman without being obliged to offer
her a furnished apartment, with flowers, powder, hairpins
and emotions. The lady always replies ' No '. If the
gentleman retires she understands that he has been very
polite. If he insists, she represses his ardour. If he
says he will die if she does not accept, she does all she
can to save his life. There, Madame, that is what is
meant by ' no '. "

" I should never say that word, " said Philis smiling
archly.

But Pausole tapped the arm of his wide sofa with his hand.

" Come, read your verses. One should never answer ladies' questions. A man asks the questions of a pupil : he asks about those things he does not understand. But a woman puts the teacher's questions and only from those pages which she knows by heart. "

" Then, sir, " said Galatée, " what is modesty ? Tell me. "

" What has given rise to this — question of a pupil ? " asked Philis laughing.

" M. Djilio apparently believes that the women say ' No ' from discretion in the first place, then from pity if not from impulse. I ask him what he knows of our modesty, and I hope he will answer. "

" Modesty, mademoiselle (we are at our lessons, aren't we ?) modesty is a word derived from the latin meaning ' shame '. It is that sentiment which a lady feels when having found out by an impartial examination the exact value of her figure, she has to reveal to others that which she would rather have lamented alone. And nothing is more natural. "

Philis and Galatée consulted each other by a glance : but while the elder did not move, the younger went out of the room in silence, with a feeling of having been challenged and put on her mettle.

Pausole put out his hand towards his page.

" Gilles, show me your book, " he said. " What is this I see on the cover ? "

And as the page handed him the volume :

" Oh ! How terrible ! " said the King. " How can you publish verses under such a cover ? M. Lebirbe was just telling me that this sort of excitement only appeals to certain old men whose hypocrisy and stupidity we both of us loathe. "

" In Tryphemia, " replied Giglio, " it may be so. But in France where old men direct morals and make the laws, it appeals to the whole people. The *retroussé* is the national costume of French women. It is worn everywhere, at public balls, at concerts, at the theatre, at the Elysée, and even in society. In foreign caricatures, turned-up clothes indicate France between the English lion and the German eagle. If I have had a woman drawn on the cover of my book, dressed entirely in black except for the upper parts of her legs it is to show at once that I am dealing with Parisiennes ."

" What a curious fashion ! " said Diane dreamily. " Why please old men and not the young ones ? "

" Parisiennes want to please everyone and they have a very special regard for elderly gentlemen. It is expressed differently according to the particular woman and the hour of the day. "

" Oh ! You don't say so ! How curious these customs of an uncivilised country are ! "

" In the lower classes, the woman shows her deference to an old man by raising her foot to the level of his eye. This gesture is usually accompanied by an ironic or insulting exclamation : but the septuagenarian is enraptured. If this scene takes place at a public ball, the police and tradition insist that the woman shall show at the same time a multitude of underclothes, a quantity of imitation lace and soiled calico. The habitué of the Moulin Rouge or the Casino de Paris only admires the elegance of the thigh and cannot distinguish the difference between linen and cotton : the more linen there is, the better he likes it. If on the other hand we are at a cabaret, or in the street at night, or in a simple family circle, no linen must be worn to delight the septuagenarian by this salute of the stocking on high. The ethnologists put on record without explanation these contradictions of the French tastes. "

" You have lived in that country ? "

" I was born there, Madame. "

" Oh ! I beg your pardon. I thought you were Italian. You were saying ?... please continue... it interests me deeply. "

" Amongst the middle classes the gesture is different. On the pavement for instance a lady feels that she is being followed by a member of the Upper Chamber for whom she can have nothing but an utterly filial veneration. She shows it by a manœuvre which is fairly difficult to achieve, and which consists of raising the skirt in such a way as to mould it to her figure from behind, whilst disclosing the left calf. It is not in the least interesting, but the septuagenarian is bewitched. "

" I don't understand... "

" Nor I. Amongst the so-called upper classes the clothes are tucked in rather from the shoulders. This is how it occurs : the old man standing up and the young lady sitting down, the latter leans forward drawing her arms together and arching her shoulders. The posture is ungraceful, but the bodice opens out and enlarges : the old man's eye beams in that direction, and when the lady's breast is sufficiently obliging to show its form, its shades and the curiosities of its point, the septuagenarian cannot contain himself for joy. "

" But what do the young men think of all this ? "

" The young men ? Most of them think like their grandfathers. They obtain more complete ' *retroussés* ', that's all... The others dare not protest... "

" And the ladies ? "

" Oh, the ladies are so used to it. And anyhow it's the fashion, they can do nothing against it. Just now I heard M. Lebirbe telling the King that in his theatre the actresses in lovers' parts undress before singing ' Ecstasy ! Rapture ! ' But in Paris, Monsieur Lebirbe, no one would in the least understand it. The uniform of courtesans is a black corset and black stockings, with or without knickers : in former times these were even kept on in bed, according to the best authors. Nowadays, they are worn only in the room and there is one point gained, but does the public of the little theatres know this ? For them all naked women represent the same person, the only one they have ever seen in the illustrated papers : that is the Truth on M. Dreyfus. If this were brought on the scene, there would be a riot. "

" Ha ! Ha ! " laughed Pausole, " you ' re exaggerating a bit. "

" I even believe that he is inventing, " said Diane anxiously. " Such customs cannot exist anywhere. "

" Please God ! " sighed M. Lebirbe. " But they have penetrated even here, Madame, and hide their insanity in the secrecy of our houses. "

" In Tryphemia ? "

" In Tryphemia. "

" Not in your home, at any rate, " said Diane with a smile.

Philis came in again without any covering except that with which Nature herself was beginning to endow her. Behind her a servant in nut-coloured livery carried lemonade with tangerine sorbet.

She seated herself next to her sister on a settee for two and Giglio became restless.

Galatée examined with her hand the tidiness of her hair.

Philis removed with the end of her finger a little surplus powder on her hip.

" Well ! " cried Pausole. " That's enough, my boy. Read your verses : we are all listening. But choose those that are more proper than the cover of your book. You are speaking in the presence of two young girls. "

" Oh, Sire ! We can listen to anything. Mamma allows it ", said Philis.

Mme. Lebirbe broke her silence to give forth this aphorism which she must have read somewhere :

" When girls understand, one does not teach them much... And when they do not understand, one teaches them nothing at all. "

But as Giglio re-opened his book the last stroke of midnight sounded...

Taxis, always punctual, announced himself.

VIII

HOW TAXIS MEANT TO FOLLOW THE EXAMPLE OF THE FAIR
THIERRETTE

> All that which makes men dependent on
> each other as regards their pleasures,
> contributes to a great extent in giving to
> their habits an impression of tenderness
> and humanity so necessary to the happiness
> of society in general; also it has been noticed
> that men ill-formed by nature are of all
> mortals the most unsociable.
>
> FRERON — 1776.

THE Huguenot, with an air both obsequious and vain, bowed with eyes closed and mouth open.

At once, Diane à la Houppe sat sideways on her chair, pretending to turn her back on him. Her right arm supported on the back of the seat, she gently raised her left hand to the page and said :

" Why don't you read ? "

" Madame, " replied Giglio, " All my verses could be given to young girls to read for they speak of precisely those things which interest them most. But they are not written for Taxis and whilst M. Taxis is there, I beg for permission not to give him cause for shame. "

" Misery to him through whom this shame is wrought, " said Taxis lugubriously. " But the shame must come ! The shame must come ! "

" Who is this gentleman ? " murmured Philis.

" He is very badly dressed, " said Galatée.

" Did you see his hands ? "

" Ah ! and his neck ? "

" His teeth ? "

" His beard ? "

" And his tie ! Oh ! his tie. "

" How terrible he would look undressed ! He is quite right to dress himself. "

At the same time, Taxis approached the King.

" Sire, " said he, loudly, " I have the honour to ask for a private audience. Most serious events are taking place. I beg leave to remind you that as from midnight Your Majesty deigns to honour me with his confidence and I insist on being heard. "

" We will retire, " said M. Lebirbe.

" No ! " said Pausole. " Stay ! "

" Then I shall have to remain silent, " said Taxis.

" Oh, what a nuisance ! " repeated the King. " What a nuisance ! Cannot you make your decisions alone without troubling me at this hour ? "

" Does Your Majesty give me carte blanche ? "

" Certainly. "

" That is sufficient. "

And turning towards the page :

" I arrest you ! "

" Heavens ! " cried Madame Lebirbe.

" One moment, " said Pausole. " You are mad, my friend. I shall be obliged to have you removed from office if you behave in this vulgar way towards my best page in the house of the worthiest of my subjects. Madame, I beg that you will forget this deplorable scene at which my mind revolts ! Taxis is a conscientious functionary, who is sometimes useful, but of an excessive zeal and with a judgment distorted by I don't know what extravagant Chinese morality. He craves your pardon for the words he has just spoken. "

All the same, M. and Mme. Lebirbe, distracted by this scene, insisted that the King finished this conflict without their presence, and they retired, taking their daughters with them.

As soon as the door was shut :

" My friends, " said Pausole, " I'm tired of separating you and giving one or the other right. Settle your quarrel between you, but above all settle it quickly. "

Then he crossed the room and seated himself affectionately next to Diane à la Houppe.

Giglio with hands folded behind him, kept silent.

Taxis remaining at a distance let fly this vibrant insult :

" Well, sir, is this a principle of yours ? Have you set yourself the daily task of selecting some unfortunate girl, servant or peasant, and having her outraged by a mob, drunk with stupration and sensual vice ? "

" Outraged ? " said Giguelillot quietly.

" Yesterday, you bound one of the King's chambermaids to her bed so as to deliver her to the attacks of a dozen blackguards in turn. And to-night it is a farm girl whom you have thrown into the wood with forty satyrs. "

" Forty men chosen by you, Monsieur Taxis ! Forty

picked anchorites. And this is what they become when a woman is put into their charge. Ah! how weak is the flesh! How very weak is the flesh!"

— "The sight I had to look upon will never leave my memory. In all probability there never has been such an orgy displayed to the Heavens since the sad age of paganism, and had I not known, I should have believed myself to have been transported by a diabolic dream to the sewers and the brothels of Capua. The unhappy girl had her four limbs spread out in the most critical position, in the centre of five or six cavalrymen who were defiling her in I know not what ways, but all at the same time, and the rest of the gang were singing a hellish song while dancing round the victim."

"And was the victim protesting?"

"No, she was stoic. Wounded, I have no doubt, wounded internally from the violences to which she was being subjected, and more so from the shame to which her looks gave witness, she showed nothing. Her bravery was that of a martyr. Suffering under the outrage, she offered the other cheek, she asked unceasingly for new tortures. Had she sins to expiate? I do not know; but in the convulsions of her agony, the sublime child rejoiced. She herself proudly told me!"

"You see," said Giguelillot, "the ladies never find that they are surrounded by too many."

At this point Diane à la Houppe gave a long sigh. But Taxis stamped with rage and waved his hands frantically.

"Laugh!" he said. "Amuse yourself. Your laugh is sinister, young man! You are evil and lascivious. You have the soul of a Borgia! of a Richelieu! of a Heliogabalus!"

Giguelillot advanced and interrupted :

" Sir, I have a boundless admiration for Heliogabalus, and I am delighted that, in your eyes, I resemble him... "

" Ah ! "

" ...But you are making your historical comparisons in a tone that does not please me at all... "

" Sir... "

" And since the King authorises us to settle our quarrel between us... "

" Certainly... "

"... I insist that you apologise... "

" Never ! "

" ...Or that you arrange with me, without intermediary and without delay the conditions of a... "

" Not that either ! "

Taxis of a quick but nervous temperament stepped back a pace at each word.   He bumped against the door, opened it and wanted to disappear.

In the room which they entered together, Philis and Galatée, close to their worthy parents, awaited the issue of a conference whose curious uproar disturbed them.

" Madame, " said the page calmly and with respect, " I certainly should not end a private discussion in your presence, but you witnessed its birth through no fault of mine and, if you deign to consent, I will present to you my accuser, the Grand Eunuch, from whom I demand reparation. "

Then turning to Taxis, who had become livid :

" Sir, " he continued, " I despise you from my heart.

You are stupid, ambitious, servile; you have neither tact nor courage. "

" Do you insult me ? "

" I don't think so. "

" I make a note of that statement. "

" We were saying, " said Giglio smiling, " that you were without both courage and dignity. Nevertheless I am ready to give you the honour of a duel... "

" But I don't demand it ! "

" I offer it you. "

" I decline. "

" You refuse to fight ? "

" Sir, the Almighty has written in letters of flame on the summit of Sinai this commandment ' Thou shalt not kill '. Christ repeated it. Paul taught it to the Gentiles. And you expect me to touch a murderous weapon. No, sir, you do not know me. I wish to follow the noble example given me this evening in the little wood of olive trees. I also, when suffering, offer the other cheek ! I, too, will drink my cup of shame to the dregs ! I, too, will spread myself on the bed of affliction ! I beg your pardon, sir. I offer you a public apology. I shall proudly emerge from the fight victorious. See, I bend my head and I feel consolation in my heart. "

IX

HOW GIGUELILLOT INTERPRETED THE ANCIENT LAWS
OF HOSPITALITY

> It is customary for young girls to allow
> the hand to wander up to a certain point,
> but moral decency forbids me to tell you
> which.
>
> FISCHER : Ueber die Probe nachte, etc. 1870°

DIANE à la Houppe and the King, guided by their hosts, were shown to their rooms which for so many years had awaited the honour of a royal visit.

Taxis possibly had the intention to separate them, but the disturbance resulting from his dispute caused him to forget the fundamental rules of his politics of the moment.

This upset the calculations of the page who was most surprised. It was still worse when, entering the room with Pausole where she was to spend her third conjugal night, Diane cast glances of forgiveness and reborn love towards her husband.

Then Giguelillot felt himself bitten by the serpent of jealousy. This woman who was being taken from him, (for they *were* taking her from him) immediately acquired in his eyes the most fascinating seductions. Inwardly disturbed, anxious to drown the recollection in reality, he resolved on a diversion.

As a practical and determined young man, he was well armed. The pouch which held his books was completely equipped for all adventures and habits, a triple indispensable holder divided into three partitions of unequal importance.

The first held :

A button hook,
Six stay laces,
Smelling salts,
An inoffensive poison,
Face powder, white, rachel and pink (in handy little boxes)
Three lip sticks, quite new.
Pins, black, white and knob-headed.
Hairpins of various shapes,
Safety pins.
A folding comb,
A hand glass,
Several pharmaceutical products,
Finally several curious objects not absolutely customary.

The second held the three volumes of verse, and Giguelillot had included as dedications, or acrostics, four hundred feminine Christian names or pet animals' names, listed alphabetically so that a search in the midst of emotion could be carried out most easily.

(" Read !   Read !   That elegy... to Miquette...   You were Miquette !   I loved you to distraction, and you did not know it ! ")

The last division was the most precious of all.   Gigue-

lillot kept there a collection of thirty notes, simple declarations of love or declarations begging a rendez-vous.
These notes by means of their variety were suitable for
all occasions, and by the supply for the greatest urgency —
one never has the wherewithal to write in such cases.
There were tender ones, respectful, excited, literary,
timid, highly improper, despairing and practical ones.
Some said " Do not give me up ! " Others " Well,
yes ! I love you ! " Others " Go for a long walk
before coming to me, to fill up the time. " Some were
almost illegible as the ink was swimming in tears.

As soon as one of these notes had been transferred
from the pouch to a fair hand which would always be
curious and trembling even in the case of a hesitating
refusal, Giguelillot re-wrote it from memory for a future
occasion and the collection lost nothing. Envelopes of
various colours arranged in a known order, easily informed
him of the subject of the letter without the necessity of
opening it to verify the choice or the carefully chosen
vague terms.

On the present precious occasion, Giguelillot withdrew
secretly the third and fourth blue notes which in different
grades developed the theme : " I adore you. I shall
come to your room tonight. Open your door even if
it is only to send me away. "

And before leaving his hosts he was able secretly to
slide first one and then the other note into the two girls'
hands so as to ensure two chances to one of forgetting
Diane à la Houppe.

He went up to his room, undid his luggage, drew out
various articles of toilet, and occupied himself for a long
time with his physical appearance more from a sense

of politeness than conceit, for truly he was neither vain nor modest when he spoke of himself and took as little pleasure in paying himself compliments as in saying disagreeable things.

If women had shown him a certain amount of kindness, it was not, he thought, on account of his charm, but because he had disconcerted them, and if the circumstances are even faintly favourable, two sexes made for union quickly forget the reasons they imagine they have found of not doing their duty.

In one hour the last sounds were silenced on the top floor.

Giguelillot, carefully turning the handle of his heavy door, slipped into the long corridor and silently mounted the marble staircase.

Philis really did not have enough experience to play the part of a lover : she was waiting for him on the top step.

" Ssh ! " she said. " Oh ! how happy I am. Come quick. "

They entered her room. She turned to him :

" You love me ? How has that happened ? "

Giguelillot had not the courage to play his ordinary role, which in any case would be useless on this occasion. He gathered her into his arms, and she was red and laughing with excitement. He planted a kiss on her eye and another in the corner of her mouth, but briskly and as a playmate.

" You are very sweet, " he said to her.

" Do you mean that ? "

" Of course ! "

" What is sweet about me ? "

" Don't you know ? "

" I have never been told. "

" Well, this and again this : and that, and that — all of you. "

She began to laugh and then said thoughtfully :

" But other girls are better than I. "

" You're mistaken. "

" Unfortunately no. I've a cousin who comes to lunch every Sunday and when she takes off her dress in my room to go to table, I want to smack her because she is so much prettier than I. That feeling is dreadful, isn't it ? "

" Yes, you're absurdly modest, " said Giglio tenderly. " What do you think you are like ? "

" I ? Like a match. "

" Because your head is red and your body white ? "

" Above all because I am thin. You can't deny that. "

" I shall deny it at once. You, thin ? You are slender, as you should be. Girls of fifteen who are like elephants sometimes find husbands because their double size gives the illusion of bigamy : but not lovers, they are too difficult to run away with. "

Philis, who was easily amused gave a ripple of laughter and then asked very seriously :

" You have already run away with girls ? "

" A whole school. "

The girl looked at him with admiration.

" Tell me about it. "

" Impossible. It's a great secret. "

" Well, without names. Where did it happen ? "

" In France. I can't tell you more. "

" Were they big or little girls in that school ? "

" Both. "

" How many in all ? "

Giguelillot searched his mind for an extraordinary yet possible number.

" Thirty one, " he replied.

" None refused ? Oh ! I can quite well understand that ! You're such a lovely boy. I said ' yes ' like they did, you see. And again they probably knew what they were doing in following you, whilst I don't know at all. Or scarcely. "

" Really ? "

" My sister will never answer me when I ask for details. All that I have learnt is from my cousin. But she hasn't told me the most important things I am sure. "

" What has she told you ? "

Philis hesitated, smiling.

" You will laugh at me if I tell you. "

" I certainly will not. "

" I've probably got it all wrong. And then I don't know all the words. Anyhow, never mind, you shall tell them to me; here goes. "

And counting them on her fingers in order to forget nothing, Philis enumerated the little things she knew in a low, slow and circumspect voice, sometimes raising frightened eyes like a wavering pupil fearing the fatal zero.

Giguelillot listened with an increasing esteem. When she had finished speaking, he said whilst folding his hands :

" But, I beg your pardon, Miss Philis, what do you think that you don't know ? "

" The harm of it, " she replied simply.

She went on to explain :

" Apparently it is shameful to receive a young man in one's room. Does the harm take place with him ? "

" No, no, " said Giguelillot.

" But yes ! Papa forbids it. He never has young people to the house and when he is asked why, he replies that there are young girls here. It is clear that everything that I have just told you is a game which can hurt nobody, therefore it is not that that is forbidden. "

" Of course. I am sure that M. Lebirbe is protecting you against ' certain ' young people : those who don't know how to play, you understand. But if he heard that you were playing with me... "

" You ! But, good heavens, you especially. I don't know what you said to him to-night, but he fears you like the devil, and he gave instructions for a maid-servant to sleep on a mattress in the passage between my sister's door and mine. You know my sister sleeps over there. Galatée has a horror of servants and hates to be watched. She gave some money to the maid and begged her to go and sleep in the out-buildings as usual. Isn't that lucky, for otherwise I couldn't have seen you ? "

This confidence interested Giglio extremely. He had had ' yes ' said to him from two sides. He looked at little Philis and felt a scruple regarding her. He thought that as he was expected by the elder, and resolved to know her, he hardly had the right to lead the younger into irreparable indiscretions and that it would be better

Discreetly he confined himself to enlightening Philis on certain subjects about which she was inquisitive. He also gave her his advice, methods of musing and easy lessons, but he suggested nothing of which she did not know the elements.

He was in fact so reserved that at the moment when she begged him to attempt with her a fatal experience, he replied that on the brink of a serious illness he had made a vow never to act thus, however circumstances might favour it, and that anyhow according to the general opinion, these violences only brought about deception.

Two hours later he left, pretended to go downstairs, but soon returned on tip-toe and knocked lightly twice on Galatée's door.

The young girl opened the door herself, in a dressing gown buttoned up to the neck. She carefully closed the door, leant her elbows on it and said in the coldest of tones :

" Sir, I know all that you did this evening in a room at the Hotel du Coq. "

" What ? " cried Giguelillot, astounded.

" And I have decided not to remain silent if you approach me without permission. Now listen. I want to talk to you. "

X

Ἐγὼ δὲ μόνα καθεύδω
ΣΑΠΦΩ.

" ARE you threatening me ? " asked Giguelillot.
" I am warning you. "
" And according to your information, what did happen
in that room at the Hotel du Coq which I am supposed
to have entered ? "

Galatée took from a drawer an officer's telescope.

" I am bored, here, " she said. " I pass all my days
in my room and not knowing what to think of, I dream.
By paying my English teacher, I have succeeded in
getting certain forbidden novels. I like them very much.
I know them by heart and I have lived them myself alone
twenty times. I know all that André Sperelli has said
to Hélène, all that Henri de Marsay replied to Mme. de
Maufrigneuse, and M. de Maupassant has clasped me so
many times that I want to send him away. Well, I seat
myself at the window and through the slits in the shutters
I look through this telescope at all that goes on at the
Hotel du Coq. "

" Oh ! "

" Yes. Lots of things go on there and no one thinks of being spied upon, but that also is monotonous. I was fifteen when I began each evening to look on this varied spectacle. To-day, I am twenty-three. During the first two nights I was quickly taught. During the succeeding eight years I discovered nothing new which I had not already seen or easily imagined. However, these people appear happy—happier than I am, believe me. "

" Ah ! " said Giguelillot in a different tone.

" For months I have not seen anything so interesting as that which has taken place during the last three days behind the windows of the big room. Those girls were delicious. I pretended to have a headache and without a pause I have stopped here following their slightest movements. I have got up at nights to see if they had re-lighted their candles, and in this way I once surprised them at their waking between three and four in the morning. When I myself got back into bed, I couldn't sleep... "

She passed her hand over her forehead.

" I wanted you to disturb their secrets and to make them go away. But your secrecy and theirs and the care you took to throw their clothes out of the window proves that they were at fault and that you are their accomplice. "

" Quite true. "

" You admit it ? "

" At once. I don't hesitate. "

" Don't you fear me, at all ? "

" Not at all ! "

" Why ? "

" Firstly because your character is not nearly so bad
as you imagine.   Secondly, because I too am armed.   Ah
ha !   Brr...   I have a thunderbolt in my hand. "

" Will you show it to me ? "

" This is it.   M. Lebirbe, your venerable parent, had
stretched across your threshold a young defenceless slave,
doubtless with the object that if a ferocious seducer
appeared, the poor girl would act as prey and would
offer herself as sacrifice to save your honour. "

" That was not quite his object, but how do you
know ? "

" Mystery and novelettes. "

" Go on. "

" You put gold into this girl's hand... "

" This is extraordinary !   Did she tell you ? "

" ...and you asked her to go into the outhouses and
find the valet or the kitchen boy she likes best, instead
of passing a miserable night with no other reason than
obeying her master. "

" And then ? "

" Then ?   Well, as a girl does not generally send away
her guardian except at the time when she has the greatest
reason for not wishing to be strictly observed, and as
my presence with you as a sequence to this manœuvre
immediately proves our understanding, you may struggle,
shout, accuse me of all sorts of crimes, and no one will
believe that I am not here with your approval, mademoiselle, if not by your invitation. "

"And you reckon on taking advantage of that ? "

" In detail. "

" You are not very gallant. "

" What a distressing mistake. "

" Ah ! Explain yourself, please. You have already given me this evening a definition of modesty which is not in the dictionaries. Continue my education. Tell me now what is gallantry. I am listening. "

" In the sense in which you understand the word, mademoiselle, gallantry is a well-known but fairly subtle game which allows one to insult ladies with impunity whilst offering them that respect which they have the thoughtlessness to expect. It is also an excellent means of disguising under the most pleasant appearances that compunction which attacks most men when they find themselves alone with the object of their desires. As I am far from experiencing these sentiments so unworthy of you, and as your beauty leaves me no leisure in which to moderate those which disturb me, I shall be very ' gallant ' soon, but in the sense directly opposite to that which you look upon as so good : for that word also may signify the contrary to what it means. "

" And if I told you that I detested you ? "

" Then all the more reason. "

" Really ? "

" Yes. To obey you would be to leave you, that is to say to renounce you, and I should thus lose all hope of making you change your mind. If I force you, there may still be a chance. "

" In the meantime, you do nothing. "

" No, no ! What I am telling you is literature. I have not the least desire to be disagreeable to you. "

He sat down, picked up the telescope and made the cylinders work with a certain application.

Galatée, disturbed and panting slightly, watched him from a distance and tried to fathom him.

Not being successful, she took the flounce of her dressing gown, examined it, stretched it, turned it inside out, looked at the light through its lace...

This indifference would have lasted a long time if Giguelillot had not had an attack of affectionate gaiety and become communicative in the midst of the silence.

" We are playing our parts well, " he said.

" We ? "

" With a lot of talent. "

" What a child you are ! "

" Let us go on to the next scene, it is so pretty. "

" What do you know of it ? "

" I guess the dénouement. "

" It is not a comedy. "

" It is a charade. I've got it ! I sent you a note (¹). A chilliness (²) followed and my whole is the celebrated verse of Paul Robert :

> Si tu veux, faisons un rêve :
> Montons sur un poulet froid !
> Tu m'emmènes, je t'enlève...

Will you act the third verse ? I am in the right costume. " And he twirled his cap on the tip of his finger.

Then suddenly rising :

" In short, why did you let me in ? "

" I dare not tell you. "

" Was it criminal ? "

(¹) ' poulet ' (²) ' froid '

" No. "

" Well — unseemly ? "

" Yes. "

" Whisper it to me. "

" I don't dare. "

" Tell me in signs. "

" It's too complicated. "

" I will help you. "

" To the end ? "

" Yes. "

" You promise ? "

" I promise. "

" Good. I believe you. "

" Now, let me guess. "

" Oh, you never could. Don't even try. "

" Is it beyond my imagination ? Are you sure ? "

" Yes. "

" Mercy ! What can it be ? "

Galatée did not answer. To keep herself in countenance under the curious and smiling gaze of Giguelillot she seized the telescope and stroked the cylinders.

Then standing at the open window she directed it on the little pavilion which led from the hotel.

" For shame ! how unseemly that is ! " said Giguelillot. " Don't look on such things, mademoiselle. "

" Do you want to take my place ? I will give it up to you. "

" No, thank you. "

" You are wrong. I am amusing myself very much. Why do you refuse ? "

" I am not old enough for that. "

" I am, however. "

" I don't say no. That type of distraction was put into the world for the delectation of baldness and virginity both of which have the same reason for finding it interesting. As for me, I assure you, it is most disagreeable. "

Galatée took up her point of vantage once more. Then waving her hand impatiently :

" But I want you. Come quick. Fantastic things are going on. Just now there was one man and two women, now I see one woman and two men. Nobody has entered or left. Do explain that to me. "

After a pause of about half a minute, Giglio gave his opinion :

" A man — with an attractive but ugly woman, followed by one who is pretty but not so attractive. "

" Ah ! but then... "

She was going to discuss it further when a sudden blush rose to her cheeks, and she said simply, whilst nodding her head :

" Yes. I see that I don't know everything. "

And as if this confession gave her the strength necessary to express what she had to say :

" Well, this can't go on, " she said. " I must speak to you, and then you will know why I want you. It is most unseemly, so don't look at me. And it may take a long time, so don't be inattentive. "

" On the contrary, I am most interested. "

" I am twenty-three. I am not married. I, like all other girls, lead a stupid life. "

" Yes, yes ! "

" You understand me, I see that. My father has great ideas upon home life and education.

" But naturally he doesn't apply them to his daughters ?'
" Naturally ? "
" It would not be humane. "
" Do you think so ? To my mind it is incoherent. "
" Humane and incoherent. Doubly humane. We agree.

" Don't interrupt me, otherwise I shall forget all I have to tell you before... "
" Before speaking frankly. "
" You're impossible. I am sure that you are going to condemn me, and you will not know why I am right. "
" I already know well why you are wrong. "
" As I said, you are not listening to me. "
" I am listening to you before you speak and I want to spare you the trouble of a conversation which embarrasses you. A gentleman I know, and who passes for an intelligent man, only speaks half his phrases because a skilled listener guesses his intention from the first few words and that during the conclusion of the sentence, his adversary being spared the necessity of listening, prepares at his leisure his conclusive arguments. "
" Then finish my part yourself. I will then at least know if you have understood me. "
" If I have... But in your place I wouldn't think differently from you. And I should be wrong. And that is what I wish to tell you in a couple of words, which naturally will not be heeded. "
" Go on. "
" Here you are. You are twenty three, you are beautiful, you have been ' grown up ' for some ten years, you cried a lot when you were fifteen, sixteen, seventeen and so on : you read passionate novels where girls of

your age, or even younger, passed wild nights with the most perfect lovers. Your field glasses proved to you that these novels were not fables, and when you compared yourself to those people you envied, you recognised from certain signs that you could give happiness to several men who could also make you happy. "

" Yes, " said Galatée, " I prefer not to have said that myself. Don't look at me in that way. You embarrass me. "

" On reading my letter, " continued Giglio, " you did not believe for one moment that I loved you, or rather you hoped that I did not love you... "

" ' Hoped ' is right. That is just what it was. "

" And as you had seen me at my work of costumier, you relied on me to help you to get away in disguise with all the art of my talents, because even if a policeman does not arrest you, you do not want to go demonstratively. You prefer to disappear, so that no one can track you down. "

" And without knowing what I was going to ask, you promised just now to help me to the end. Don't forget that, my friend. "

Giglio took her hand and said most affectionately :

" You are wrong. "

" No, no. "

" You don't know the life you are running after. There everything goes on as usual and as in any family. That is to say that happiness is divided into two portions : practically all for the man and nothing for the woman. That follows, it is said, on certain events which took place in earlier days and concerned with a serpent and an apple. Women are in the world to be very unhappy — often without any reason : but when a cocotte weeps, I assure you she knows why. "

" Will you tell me ? "

" Because she plays with a love which always escapes her. Because from twenty men she detests she chooses one whom she loves, and that one has but a single wish and that is to get away from her as quickly as possible. For there is no sadder comedy nor one more difficult to play than that of affectionate feelings. Because... "

" But, at least, this woman sees life ! She is not a useless chattel, a solitary in spite of herself, leading an aimless existence, without joy, without liberty. "

" Could you get your father to make you an allowance, and to let you live your life without any restrictions whatever, as he would have done at once had the gods wished you to be a son ? "

" He would never allow it. "

" The man's law ! Always the man's law. "

" As a matter of fact, it would be only just. "

" Be a boy, like that lady you were looking at just now, and M. Lebirbe will find it quite natural for you to come back home in evening dress about ten or eleven o'clock in the morning with your eyes the colour of a storm and with legs like a convalescent. Even if you were a little drunk, I believe he would make allowances. "

" Ah, but you aren't serious, "

And the young girl smiled sadly.

Giglio continued :

" Nothing that I have told you about the life of pleasure has convinced you, then ? "

" Nothing. "

" I thought not.   At what age did you first have the desire to leave ? "

" I don't know.   Always. "

" Then it is not a caprice ?   You have thought it over, you know what you want and you are sure that you do want it ? "

" Heavens, yes ! "

" These women you watch in the delightful surroundings with which your father has provided you, you envy them ?   Look at them once more. "

And whilst she picked up the telescope and directed it on the distant prospect, Giguelillot thought how lucky he was that he did not love this girl at all, so that he could speak freely to her.

" I envy them, " said Galatée.

" Both ? "

" Both equally.   I should like to be a maid in the hotel. I should like to be the little beggar girl who at this moment is sleeping in a ditch by the side of the road and who will soon be strangled, but not before she has been possessed. "

Giglio bowed.

" I have nothing more to say, miss.   And if you wish me to help you to get away from here, I am ready. "

" What ?   You are willing ? "

" Perhaps it is absurd : I don't know.   In any case, it is not my business.   You certainly have the right to express a wish after ten years of reflection.   I have said what I had to say.   Now, if you are determined, I do not press it any more.   Further, I am living up to my repu-tation of a young man bringing confusion into the midst of a family, and upsetting the intentions of a father.   And

I believe that I promised to obey you? That fits in admirably.

Galatée seized his two hands.

" Oh, how good you are, and I received you so badly. Forgive me if you can. I love you with all my heart. Listen. What time is it? Ten past four? The servants never wake before half past six. We have more than two hours to ourselves. I give you permission not to dress me at once. "

XI

HOW PAUSOLE'S SCHEMES AND DIANE A LA HOUPPE'S DREAMS CORRESPONDED EXACTLY

> It is said that it is better to lie on the
> leaves of the banana tree with two men at
> the same time than to sleep alone.
>
> Popular Annamite song.
>
> (Trans : DUMOUTIER — 1890)

PAUSOLE standing in his room, folded his arms and shook his head.

" What have I come to do so far from home ? " he said aloud. " Into what escapade have I thrown myself ? Here am I travelling more than 3 kilometres from my palace, prepared to sleep in any bed that chance throws in my way, without any of my comforts nor my familiar surroundings. What madness this adventure is ! "

But Diane who had very good reasons for wishing it to appear good and to last as long as possible, led the King to a large sofa, and knelt at his feet.

She possessed a simple mind in regard to the complexities of life and it would have shown ignorance of her character to see in her a brain worker : but by intuition she was expert in regulating her politics by the psychology

of love, the only portion of learning on which she had
received any illumination. No advice other than hers
had led the King to put off his departure at the moment
when she did not wish him to leave the palace. Now
it was necessary that she should prolong the excursion,
and above all share it, that is to say, be pardoned for
her pursuit both inopportune and against all rules.

On this last point she considered that silence would
be of more use to her than contrition, for excuses recall
the fault rather than mitigate it, and they provoke resent-
ment even though they obtain words of pardon.

Diane made no effort to excuse herself. She relied
solely on the influence of her own good luck to appease
the mind of the King, and she raised to him a face whose
serenity was troubled only by the lustre of a frown.

" How happy I am here, " she said, " and what adorable
memories I shall have later when dreaming of this strange
room. See, our host has arranged for everything as you
like it best. It is comfortable and cool in this house.
Here is a low divan, another higher but not so firm.
This one is so wide and that one is so well placed in the
fresh air coming from that large window. Here are
lemons and sugar. Here is your port wine. I brought
it with me in case they forgot it. "

" Is it possible ? " said Pausole.

" Will you have some now ? "

" No. It is enough for me to know that it is within
reach. But it would have annoyed me not to have been
able to see it before I fell asleep. "

" To-morrow morning you shall have your Spanish
chocolate which I have told them to make black and of

even thickness, because the Master of the Kitchens had not given the instructions. "

" That is good. "

" I asked above all that the house should be as silent as a church until such time as you deigned to announce your awakening. "

" That, in fact, is most important. "

" Your own chambermaid is here. To-morrow at the moment when you tell me to ring, it is she who will appear and I sent her word to remain silent : I heard that she annoyed you this morning. Finally, I asked Mme. Lebirbe for two hair pillows because I know that you don't like those stuffed with feathers. "

" That's perfect. I want to kiss you, Houppe. Come on to this low divan. The seats are truly comfortable here, which reconciles me to my new room. Tell me, did you talk much to Mme Lebirbe. "

" A lot. We are distantly related. Her sister who married a doctor was Papa's mistress for three years. Mme. Lebirbe reminded me of that at once. "

" Is this sister of hers a widow ? "

" No. First of all she had a child by her husband and then two sons by my father. "

" I don't like that, " said Pausole. " Why did she not frankly divorce him ? "

" Because my father was married also, and mamma had a very trying character. With her, there could be no question of polygamy. I remember that when papa brought his mistresses home, there were endless scenes. He could never keep one for more than a week. "

" You take after your mother, " said Pausole, " for

you badly scratched poor Denyse whom I saw this morning. "

" And whom you sent away, Sire ! Oh, how pleased I was when I saw her return to the harem. I shall remember that joy also... but my recollection of this evening will be the sweeter. "

Pausole put his hand on her shoulder.

" You lead an unhappy life in the Harem then, my Houppe ? I see that behind all your speech. "

" Oh, yes ! very sad during the last year. Very happy for the last two days. "

" It's sad. What can I do ? I don't want to put any constraint on you or any of my wives. If I have the Harem guarded so strictly it is because it would be personally disagreeable for me to be deceived. But I hold nobody with force. "

" How can you speak so ? You love me very little ?" said Diane, very pale.

" Houppe, I love you very much and that is why I will give you your freedom on the day you ask for it. "

" I shall never ask for it. "

" And you look forward to unhappiness ? "

" Yes, but less unhappy for one day in each year. "

" It's sad, " repeated Pausole, " it's sad. "

Diane, dissatisfied of the point to which she had led the conversation, wondered how she was going to persuade the King to see in her, three hundred and sixty five different women. But Pausole was turning over in his mind doubts of quite a different kind.

" Perhaps I ought to go further, " said he. " I had already thought of it. Oh ! how embarrassing it is sometimes to suit one's own happiness and liberty to the

happiness and liberty of others.   It is an impossible ideal;
one must always go as far as sacrifice.   And then the
question arises whom to sacrifice.   I would like to solve
that question against myself, if in this way it approaches
solution. "

" Against yourself ? "

" Oh, yes !   I realise that in compelling the young
women to keep absolute continence during their adolescence, I make them pay too dear for the satisfactions which
the title of Queen could give to their tenderness or more
often to their vanity.   They adapt themselves to it, I
know.   It is, however, contrary to nature, and I have
asked myself sometimes whether I ought not to let the
pages loose in the harem, night and day, closing my eyes
to that which would very probably happen.   I have not
decided, but neither have I given up the idea.   They
are only beardless children of whom one could not
reasonably be jealous.   And if I foresee that their games
would cause me a certain amount of anxiety, I should at
any rate be able to be resigned to it as the least shocking
solution of all, with the satisfaction of having given a
little joy to the voluntary captives who beat their wings
round me.   Houppe, it is late.   I have travelled a lot
on mule-back, and I'm tired.   Let us rest. "

Towards six o'clock in the morning, a ray of sunshine
already warm woke Diana à la Houppe.

Pausole was sleeping on his back, his nose in the air,
his mouth wide open.

She turned over, spread her legs, stretched herself
with clenched fists and chest thrust out, then lay back
frowning.

Was she still dreaming ? Almost certainly, for her
spirit haunted, no doubt, by the last words of the King
had the following vision :

The door, left ajar to cause a draught during the too
hot night, opened slowly by itself... A page entered,
timidly at first, then reassured, then boldly. Two light
hands passed deliciously over her hot moist skin. A
soft caressing cheek brushed her left breast. Then a
licentious smile appeared and she murmured (in her voice
of dreams) " Take care, " and she believed that a reply
was made, " Nothing awakes the King, madame. " Then,
as she turned over on her left side in order to keep the
sleep which she felt was about to be interrupted, it seemed
to her that the page behaved towards her much more like
a husband than a faithful servant. She trembled three
times, lost consciousness and fell from the height of her
dream into black nothingness.

BOOK IV

I

HOW DIANE A LA HOUPPE EXPLAINED HER DREAM
AND THIERRETTE HER AMBITIONS

> " Generally you will find that women
> prefer a fop to an honest man, a libertine
> to a moral lover... This preference on the
> part of women follows in nature the sexual
> proprieties which they imagine in a more
> interesting bearing, and in morals to that
> innate sentiment by which each seeks that
> which is most identical with himself. "
>
> Woman in the Social Order and the
> Order of Nature, 1787.

THE Whitsun bells were ringing a full peal at half
past nine in the morning, and Diane, who had
forgotten to warn the bell ringers, awoke for a second
time. Had she really been dreaming?

At first, she didn't doubt it. The dreams of Diane
à la Houppe easily became voluptuous and even imagi-
native. They had often suggested fancies which occasionally kept her thoughtful for a whole day, and she
pondered over them with a sort of respect, for she would
have been incapable of building them up whilst awake.
Their recollection stood out as landmarks in her monotonous existence. She knew exactly when she told

herself that such an event happened before the dream of the drum-major or after that of the little negro between the governesses. Thus was she about to join the dream of the page to a string of others when, having discovered reasons for doubt which did not come to her by reflection only, and, on the other hand, not being able to accept such a fantastic event as true, she was plunged into perplexity.

Pausole, who was eventually disturbed from his heavy and sweet sleep by the crashes of bronze, sat up and shortly afterwards rose from his bed.

This was the hour when he attended to business.

He must have a counsellor.

He asked for Giguelillot.

The little page kept him waiting, for he had slept little after his boisterous day. First of all Rosine, then Thierrette, then Philis, then Galatée, and lastly Diane à la Houppe had experienced in turn all that he could offer in energy, perseverance, and good conduct, but it had not left him without a little faintness and prostration. So, when he answered the King's summons without having rested for more than two and a half hours, he was twenty minutes late. Pausole had left his bed-room for his dressing room.

Gilles entered, and, as he was extremely badly trained, Diane saw at once from his smile that manifestly he had at least shared her dream.

After a moment's confusion, she took her part in an adventure in which she had so little responsibility and which was much more burglarious than adulterous. From her bed she made a sign to the page to approach

placed a bare and languorous arm round his right leg
and said slowly and softly :

" Brigand ! Scoundrel ! Rascal ! Little germ !
Gallows'-bird ! "

He replied in a virtuous voice which might have
belonged to a child of five :

" I beg your pardon, Madame ? "

" I hate you. "

" Yes, Madame. "

" Who taught you that ? "

" My little sister. "

" Never do it again. "

" I will never do it again. "

" At least... not so imprudently. "

" Very well. "

" Not with anyone ? "

" Nobody, nobody, nobody ! Never, never, never ! "

Diane laughed, tapped his hand and went on more
seriously :

" I hope we shall not find the fair Aline this evening. "

" Ah ! Don't you wish it ? "

" I'm in no hurry. "

" All right. "

Then, to please the young woman by a confidence
which in any case didn't mean anything to him :

" There is a second fugitive, " he said.

" Who's that ? "

" The elder Mlle. Lebirbe. "

" Since when ? "

" Last night. She explained to me that family life
did not lend itself to misconduct, that she was experiencing in herself all sorts of frenzies and that mysterious

voices were calling her to the lowest prostitution. So I sent her off... "

" Oh, how dreadful ! "

" I sent her off to a respectable lady who keeps a private hotel in Tryphemia, where large numbers of married ladies meet gentlemen — often married also, but, as a rule, not to them. "

" You little bandit ! How disgraceful ! "

" It's not so bad as all that. M. Lebirbe is president of the *League against Domestic Licence*, an admirable society whose work is slackening somewhat, I believe. When he learns that his eldest daughter, in a well-known private house, allows all licence, and takes them each in turn, he will be inspired with zeal and spirit for the good cause. "

Diane's burst of laughter was heard by Pausole, who, fresh from his bath, entered in morning clothes.

" Ah ! It's you, my boy ? I only have a few words to say to you. Yesterday, you made an inquiry, which must have been clairvoyant, and of which I do not ask for an account. I have just read the little letter which you found. It is most affectionate, but does not give any details. Do you know what has become of my daughter ? Where is she to-day ? That's all I want to know. "

Giguelillot gladly consented to save the fair Aline, but for divers reasons he wanted at the same time to be reconciled to her. So, making a slight sign to Diane which spared her anxiety, he replied :

" In Tryphemia. "

" That's enough for me. Do you think we ought to

leave to-day on another stage of our journey ?   I will
consult Taxis as a matter of form because he is my
counsellor, for the morning, but I have more confidence
in you. "

" It is better to go. "

" You are right.   And at what time, do you think ? "

" In the middle of the afternoon. "

" How far must we go ? "

" Tryphemia is four kilometres away. We could cover
that in three quarters of an hour. "

" It's a lot, but we will do it.   I am feeling very fit
this morning.   Go and tell Taxis to come and speak
to me. "

Taxis appeared, very agitated.

" Sire, " he said, " a fresh crime has been committed
this morning.   A virgin has been abducted from the
affection of her parents. "

" What ? "

" By an unknown suborner.   The elder daughter of
our host is no longer in her rooms. "

" Ha ! Ha ! Ha ! " laughed Pausole.   " Poor Lebirbe !
It would happen to him. "

" I cannot prevent myself from establishing a corre-
lation between the extraordinary events which have been
occurring for some days, and which are all connected
with rape or clandestine seduction. "

" The comparison is unwarranted, " said the King
peevishly.   " Further, I have reasons to find it highly
out of place.   It is pure common sense that one individual
would not be able to seduce and abduct more than one
young girl at a time.   You are really too ignorant in
matters of gallantry.   Even the father confessors consider

it their duty to become erudite on these points. But let us say no more on the subject. Have you no other report to give me? "

" The unknown, whom I persist in considering as the sole author of all these crimes committed during the last few days, has been arrested, Sire, or is on the point of being. Here again, I only await a word from you. "

" Oh, if that is the case, I give it, " said Pausole. " Since it will render unnecessary a journey which I am beginning to dread. Let's finish this business. Where is the guilty one? "

" On the road to Tryphemia. "

" And who is with him? "

" Princess Aline. "

" How do you know? "

" In carrying out a search of the apartments of Mlle. Lebirbe, I found a powerful telescope, of which doubtless the studious child made use for astronomical purposes, so as to contemplate each night the unfathomable work of the Creator which the firmament... "

" Cut it short, Taxis. You are verbose. "

" I therefore seized the telescope and used it to search the neighbourhood. Providence willed it that this object should be an instrument of discovery in my hands. Two hundred metres away on the road to Tryphemia, I saw a young man whose costume corresponded exactly with that which my police had informed me clothed the mysterious culprit. Close to him, in a green dress well-known to all at the palace, since the last fortnight, was Princess Aline. Such is the result of my efforts. I consider it my duty to warn Your Majesty that speed in decision and action is absolutely necessary for the success of your projects whatever they may be."

"My instructions," said Pausole, "are firm on one point. No one but myself shall detain my daughter. I will not alter my decision : I have had too much trouble to make up my mind on that point."

"In that case, we must leave immediately."

"Let us go, then. Is the luggage ready?"

"Most of it. And the rest can follow. I have had the horses saddled, including my faithful Kosmon who has been made to suffer the most scandalous outrages by some stupid malefactor."

"What, he also?"

"Pardon. My thoughts..."

"It is madness," said Pausole. "Here, in the open country, in a simple and free land, where anyone can make love to pretty girls in the fields without the slightest trouble, to go and take as a lover a knock-kneed and broken-winded nag such as you bestride. That is a depravity which I should never have imagined."

"I never said anything like that..."

"Your malefactor is a man more to be pitied than blamed. I oppose any prosecution. We will say no more about it."

"Let me explain..."

"You shall explain on the way. It is of no interest to me. Hurry, Taxis, and take your leave."

The assembly was carried out in the courtyard, where the guards formed a line from the main stairway.

Giglio, already mounted, was showing himself to the

16

curious populace, when Thierrette separated herself from a group of peasants.

Smiling, with tired lines round her eyes, she advanced painfully but not without courage.

Although she had proved herself ready to fight a whole armed escort, she was intimidated by the silence and space surrounding the horsemen, and she approached Giguelillot blushing.

" Thank you very much, sir. Thank you. You have been very good to me — and to these gentlemen too. Thank you all. Thank you for your generosity. Again thank you. Thank you. Thank you. "

Then, with a sigh, full of sincerity, and nodding her head, she spoke these simple words :

" I shall not forget. "

But Giguelillot, bending down from his zebra, asked :

" What are you holding in your hand ? "

" It is the fortieth tulip, sir... I kept it for you... so that it may bring you good luck... "

" How kind of you ! I shall keep your fortieth tulip. What can I give you in return ? Tell me. "

" Sir, they have been very nasty to me at the farm. The owner said that I was going mad, that I was associating with men, and that I had not done the evening milking, and that two pails were missing. And then what ? I was thrown out with six francs in my handkerchief, and am without employment at the moment. "

" But, my poor Thierrette, I have none to offer you. "

" Oh, yes ! I know of some. These gentlemen have no *cantinière*. The work is hard, I know, but I will do it well and willingly. I will do what I can, you know. "

" What ? You would... "

" Yes, for the first days, I would follow in the luggage-cart. A little later, I would mount a horse, if you don't mind. "

" Right. Go into the luggage-cart; it is an excellent precaution. Hide till mid-day. Don't show yourself any sooner. Do you understand ? "

" Quite. At the moment, sir, I want to sleep rather than to deck myself out. Thank you once more. Thank you. You have a good heart where women are concerned. "

II

HOW PHILIS FOUND A HUSBAND

> Father, marry me, or I am a ruined girl.
> If you don't marry me, I must go on the
> street, either in my chemise or quite naked
> doing the worst I can.
>
> There follow Several
> fine new songs — 1542.

THREE vases from the royal manufacturies, an auto-
graphed portrait and liberality to the servants,
marked the Stay of Pausole with the unhappy M. Lebirbe.

But the old man lost both his daughters at once.

The King, not knowing how to console his host
after the flight of Galatée, and believing to have learnt
by his experience of the human heart that in most cases
personal vanity outweighs affection, thought he might
alleviate all griefs by informing him point-blank that,
charmed by the young graces of the little Philis, he was
placing her amongst his Queens and taking her with his
convoy.

Then the whole cortège started off, Philis in blue on
her pony on the right of Pausole mounted on his mule :
Giguelillot on the left on his zebra : Taxis scouting on

the shabby Kosmon, still stumped and branded, whilst further on, gently rocked by the nautical stride of her camel, Diane à la Houppe, sleepy-eyed, stretched on her left side, picked up the threads of her dream.

III

WHEREIN PHILIS PRATTLES, LISTENS, AND LEARNS

> She resembles in her little bustle the
> lavender girls in garden alleys. She
> challenged and wheeled before the gallant,
> her slave, like a fly playing on a dessert cloth,
>
> SYGOGNES — 1609.

PHILIS could hardly believe it.

" Sire, " she asked, " I shall really be a Queen like all the others ? "

" Assuredly. "

" Like the three hundred and sixty six ?   And I shall live in the harem ?   And I shall have as many friends as that ?   Oh ! how I'm going to enjoy myself ! "

" Good, " said Pausole.   " That's the right intention. "

" Are there any Queens of my age ? "

" About thirty. "

" As many as that ?   And are they nice ? "

" Very nice. "

" Are they fond of each other or do they quarrel ? "

" I think they are rather too fond of each other. "

" One can't be too fond.   Are they serious minded ? "

" Not at all serious. "

Philis, with a little gay cry, stood up in her stirrups and sat down again several times, which was her way of expressing a lively joy when riding.

" But, " said the page, " you will have one wife too many, Sire, one more than the year has days. From today onwards you will feel wealthy in love. "

" No, no ! " said Pausole. " I have dismissed Queen Denyse. The harem is pacified. Each Queen has equal rights which are asserted once a year. I shall not be forced to compromise by caprice an order of succession which should be perfect, since it is modelled on the revolutions of our planet itself. "

" What does that mean ? " asked Philis.

Then she went on quickly :

" I beg your pardon, Sire. I have often been told that one must not ask questions. It isn't my fault. I know nothing. "

" I am enchanted, " said Pausole. " But, tell me, what do you call nothing ? "

" The list of the Kings of Tryphemia with the sub-prefectures, and the participle rule. "

" You know all that ? It's wonderful. "

" I know it all — but not very well. "

" And what more do you want to know ? "

To this question Philis replied so frankly that Pausole had a start.

Confused, and with lowered eyes, she continued :

" Pardon, Sire, I have said a silly thing. I ought not to have said it ...especially before you... But it's always the same... Papa was right... When I have been on horseback for five minutes, I'm no longer responsible. Another time I'll be more careful. "

Pausole reassured her with a gesture.

" It is I who was wrong, my child, if I led you to believe that I disapproved, for you answered well. "

" Really ? "

" Truly.   Firstly you spoke from the bottom of your heart. "

" Oh, yes ! "

" And one must always tell the truth. "

" Even that truth ? "

" It is a woman's greatest truth, and the greatest ambition that she can express decently.   If you had answered that you regretted having so little knowledge on celestial mechanics or differential calculus, I should have been less satisfied : not that there aren't in the world female mathematicians and astronomers fulfilling well their petty callings : but simply because these become like men and take pleasure in the faults of half the human race that inspire me with antipathy. "

" Oh, not me, " said Philis.

This time the word sounded trifling.

Giguelillot, always obliging, hastened to break the silence.

" Have you noticed, Sire, " he said bluntly, " how similar the Tryphemians are to the French ? "

" What a curious question !   How should they be otherwise ?   They are a mixture of Catalans and Languedocians, a Gallic Roman race. "

" Yes, but that isn't what I meant.   I came from Paris expecting to find here totally different surroundings. You had had a revolution, proclaimed moral liberty... "

" Oh, " said Pausole.   " That is nothing, my boy. The importance of revolutions is gauged by the interest

which the government has in retarding their success.
There has only been one revolution whose success was
doubtful, and whose recollection is extraordinary and
that is the one which gave one religious liberty, because
in surrendering to divine right, one's will was deprived
of a fundamental support with which till then it had been
assured of a stability often secular. But moral liberty?
You can have it for the asking. "

" What is it ? " ventured Philis.

" You may imagine, my Gilles, " said Pausole, without
answering her, " that the day when the people of Paris
take the trouble to demand a naked dancing girl at the
Opera, she will be given to them at once, because the
Ministry will not be overthrown, especially if the seat
holders know that the dancer is good. "

" It's possible, but I thought that I should find here a
different world to mine, something confusing, unpre-
cedented, an absolute contrast. And everything happens
as in the neighbouring country. The roads are quiet,
the harvests flourish, the farmers turn out the girls who
misbehave themselves, the evening parties are conducted
gravely, and the young girls are apparently brought up
strictly. "

" Certainly. Nothing changes in mankind, my boy.
One can only make life a little easier and sweeter by
giving freedom to do anything that harms no one.
And that is what I tried to do. I believe that for many
centuries I am the first legislator who has taken as a
principle that the people should not be worried. "

Philis became restless on her saddle.

" Then, Sire, they do all they want in the harem ?...
There, I've asked another question... If you can't put

up with me, you must tell me. I'm used to it. I am always being scolded. "

" No, I can put up with you, " said Pausole. " And I like you like that. I hope that in the harem you wouldn't ever want to do what wasn't allowed. In any case, it isn't a prison. So long as you are happy, I will keep you. The day that you wish to go you will simply say to me : ' Good bye '. "

" And you wouldn't restrain me ? That is unkind of you. "

Pausole turned to Giguelillot.

" You see, " said he, " One never gets out of the habit of complaining, and as soon as one has got one's liberty... "

But Taxis was galloping back.

" Ah ! we are about to hear some news, " said the treacherous and waggish Giguelillot. " Here is the Lord Grand Eunuch returning after a fruitful beat. He has found the Princess. Let his clairvoyance and his tactics be praised on earth and in heaven. "

" Which Princess ? " asked Philis.

" The culprits have been arrested ! " cried Taxis from as far off as he could.

" What ? My daughter ? You have dared to arrest my daughter ? "

" Oh, but this is interesting, " said Philis quietly.

" I have not been so rash, " replied Taxis. " I have only seized the accomplices who are over there under guard. They are two little peasants from the hamlet. Without doubt, they are mixed up in this abduction for they are wearing the clothes of the Princess and the Unknown Person. "

" Have they confessed ? "

" They deny everything. It is just that which condemns them. The true culprit is recognised by a striking sign; he always begins by protesting his innocence. As soon as they had declared their innocence, the police put them in gaol. In my opinion, there is more than a presumption in this : it is almost a certainty. I would even go so far as to say that, in the absence of other proof, I should be satisfied to condemn them on that alone. "

" Send for them here, " said Pausole.

And there appeared, hand in hand, a young peasant girl and her brother, in tears and livid with fear.

They stammeringly explained that they had found this beautiful dress and these smart clothes in the courtyard of their cottage. That as it was Whit Sunday, they had thought that the Blessed Virgin had sent them this finery as a recompense for the many troubles of the previous year. That they had seen here a miracle, that is to say something quite natural; and that had they imagined what was awaiting them, they would rather have thrown the clothes in the fire than have put them on for one moment. Finally, their bearing was so humble and candid and so simple, that Pausole shrugging his shoulders cried :

" Taxis, you're a fool ! These children are absolute idiots, and therefore incapable of doing wrong. Crime si one of the privileges reserved to intelligence — at least I am referring to complex and clandestine crime such as that we are investigating. I hope that for my daughter's honour she has been abducted by someone

sufficiently subtle to be able to dispense with the help
of ragamuffins such as those you have captured. "

" Nevertheless, I ask that they be searched, " said
the Grand Eunuch.

" Very well. But you won't find anything. I'll
guarantee that. "

Taxis, with his own hands, undressed the bashful
brother and sister, who clung to each other and put their
fingers in their noses.

He laid out their clothes on the dusty slope of the road,
searched their pockets, folds and pleats.

" Nothing ? " said Pausole, " I thought not. "

" Four letters, " replied Taxis.

And with a deference which was not without pride
he held them out with a quick movement.

" Where were these letters found ? " said Pausole.

" In the left inside pocket of the waistcoat ".

" Read one to me — whichever you like. "

And while Philis, greatly interested, guided her horse
behind him so as to follow over his shoulder, Taxis read
out the first letter.

" My little Mimi,

" Wake up. I shall be with you at half past
ten. My old ape is carrying out an auction in
the country. I am as free as a swallow, and
feel so full of tenderness that my eyes droop !
Send anyone away whoever it may be, if you
are not alone ! I am dressing and am hurrying.
I kiss your lips.

CAMILLE. „

" The letter is extremely odd, " remarked Pausole. " Who can this Monsieur Camille be who stupidly compares himself to a swallow and possesses an ape which carries out auctions ? Amongst what people do the old notaries sell their practices to monkeys ? That's what I don't understand. "

" I say, " whispered Philis in the page's ear, " it's a woman's writing, you know. I think there is more behind it... "

" Ah ! Ah ! "

" Ought I to say so ?

" No ! It would have a bad effect. "

And suggesting to his zebra his wish to turn round, he said to the King :

" Precious time is being lost in reading this correspondence. It can teach us nothing. I have known since yesterday who is with the Princess. "

" I also know, sir ! " cried Taxis. " My discovery corroborates all my deductions. These four letters are addressed to ' Mlle. Mirabelle. ' Once more I affirm that this precocious intermediary has served as messenger, and that the culprit is her friend who confided in her and paid her. "

" I believe, " said Giguelillot, " that the truth is quite different. " And, certain of the reply he was about to receive, he added :

" It is what I shall have the honour of explaining to the King if he will grant me here an interview of three hours during which I will faithfully give an account of all the researches I made yesterday. "

" And why ? " asked Pausole. " It is quite useless. I am not a chief of police and I have no intention of getting mixed up in your work. Do you hear, I repeat? Your explanation of yesterday, although lively, may have brought you together. Carry out your inquiries together or separately. It is a matter of complete indifference to me. I shall only intervene at the end to fetch my daughter from the retreat in which I trust that you will find her. "

" Your daughter has gone, Sire, like Galatée? " asked Philis.

" It is not at all the same thing, " said Pausole.

IV

HOW TAXIS LEARNT AT LAST THE TRUTH
ABOUT THE WHOLE AFFAIR

> " I have in my repertoire several remedies,
> *Pulsatilla, Natrum muriaticum, Belladonna*, all
> efficacious for those folk who believe
> themselves damned. "
>
> Dr. GALLAVARDIN (of Lyons), 1896.

THE two young peasants having been freed, the whole
cavalcade got under way again in the direction
of Tryphemia.

Giguelillot had no wish to mystify King Pausole, for
he liked him too sincerely, in spite of having cuckolded
him. But his scruples were less lively as regards the
seigneur Taxis. And as it was necessary to palliate
the unfortunate episode of the letters, he rejoined the
Grand Eunuch and said to him confidentially :

" Sir, for my part, I will pursue inquiries pitilessly :
but I think it my duty to tell you that the culprit is unfortunately one of your co-religionists. "

" What do you say ? How scandalous ! "

" Don't be afraid. His actions are honourable and

only apparently misleading. This then is the truth of the whole affair : a young man chosen from amongst the most chaste of an important society, has been charged with a moral mission in Tryphemia by a group of Protestants living in Alais. "

" Alais is a city without blemish, " said Taxis.

" You know, sir, that I do not share your views, " replied the imperturbable Giguelillot, " but, in spite of that, I find a certain grandeur, a general disinterestedness in the visits which your friends pay to the courtesans of our great cities, doubtless to purify them. "

" You need have no doubts in that respect. "

" Such precisely was the aim of the young man we are seeking. For five months, if I may believe his own words, he has passed all his nights and often even his days in the beds of these lost women, going ceaselessly from couch to couch, from repulsion to repulsion. "

" The noble fellow. "

" His own particular method was to show his naked body, which in fact is without charm, unpleasant and malformed. He shed his clothes, approached the sinner and speaking in a sorrowful voice said, " Such is the flesh ! Are you not disgusted ? "

" And he converted many ? "

" Not one. The majority protested at once that they had never encountered anything so tempting as his body, and that they liked blondes (for he was fair). Others explained with a smile that they were no less partial to second-rate beauty, and that for double the price they would double the endearments. Those who remained sufficiently outspoken to tell him what they thought, refused to abuse the rest of their lovers in the face of

such contempt. These latter were the younger ones.
In short, he was about to leave, very disheartened, when
he learnt that the Princess Aline lived not far from the
harem and thought that no soul could be in greater peril
than hers and that he would have the glory of saving her. "

" How did he reach her ? "

" That is a secret. Concurrently, sir, he saved from
a nest of vice a poor dancer named Mirabelle. "

" Ah ! Now I see. "

" But this dancer had not sufficient money to return to
her own country and forget her riotous youth. Her
adviser did not care to give it to her, as he had a horror of
all prodigality. Princess Aline took in hand the matter.
And so it was that on one and the same day she was able
not only to save herself but to rescue another lamb from
the abyss. That was why she wrote and had carried, as
you know, by the hand of a lady-in-waiting the letter
that alarmed you. "

" Everything is explained ! And those letters that
we found... "

" Were the last witnesses of a mad existence. Mirabelle
wished at first to destroy them; then she gave them to her
priest to prove her sincere repentance. "

" And the clothes themselves... that blue jacket... that
green dress... "

" A free gift for the poor peasants. Princess Aline
and her companion wish to dress in black only from now
on. "

Taxis looked fixedly at the little page.

" Sir, " said he, " (I apologize first for what I am
about to say). I have reasons to believe that you would

17

laugh at me if I gave you the opportunity. But to-day I believe you! Oh! I believe you. Truth illuminates what you have just told me. I feel it! I know it!. I announce it publicly! One does not invent such things! And now a frightful battle is taking place in my heart between my moral and my public duty. If I protect the Princess, I betray my King. If I give her up, I deprive virtue of a soul. On one side is grave transgression; on the other is guilt. In both cases Hell is lying in wait for me. What shall I do? Where shall I go? What will become of me? Sentry! Sentry! What of the night?"

Philis's pony dashed into the midst of this despair. Flushed and panting the little girl cried:

"Don't you see anything? Look ahead of you. Look! Look! There on the road..."

V

HOW KING PAUSOLE WAS RECEIVED BY THE PEOPLE
OF TRYPHEMIA

> "On the 30th January, 1589, several
> processions took place in the town, in
> which there was a large number of children,
> as many boys as girls, men and women, more
> than five or six hundred people, all naked.
> Never had such a beautiful thing been
> seen. Thank God !"
> *Journal of Events in Paris since the 23rd
> December,* 1588.

ALONG the road in the June sun the whole cavalcade advanced slowly, heralded by an uproar of
voices, songs and music.

The page and Taxis stopped.

" What is all this crowd ? " said Pausole who had
joined them.

" I think, " said Giguelillot, " that Tryphemia is
preparing a triumphal reception for its good monarch. "

" What ? A reception ? But I am making a secret
journey ! As a fact it is possible that I may not have
preserved a strict incognito, because I am wearing my
crown. However, I have told no one and am dumbfounded
at what I see. "

" Tryphemia is seven kilometres from the palace.   On a bicycle this can be covered in a quarter of an hour. The whole town knew of your departure yesterday, before twelve.   It has had plenty of time to prepare a cordial and pompous welcome, and I think, Sire, that we shall have to submit to it, whatever our feelings may be. "

" Never mind, " said Pausole.   I am resigned.   Let us bear with a pleasant face whatever they want to inflict on us.   Popularity is a heavy burden : but only a fool would be sullen towards it. "

In the centre of a shady circle, where the road broadened, the head of the procession halted within six paces of the King.

It was formed by two young girls astride Arab mares in white trappings and with long tails.   Their black hair was crowned with feathers.   Their brown legs looked even darker against the glistening coats of the animals and their little feet fell straight as they had neither saddles nor stirrups.   One hand held the silken reins and the other held the bamboo staff of a light banner which stretched between them raising to heaven the words in silk and silver :

LONG LIVE OUR GOOD KING PAUSOLE !

Further on two other girls held a second banner on which one could read :

TRYPHEMIA IS HAPPY

A third couple followed with this inscription :

TRYPHEMIA IS GRATEFUL

Then followed long lines of women carrying baskets of flowers on their heads, encircling first the band then the municipal authorities, bearded men or clean shaven patriarchs all clothed in white drill.

Behind came an enormous crowd.

" Oh ! how beautiful it is. How beautiful ! " said Philis, her hand to her chin. " All that is for us ? For us two ? Is it a marriage feast for me ? "

" Yes, " said Pausole. " You have guessed it. "

Then Philis cried :

" Long live the Tryphemians. "

Her shrill voice sounded above even the fanfares, and the crowd replied :

" Long live King Pausole. "

Then the ophicleides, having finished their march on a dozen perfect cadences repeated according to custom, blared out the Pausolian Hymn with a hundred voices singing the words.

Pausole did not listen to it standing up. A very busy gentleman with feverish hand and worried eye having formed the whole procession into a circle led the King to a platform hastily erected in the green shade of the open space.

Philis, finding no seat provided for her, laughingly seated herself on a little cushion. Diane à la Houppe less jealous than the previous day, and with every reason, contented herself with a similar cushion. Thus, flanked by his two wives, like a marble statue surrounded by allegorical figures, Pausole spread his arms and bowed his head to express to all that he felt overwhelmed by the honour, and gently took his place on the throne.

Alas ! he well foresaw that the official eloquence muſt on that day be borne as a divine scourge.

But the town meant to flatter his wishes and the firſt of all the speeches was made by a man of the people.

" Sire, " said this orator, " we love you, we, the beggars, the homeless people. When we are found ſtretched at the foot of a wall or on the green plank of a seat, sleeping or loving, we are not sent to prison in order to punish us for not being rich. When we only have two sous with which to buy bread, the law does not force us to ſteal six francs to buy trousers. When we have neither money nor rags, we know that we can enter the royal bakeries where you have the wherewithal to live given to us poor wretches racked with hunger. In short, whilſt we do no harm to those who leave us alone, we have the right to be beggars without having to die. This is found only in our country. King Pausole is a great man. "

Pausole held out his hand.

" That speech pleases me greatly. Let this poor wretch be given a house and a pension with tobacco, wine and two or three ſtrong girls to warm his sheets in December. Let the same be given to the twelve beggars whom he shall nominate. I will bear the coſt of their maintenance from my privy purse, and if they have children I will double their income. Finally, have all the other beggars collected and give each a gold piece. It is my gift to celebrate my joyful entry into the good city of Tryphemia. "

The crowd cheered.

Another orator advanced.

" Sire, " he said, " we bless your name, we the retailers,

for you leave us alone and we sell what we please, without licence or privileges. No one has the right to come to us on behalf of the government. Our matches, our cigars, and even our playing-cards bear no stamp. If a buyer scorns our scarves but is attracted by the saleswoman and declares himself then and there, we can shut our eyes to what occurs in the inner room without the State opening its eyes when no one claims its support. If, in order to make ends meet, we decide to dye or bleach the handkerchiefs that we sell, they don't come and treble our taxes so as to break us and at the same time ruin twenty five poor people. It is to you alone, Sire, that we owe this lot which is the envy of Europe. In the name of the retailers, I thank Your Majesty. "

" My friend, " said Pausole. " you do not wish that I grant you largesse, for you have no need of it, but I give ten hectares of Crown lands with the necessary money to build thereon a rest home for unfortunate retailers. Could I add the slightest liberty to those you have just mentioned, I would freely do so, but the code of Tryphemia not allowing me the right to add a burden (and I would wish it so), forbids me at the same time the pleasure of giving you one more liberty. Appreciate your privileges, since you say they are real, and overthrow my successor pitilessly and without scruple, if he tries to restrain by one line the freedom which I bequeath you. "

" You will live for ever, " cried the people.

" I do not like to doubt it, " replied Pausole.

A third person came forward.

The sense of his speech could he read in his eyes, and still more in the gesture by which he announced the spirit of the first section. In the name of the directing

classes, he wished to thank the King for the benefits
which his friends, even they, received from the law of
Tryphemia.

But the King interrupted him.

" Sir, first of all it is not for you that I altered all the
customs. If my rule pleases you, I am delighted, but
you will agree with me that you could reach happiness,
within the limits of human joys, without my troubling
myself to tap your cheeks to prevent you crying. The
stupid burden of laws was no less on your head than on
that of my lowest subjects. Their interest, however,
was studied before yours, and I do not trouble about
you except as one of the whole lot. This by no means
prevents me from feeling deeply sensible to your homage
and touched by your gratitude. You are a man and like
all men you have the right to regulate your life with
independence. I am pleased to salute you. "

The shouts were redoubled.

" Good. Good, " said Pausole. " That's enough.
I declare the meeting adjourned. Is the Chief of Police
here ? I have a few words to say to him in private. "

Pausole and all his companions remounted their various
steeds. The cortege, the banner-carriers, the crowd,
the baggage, the forty lancers, all followed in disorder as
desired by Giguelillot who had taken over the command.

In due course the Chief of Police was taken aside
by the King, who addressed him in the following words :

" I would have preferred, sir, to have entered the
gates of Tryphemia, without being recognised or known,
for I am travelling with an object where mystery and

silence cannot be too greatly emphasized. But since my presence is no longer secret from anyone, there is no reason to hide my purpose from you, depriving myself of your devoted services. Let me have your assistance."

" It will be my duty and my honour, " replied the faithful officer.

" My daughter, the Princess Aline left the palace on Thursday. She had her reasons for doing this and I allow no one to question them. A young man is advising her, accompanying her and protecting her. I do not know where he has taken her, and this is the first point upon which I wish enlightenment. Neither do I know who he is, and I would like to have this second uncertainty cleared up. "

" Could Your Majesty give me any description ? "

" Taxis ! " cried the King.

Taxis appeared, very pale. Pausole said to him in a whisper :

" The Chief of Police is asking for a description of the unknown man we are pursuing. "

" Ah ! "

" Well ? Answer ! Have you one ? "

Torn by the necessity of obeying, Taxis plunged a trembling hand into his pocket and withdrew a paper which he held out.

" The description ! " he said, " the description !... Oh ! unhappy young fellow... Admirable martyr ! He will be recognised at once and it will be I who have given him up. "

The details were as follow :

Figure .... Normal
Hair .... Auburn
Beard .... None
Eyes .... Grey
Forehead .... Normal
Nose .... Ordinary
Mouth .... Normal
Chin .... Round
Face .... Oval
Special Features........... None

" That is perfect, " said the Chief of Police. " With this characteristic description, we can start our pursuit. But what age ? "

" About sixteen, " said Pausole.

" Oh ! " said Taxis. " Sixteen... or eighteen... Under thirty. Probably under thirty. He hasn't been seen at close quarters. "

" Well, how is the colour of his eyes known ? " asked the officer.

" Oh ! It is known... it might perhaps be more correct to say that it is presumed. "

" Has he a beard, anyhow ? The description says ' no '. "

" Only a little beard... a little... but a little... "

" Anyway, that is not important. Such as it is the document suffices. "

Taxis withdrew hastily.

" Chief, " continued Pausole, " please be good enough not to worry me with questions or accounts. Remember, further, that your mission is to discover, but not to arrest. All I give you is a search warrant. As soon as you have found out how to execute it, make your report and give it to my page. You'll see him over there mounted on a zebra, next to Queen Philis who is laughing and talking to him at this moment. If, however, your pursuit succeeds between the hours of midnight and midday, you will have as your superior officer my counsellor, Taxis, who has just left us. For my page has authority for only half the day. Go! I have told you all that it is good for you to hear. "

During this conversation Giguelillot approached Philis.

" Go away, " she said with a pout that was meant to be severe.

" Why ? "

" Because I am beginning to find you nicer and nicer. And apparently I must not say so. "

" Well, don't say it. "

" But it is what I think... Go away !... I want to kiss you. "

" No, no. "

" Yes... there on the neck, behind the ear where you kissed me so well. I will give you one on my own hand. Look out ! it's for you. "

" I felt it. "

" So did I. Go away. "

She blushed furiously, feeling Giglio's glances on her. There was silence.

" But do go away, " she went on. " You are making me say dreadful things. "

" I don't think so. "

" Really ? Oh ! but it is so, all the same. You mustn't listen to me. I never know what I shouldn't say. "

" Nor do I. "

" Well, I thought of you all last night after you had left. May I say that or not ? "

" If it is the truth. "

" Oh ! I've pleased you. You're confused. You're happy. Ah ! Ah ! Stop there. I forbid you to follow me. "

Instinctively knowing that she should leave at this stage, she kicked the flanks of her black pony which, in a few strides, came alongside King Pausole.

They were now entering the suburbs.

On all sides, at the windows, the doors, the roofs, the trees, an exultant populace was thronging, laughing, raising excited arms and throwing bouquets with joyful cries.

Workmen in coloured shirts and blue linen trousers, citizens in clothes suitable to the heat, little naked girls, street arabs in red stockings, women in striped petticoats, all pressed to the side of the pavement with flowers and green branches.

On all sides could be heard cries and sudden shouts :

" I see him !... It's he !... There he is !... Mamma, mamma, ...There he is !... Oh ! I saw him well !... I have a good view of him !...

Others cried plaintively :

" Papa, lift me up !... I'm too small !... Where is he ?... Pick me up under the arms !... Higher... Higher... Still higher. " A baby girl of three years old cried out, whilst brandishing a pink doll by the arm :

" Ong ive the King... King Paupaul ! "

And Pausole picked her up by her arms and kissed her on both cheeks.

Everywhere triumphant arches built up in a night stood at street corners, at the entrances to the squares and at cross roads. Every window was decked in bunting. Coloured materials, foliage, waving branches, or roses covered the houses, pavements, roads and even the sky itself. From the city gates to the Grand'Place eighteen hundred naked girls formed a brown hedge and flung a stream of red roses beneath the feet of the King and his Queens. Innumerable June flowers fell from the windows to the streets like a waterfall in flood.

Pausole bowed, bowed, opened his arms, bent his head, sometimes raising a hand as if to say " It is too much. " And his beard and good natured eyes gave by their soft expression to the enthusiasm of the crowd a paternal affection which enchanted the onlookers.

Philis, close to him, held herself very upright, conscious of her newly-acquired rights and of the part which she herself might take in these public acclamations. Her appearance was severe and dignified : but in order to keep in the fashion which she saw was general, she had removed the pin which held her bodice together, and she showed to the people her breasts raised to the shadows, being proud of their pale points and transparent skin.

Taxis searched in his Bible for some sane distraction from such a sight; but fate having willed that he should open it at the second chapter of Chronicles, he only found in the biography of Solomon examples, even more scandalous of the ignominy to which royal profligacy can sink.

Diane à la Houppe, raising the curtain of her palanquin, looked at the crowd.

Giguelillot, sitting the wrong way round in his saddle, held by the hands two young girls, each of whom drew behind her a dancing line of sisters, friends and strangers. What he said to them must have been peculiarly interesting for, as soon as he had spoken a word, it was repeated from one end of the line to the other with deafening bursts of sound; and the procession continued to advance, drawing in its wake where Giguelillot was the attraction a double trail of laughter.

VI

REGARDING THE WALK TAKEN BY PAUSOLE
THROUGH HIS CAPITAL

> " Two desires which always unite men
> in fellowship, the desire for order, and
> the desire to be perpetuated, determine the
> new dwellers to seek a leader, and women. "
> BARON DE WIMPFEN — *Journey to Saint
> Dominique* — 1789.

THE Prefecture and the Town Hall being, as it happened, prepared to divide the high honour of the
royal presence, Pausole accepted the entertainment of
the municipal counsellors and had his luggage taken to
the apartments prepared by the Prefect.

There was, it is true, a royal palace somewhere, but as
Pausole never entered his capital, he had consented to the
old residence being transformed into a popular museum.

Immediately after the banquet, Pausole, enlivened and
not at all fatigued by his two days' journey, decided that
he would make a tour on mule-back of the lower districts
of the town.

Macarie, with a patient air, received him once more
on her back and lowered her ears resignedly.

The King, Taxis and Giguelillot went off with no other escort.

Round them the people, still eager but a little less uproarious than before, filled the roads and the windows. They still cried " Long live the King " to which Pausole replied, " Good day ! Good day, my friends ! "

Newsboys ran through the streets, calling their papers fresh from the press.

" *La Paix* ! *L'Indépendant* ! "

" *La Nudité* ! Five o'clock edition. "

One mistaken youth shouted in the ears of Taxis :

" *Le Moniteur général des jeunes filles à louer* ! Twenty five centimes complete with prize ! "

" What is the prize ? " asked Giguelillot.

" A coupon for a kiss lasting one minute to be cashed next Sunday. "

But the boy quickly stepped to one side to let an advertising cart pass, on which two Tryphemian girls of about twenty extended the pure lines of their velvety bodies on a streamer carrying in huge letters the advertisement of a scent shop.

" Those girls are pretty, " said Giguelillot now thoroughly awake.

" Nonesense ! " grumbled Taxis.

" What woman ever pleases you ? "

" There was one, once. "

" Oh ! Tell us about it. Nothing is more curious. "

" What ? " said the King, almost seriously. " But you astonish me, Grand Eunuch. You have been in love ? What does that mean ? "

" In love ? No ! I have never been in love, except with God the Eternal. Your Majesty does not know;

but one day I experienced the perfection of the divine creation before a creature of sex. In a word I met a woman who realised perfectly my ideal of beauty. To be more precise — my *physical* ideal of *moral* beauty. Do you understand ? "

" Not in the least ! But that doesn't matter. Go on ! "

" Right ! This woman was the only tenant that my father had. She managed a little house that was always closed and from outside most respectable : one of those establishments that M. Lebirbe condemns but which I applaud as being excellent in that they concentrate at one point all the impurities of a whole town, and also that they are the enemies of scandal. On this question, you know, the Protestants are unanimous. This good and worthy woman often received me. My father knew that my principles and unaffected chastity would allow me to enter the house without running the slightest danger. On Sundays, on coming out of church, I used to go and play with her children. One day then, as I imbibed a salutary horror of vice by its actual contemplation, we saw this worthy person enter. My father held her in high esteem because she brought him in five thousand francs a year. She had not even a chemise on and I was greatly impressed. Her majestic obesity commanded in the first place respect. One would have thought that she was *enceinte* with six children, and that she would have been able to nourish them all, so vast were her breasts. One could not see them without appreciating that maternity is the premier mission and the supreme glory of womanhood, sir. Finally to crown her beauty — her moral beauty, I mean — her belly fell before her with a charming modesty half way down her legs. Her breast was a scarf : her stomach a skirt. Her children could look at her without sin : even nude she was veiled. "

Giguelillot seized his hands.

" Ah ! Sir, I have a violent desire to make you my intimate friend, for we should never quarrel about any passing woman. And any other quarrels don't count. "

Pausole, who was no longer listening, pointed to a shop before which were the words, decorated with a palm, " Société Lebirbe, Grand Prix d'Honneur. "

" Is it here, " he asked, " that the decorated one lives ? "

" Yes, Sire, " said a neighbour.

" Where is this child ? " continued the King. " I would like to congratulate her. As a matter of fact even if M. Lebirbe does sometimes express wishes, whose realisation would be the death-blow to public liberty, he has plenty of sense and he has principles on the subject which are good to be scattered around. I feel sure that he has made an enlightened choice from amongst all those girls who could aspire to the crown of roses. Where is the happy *rosière* ? Tell her that I am calling upon her. "

The young girl came down quickly and as soon as she saw the King, she took off her skirt and scarf, as one takes off an apron to make oneself more presentable at home.

She was beautiful from head to feet.

" You have been crowned ? " said the King.

" Yes, Sire. They have been very good to me. "

" Did you deserve it ? "

" Just as others did. I had luck; that was all. "

" But what did you do to be crowned ? "

" Sire, my parents are confectioners. The four cooks asked my hand and each said he would kill himself if I refused. "

" That was a difficult proposition. What did you do ?"

" Oh, I didn't want any suicides in my young life. I married all four. One must be good, Sire. Men are so unhappy if one leaves them. They want so little. Why refuse them ? "

" Well, if a fifth came along, you would have to say no. "

" I have never said no to anyone, Sire; it is not in my character. My husbands understood at once that I was kind to them and that I had no reason to be unkind to others. Everyone thinks I am pretty in this neighbourhood. I don't say that everyone pleases me, but what can I do ? Each one practises charity as it occurs to him. We are not rich at home; I give what I have. I like to give pleasure, and at nights I sleep happily when I can tell myself that I have had a good heart for all those who have held out their hand. That is my little virtue. "

Pausole was thoughtful.

" I should have had nothing to say, if you hadn't been married. Marriage is a voluntary renunciation of liberty. It can be revoked, but then one must separate. "

" Oh ! we don't look at it like that. I married my fathers's cooks. They pay for the upkeep; and I look after the house. It's to our interest to keep together and as we love each other, everything works out very well. After the night has passed, and the house has been attended to, I'm alone and I've nothing to do. My husbands are at their work. Then like so many others, I might go from door to door chatting with my friends and talking scandal about the neighbours. I find that at twenty years of age one can occupy oneself in a better way. As soon as I have put on my skirt I go off with someone or other. At any rate, it isn't time wasted. "

" Well, " said Pausole, " I'm getting old. I see that I am reactionary and that the customs are ahead of me. I don't condemn you, my girl. In fact, you act on my laws better than I should know how. Up till now I always punished adulterous women who strayed from home. In olden days a god showed himself more indulgent than I. Liberty must not be renounced even by mutual consent. Your example impresses me, my child, because you follow my principles and you have, as you say, your own little virtue, which may quite well be a great one. Give me your hand; I congratulate you. "

Pausole continued his visits. He entered studios, shops, sheds. He questioned vagabonds who slept under walls; he shook many grimy hands, and saw many smiling faces. No one complained of his life to the point of attacking the government.

When he returned to the Prefecture, he underwent a second banquet, listened anew to speeches and once more shook fresh hands with an increasing fatigue.

As the guests formed themselves into groups in the prefectorial salons decorated with portraits of Pausole and his favourite queens, the Chief of Police appeared at the moment when the King had led Giguelillot into a corner apart, by the left elbow, in order that he might talk poetry to him.

Bowing with a deference which indicated the pride of a task accomplished, the Chief slowly spoke these words :

" I have the honour to announce to Your Majesty that his august daughter, the Princess Aline, has been found safe and sound. "

" Already ? " cried Pausole.

" Yes, Sire. You are obeyed. "

VII

WHEREIN THE READER HAPPILY MEETS THE HEROINES
OF THIS TALE ONCE AGAIN

> As soon as I had lain down, I said to her
> " Come close, my heart. "   She did not
> need to be asked again, and we kissed most
> tenderly.
> *History of the Comtesse des Barres* — 1742.

ALINE and Mirabelle, leaving the Hotel du Coq
arrived in the town about ten o'clock in the
evening.

Tryphemia, sleeping during the sunny hours, becomes
animated at dusk and stays awake late.   All the shops
were open along the streets filled with people when the
two friends mixed with the crowd, and Mirabelle took
the opportunity to dress herself without waiting any
longer.   The sense of her nudity was the most disagreeable that she had yet experienced.   Although she was
elbowing several other girls as unveiled as herself, she
believed that all eyes were fixed on a certain point of her
body, and that was unbearable at least on the part of a
crowd.

So she entered a shop and explained what she wanted.

" Oh ! Madame, " said the proprietress, eyeing her from head to foot. " It is not in my interest to say so, but what a pity to put on clothes. When one has so young a chest, so fine a belly, such well made legs, can one hide such things ? "

" It is my whim, " said Mirabelle.

" Well, put on transparent clothes. I can make madame a little Empire dress of white linen, unlined, and clinging round the hips. From afar it looks as though you were dressed and close to it looks as though you had nothing on. I have here some of the very finest linen. You could read a paper through it. Will madame try it ? Or perhaps madame prefers black tulle, but that would be more for a ball dress. "

" No, none of those. I want batiste, cotton stockings, a complete cloth dress and a blue shirt, that's all. Give the same to my sister who wants to dress exactly like me. "

" Well, I will, " said the woman, " but it's a sin to obey you. "

Having dressed, they bought some sort of straw hat, but of similar straw and trimmed with the same ribbons. Mirabelle insisted on that.

Then they went out.

" Big sister, " said Line, smiling, " where are we spending the night ? "

In spite of Giguelillot's advice, Mirabelle quickly answered :

" At the Hotel. "

" Why not at the house whose address the page gave us ? "

" I'm frightened of it, all those boys and girls together. "

" They must amuse themselves so. Don't you want
to go and see them ?

" They might keep us. I'm not too happy about it.
The hotel is safer. "

" The page said the reverse.   And he is so intelligent...
Isn't that little page nice, Mirabelle ? "

" Ah ! Do you think so ? "

" Yes, I like his eyes so much. "

" I don't. "

" Oh ! I've upset you. You went quite white. "

" Not in the least. I don't agree with you. That's
all. "

" But how nervous you are. Why did I say that to
you ? I'm so sorry, Mirabelle, I won't say it again.
Come into a dark corner at once. "

" Why ? "

" Because I want to kiss you... If I may. "

They turned down a dark road and found the shelter
they wanted. Behind a sand-cart left at the side, the
two girls mouth to mouth evinced a faithful tenderness.

" Come, " sighed Mirabelle. " Let us hurry, it is late.
We must find a room, you know. "

" Yes, " said Line. " I'm still quite sleepy. For
three days I have slept so little. I am feeling weak, so
weak to-night. And my legs hurt me. Why is that,
I wonder ? We haven't walked much. "

" It is because you are growing up. I am pleased to
know it. It is a good sign, darling. "

Line believed all that was told her, and did not worry
any more.

In a quiet avenue, they stopped before a hotel which appeared to be most respectable and which was named *Hotel du Sein-Blanc et de Westphalie*.

They entered. Mirabelle chose a room with a huge bed and large windows which ensured plenty of fresh air.

Just as they reached the lift, the manageress took Mirabelle on one side and made many excuses. There were six men attached to the hotel for the night service of those ladies who travelled alone. But yesterday afternoon a family of seven English girls had arrived, who had engaged by telegram all that portion of the personnel, and the hotel thus found itself unprovided for forty-eight hours. The manageress offered to replace them as far as possible by waking up the two page boys who doubtless were a little young, but were supposed to be very nice. Further, she asked if the ladies were stopping for several days, should she put them down at once for the first *attachés* available.

Mirabelle let her talk : then she replied quite simply :

" My little sister and I, madame, require nobody. "

As soon as they were in their room, they wearily undressed, and Line fell asleep while making her toilette with her fingers in her hair, without being able to finish her plait.

Mirabelle, melancholy, but patient and resigned, put her to bed like a child.

" Good-night, Mirabelle... Sleep well... " murmured Line giving her lips but unable to open her eyes.

" Good-night, darling... I shan't wake you.

" You're very kind... Good-night. "

Mirabelle lay down next to her friend, tenderly took

the little body between her beautiful jealous legs, placed
the blonde head on her breast and could not sleep till
long, long afterwards.

However, she was the first to wake, rang, jumped out
of bed and went out in the passage so as to give her
orders silently.

She wanted flowers, bundles, armfuls, boxes of flowers.
She placed them everywhere, on the tables, the mantelpiece, the divans, the chairs, the chests. She placed
them behind the picture frames, in the framework of
the mirrors, and even in the hinges of the big open
windows. She scattered them on the carpet, she strewed
them on the bed. Round Line's beautiful face she
reddened the white pillow with them and Line was
awakened by their strong perfume.

Her two hands joined under her cheeks, smiling with
eyes and lips, her plait falling over her chest and one
breast in the angle of her elbow, she called Mirabelle,
who fell on one knee as though acting a love ballet.

Line had a grateful heart. She clasped her bare arms
round the neck of her friend, gave a few kisses more
sonorous than voluptuous; then slowly turned Mirabelle's
head so as to place the ear on her mouth and offered her
without any preamble all that the girl could want to
satisfy her temptations.

Mirabelle needed no further pressing. Having shown
for twelve hours all the discretion of which she was
capable, she believed she had reached the extreme limit
of reserve and that now she could be allowed to show
herself at last just how the gods had made her.

Her frankness, for four hours, showed itself in all

aspeâs. After several endearments which shook the foun-dations of her young and ready emotion, Line stated that she was decidedly exhausted, and that she would not have the strength even to get up for lunch.

She took her meal on the edge of the bed.

Meanwhile the day was passing. Mirabelle wandered round the room, picked up their clothes, folded them carefully as she had been taught and, as it was also necessary to consider the exigencies of praâical life, examined their purses and counted their combined wealth.

Two days in the village inn, the purchase of clothes and flowers had absorbed three quarters of what the purses had contained.

Smiling all over, Mirabelle made some calculations.

" What are you thinking of ? " asked Line.

" Of you, darling. I must go out. "

" You think of me and you leave me ? "

" Not for long. Two hours, perhaps. If I am not in by dinner time, don't worry. Promise me ?

" Oh ! But how bored I shall be. Why must you go out ? "

" Don't ask. It is for both of us. As soon as I have left, shut the door firmly, won't you; and don't let any one in. Since you are tired, you must have a long rest while you are waiting for me. "

She took a pair of scissors and cut a brown lock of her hair and fixed it on the second pillow with a hairpin.

" Look, my love, here is a little bit of me so that you shan't feel too lonely... "

VIII

WHEREIN EVENTS RUSH FORWARD

> " Ich lieb' eine Blume, doch weiss ich
> nicht welche. Das macht mir Schmerz. "
> H. Heine.

MY daughter has been found ? " said Pausole. "That is most fortunate for her. But what a curious time you have chosen, sir, to make such a discovery. "

" Sire... I am amazed... We don't scarcely choose the... "

" How do you expect me to go running about the streets just before midnight on a night of feasting, with all the crowd in the midst of its pleasures and probably the excesses which a feast permits and even facilitates, for such an intimate and delicate and even improper mission as to penetrate in person the secret apartments of a Royal Highness with the paternal design of recovering her affections ? The Princess Aline retires to bed at nine o'clock, my good Chief of Police. She is certainly asleep at this moment. I should arrive like a character in a comedy, catching her in the very act, and such an idea alone is odious to me. You see me revolted. Go away, sir, you are stupid. "

" But, Sire, it was your minister, the honourable lord
Taxis who advised me to... "

" He, again ! Always that man ! I never hear
anything that is unfortunate, blundering, or indiscreet
without he has some part in the responsibility. He is
becoming unbearable and I really don't know that I
shan't end by depriving myself of his services from which
I derive nothing but trouble and annoyance. Go, I tell
you. I am most displeased. Settle matters with my
page. I do not wish to be bothered any more. "

Giguelillot led the unhappy man away.

" Why go and speak of these matters to the King ? "
he said. " If you had called me aside, I should have
warned you at once. Now, tell me what you know.
I will try and arrange things. "

The Chief of Police explained that the Princess Aline
had been found, not with a young man, as was supposed,
but with a girl a little older than herself at the Hotel
du Sein-Blanc et de Westphalie. He added that two
policemen who had listened at the door for two hours
had made a report which was the most extraordinary
that he had ever heard. He begged to be allowed to
make a prompt arrest, saying that from all accounts Her
Highness was complaining of an extreme lassitude and
that the care of the august health appeared to him to be
above all other considerations.

" Do you know nothing else ? " asked Giguelillot.

" The unknown woman spoke of a time she was away
during the afternoon and which was confirmed by the
hall porter of the hotel. "

" Where could she have gone ? "

" She refused to say : but she brought back two

hundred francs from a mysterious origin and a ring which she wanted to sell without keeping it for a single day. "

" Is that all that is known ? "

" To-morrow, Monday, between four and eight she will be going out for a second time. "

" Ah ! That's most interesting. "

Giglio thanked the officer, ordered him to cease his watch at four o'clock precisely the next day, and above all not to have any communication with Taxis on the one hand and Pausole on the other.

He had hardly spoken when there was a stir around him. The King had made known to the Prefect that he wished to retire to his apartments with the young lady he had married that very morning.

Giguelillot quickly crossed the room, approached Diane à la Houppe and inclining his head on his shoulder put on a suppliant and tender look.

Diane frowned without at the same time being able to hide a smile and putting her head forward she said simply : " Yes. "

Then laughing quietly she murmured, not without bravado :

" Don't say, little monkey, that you have never heard that word. "

He rejoined her an hour later. She was waiting on a couch; her black hair fell on both sides of her face and covered her to her hips. All he could see of her expression were two bright eyes and a moist mouth.

" Well, Madame, " he said. " I have obeyed you. The Princess Aline has not been arrested. "

" How kind you are ! You're so kind. "

" What reward shall I have ? "

" All that you wish. "

She shot the bolt of the door, whilst he put out all the lights, except one which he placed on the ground so as to leave the top of the bed in semi-obscurity. He took off his yellow and blue costume in the dressing-room. A bottle of perfume was there; he recognised it at once and poured some out for his own use.

But when he finally thrilled in the arms of the young woman, he felt himself almost humiliated, or, if one can say it, inefficient. His gracious talent served him nothing. Diane obeyed his caresses with such haste that all subtlety was wasted art. Already she knew what he was about to suggest with more method than she had patience. So, many times she disconcerted him.

In the middle of the night, as if to dominate and to keep him at the moment when she awaited responses almost solemn, Diane à la Houppe stretched herself with a sigh on him she cherished so, leant on an elbow on either side of him, rubbed him regularly with her supple and swollen breasts, whose caress was warm and said with an effort :

" Do you love me ? "

" Yes. "

" How long will you love me ? "

" Always. "

" Well then, may I confide a secret ? "

" You may. "

" The King told me that he is thinking of allowing the pages to enter the harem, and that he would shut his eyes to... what would happen... most probably. "

" What an admirable inspiration. "

" Oh ! don't laugh. I am so happy. We can see

each other again. Now I don't care whether the fair
Aline is taken or not, because it won't separate us any
more. "

" My love ! "

" But will you swear something ? "

" Anything you want. "

" There are so many women in the harem. How do
I know that someone won't make love to you ? Remember, Djilio, remember that I gave myself to you first...
and swear that the others will get nothing from your
lips... Swear that no one will clasp you as I do... with
my body and soul. Swear, Djilio. Give yourself as
I give myself. "

Giguelillot had not the slightest difficulty. He swore
according to tradition and assumed the tone suitable to
the circumstances. Then he left the beautiful Diane
" so as not to compromise her " as he explained to her —
and also that he might sleep quietly (but he didn't mention
that reason).

The next day, as he was passing along the prefectorial
corridor, a murmured but urgent whisper caused him to
turn his head.

The little face of Philis peeped timidly from behind a
half-opened door.

The door opened fully and then closed on the two
of them.

" The King sleeps, " said Philis. " Let us stop here.
We shan't be surprised. "

" What ! The King still sleeps at half past twelve ? "

" He hasn't been asleep long ! " Philis explained not
without a certain pride.

" And you ? "

" I ? I am not sleepy when I think of you. I have been waiting an hour for you behind this door. "

" What did you want me for ? "

She bent towards him.

" A little lesson, sir. You have given me only one and I learnt it quickly by heart, but I shall never progress if you teach me only one out of every four rules. "

Giguelillot congratulated her on her studious disposition.

All the same, as he didn't find the role he had to play pleasant nor decent, he decided that, if only in his pupils' interest, the second lesson should be more experimental than theoretic, and consulting his inclinations rather than his duty, he abused in a variety of ways the previous willingness which Philis expressed with a youthful dash and even curiosity.

Philis learnt the four rules. Her spirit opened gradually to all the new lights of a science which delighted her and which, she thought, was never too difficult for her young intelligence. However, after an hour and a quarter, Giguelillot told her in a friendly way that her delicate little brain had worked enough.

She tried to keep him back.

" Are you going ? "

" Till this evening. "

" Are you going into the town ? "

" Yes. "

" Will you do something for me ? "

" What ? "

" Listen. My sister is not always nice to me, but I

love her all the same, and I am miserable that she has gone. You are so clever, you might find her address and see her for a moment and speak of me. Look for her, and you will please me. Keep her secret; I don't want it. But tell me if she is well. I don't ask any more. "

" You will have news to-night, " said Giguelillot.

" How sweet you are. One word more : you will speak to her. Don't kiss her. "

" I promise. "

" Even if she looks as though she wants it ? "

" Girls never look like that. "

" Oh ! Now one can see that you don't know them. "

Giguelillot breakfasted quietly, told several friends confidentially that he was going on an investigation so that it might be repeated immediately to the King. Then he went out alone and without a cane.

In front of the Prefecture, on a public seat, he saw the beautiful Thierrette, who with folded hands, body bent, posed unconsciously for a monument to Silent Despondency.

He raised her chin.

" Well ! my poor Thierrette, aren't things going too well ? "

" Ah ! sir. I'm inadequate ! It's not for want of willingness. I put my heart into it, you know. I divide myself into four to give satisfaction, but it is too hard work. I am going to ask for my wages. "

" Already ? What, you, a strong girl, with your muscles and health, cannot cry ' Long live the army ! '

two successive days ? Heavens ! What has made you such a weakling ?

" Weakling ? I wish some one else were in my place. Sir, they are bringing their friends now. A regiment I can manage, but a whole town — no ! Well, I have come to beg of you, if you know of a quieter house, even if there are several masters, so long as there are not more than fifty... "

" Now, be comforted. I know what you want. On my own responsibility I appoint you ribald in ordinary to the corps of pages. There aren't more than fifteen. "

" Oh ! if that's all. "

" And we have lots of girl friends, but we miss — how shall I say it ? — someone who is always at hand. The King's waiting women are never alone when one calls on them. One can never rely on them. You will be our own special harem. That's fixed. Dry your tears. "

The girl was overwhelming in her gratitude and remained riveted to the spot.

Leaving her with an encouraging and hearty wave of the hand, Giguelillot first of all went to buy some cigarettes and then betook himself to the place where he knew he would find Galatée.

It was a little white hostel, apparently most respectable, and giving no indication of the life that went on within.

The page rang. He was conducted to an elderly lady with perfect manners, who immediately inquired as to his preferences, that is to say she asked whether she should advise Mme. X, the wife of a magistrate, blonde and very shy, or Mme. Y, whose photograph was on the mantelpiece.

But Giglio, without actually giving too many details, sketched in a few words the portrait of his ideal of a young girl which resembled Galatée as Galatée did her mirror.

He was left alone in a room, and after about twenty minutes' wait, during which pretence was made to send for the girl, Mlle. Lebirbe entered, coming simply from the next room.

As soon as she saw him, she uttered a cry and, turning her head, started to weep.

Instead of triumphing with an " I told you so ", which would not have consoled her in the least, Giglio approached her and took her hand.

" What is the matter ? "

" Oh, it is sweet of you to have come. "

Her tears redoubled.   She continued :

" You were right.   You spoke like a friend.   I was wrong not to have believed you.   If you only knew how rude they have been to me.   I am no happier than when I was with my family. "

" Will you go back to your father ? "

" Oh ! no.   But I want to get out of here. "

" No one has the right to detain you.   Where will you go when you leave ? "

" I don't know. "

Then, becoming more and more desperate, she sobbed :

" I'm in love. "

Giglio didn't understand.

" What did you say ? "

She did not answer.

" In love with whom ? "

She hesitated again, smiled slightly, sighed and said at last : " With your girl friend. "

Very seriously the page asked :

" Could you not give me closer details ? "

" Your friend of the Hotel du Coq. The elder of the two girls. She came here. It appears she wanted money. Oh ! If you could have known my delight when I saw her. There certainly are providential accidents. We were destined to find each other one day, and possibly for a long time. "

" There is no doubt about that, " said Giguelillot, who had a glimpse of the Machiavellisms.

" I'm mad about her, " continued Galatée. " I now understand all that I saw from my window through my trembling telescope. We remained alone in a waiting room for half an hour. I know that she loves another, but nevertheless she loved me... to purify herself, she said, from what she was going to do in this horrible place where I am still. When I think that she will come back in half an hour and that possibly we shan't see each other... "

" You will meet again, " said Giguelillot, " this very evening and for a long time. "

" I asked her and she didn't want to. "

" She will want to. Believe me to-day, since you regret not having believed me the day before yesterday. Come and write a letter. Ask for all that you need for that. "

A slave brought a writing case.

" Write, " said Giguelillot, " to the girl you are longing for and say that you are waiting for her here. "

" Why ? "

" First of all to tell her what you think of her. "

" She knows it. "

" She does not know it. Nothing is so good as a written declaration. Tell her in the letter all that you have told her in your thoughts since she left you. And then... "

" But if she is coming ? "

" Oh, you mustn't mention that. That's most important. It would spoil everything. "

" All right. "

" Tell her your thoughts and that you will meet her this evening in the Jardin-Royal under the monument to Felicien Rops.. "

" Will she be there ? "

" She will be there. I promise. But, hurry, there is not much time. "

Galatée wrote her letter and then holding it out, she asked : " To what address shall I send it ? "

" I will see that it is delivered. "

" And the result ? "

" This evening you will be quite alone with this girl and you will take her where it pleases you. I should advise you to go to France. "

" You aren't laughing at me, are you ? "

" Why should I laugh at you ? Have I led you to believe that up to now I have been playing a hoax upon you ? "

" I'm so sorry, my friend. Thank you with all my heart. Shall I see you again ? "

" No, or at least not this week. One always meets again. The world is so small. But I am sending you away and am not going to arrange another meeting, It is the best proof that I can offer you of my respect and affection. "

IX

WHEREIN GIGUELILLOT ALSO FALLS IN LOVE

The boy is for the girl,
The girl is for the boy;
Whatever one does or gossips
Mefaith ' tis but a straw
But mystery and but goings on.
The net is for the eel
The hole is for the peg
The slug is for the shell.
The shell for the snail.
The boy is for the girl
The girl is for the boy.
The handle is for the sickle
And the ball for the grate,
The thread for the reel

And the pommel for the saddle
The bait is for the hook,
The nipple for the nursling,
And the bird for the bush,
And the boy is for the girl.
The horse is for the comb.
And for the caparison
The deck is for the keel.
The cage is for the chaffinch,
And the pond for the fish,
And the graft for the escutcheon,
And the blade for the harvest.
The rock is for the eel,
The girl for the boy...

Virelay of CLAUDE LE PETIT — 1660.

WHEN Giguelillot at last arrived at the Hotel du Sein Blanc et de Westphalie — for you can imagine that he went there as fast as he could — Mirabelle had just gone out.

He gave three discreet knocks on the door and waited.

" Who's there ? "

" I. "

" You ?   Papa's page ? " said Line softly, through the keyhole.

" May I come in ? "

" I've been forbidden to open the door. But since it is you, there is no danger. "

She opened the door and, standing on tip-toe, offered her cheek.

" Kiss me, " she said, " I permit it. Now, on the other cheek. Now yours. "

She sighed.

" I've got lots to tell you. Let's sit down close to each other on the sofa. What is your name ? "

" Djilio. "

" Oh ! What a pretty name ! " said Line.

And Giglio thought once more that if every woman uttered diverse banalities according to the lovers she meets, each man does not hear more than ten phrases from all his mistresses, as if they were secretly repeating the same rôle for him only.

" What luck ! " cried Line. " I was just thinking of you. Let me look at you. I almost quarrelled with my friend over your eyes. I thought they were so beautiful. She did not. But I am right, Djilio. Your eyes are lovely. "

" Moderately so, " said Giglio. " If they sparkle when they look at you, Highness, it is due to yourself only. "

" Don't call me Highness; you frighten me. Call me Line, it's nicer. "

But he did not call her anything, for with obvious confusion which on this occasion was not voluntary, he found nothing that seemed worth saying to the fair Aline.

On the first occasion on which he saw her in that other

hotel room, where events were so rapidly precipi-
tated, circumstances scarcely lent themselves to tender
contemplation. Mirabelle present and jealous, did not
let herself be forgotten. Aline, worried, showed an altered
face. An amazing and short scene, this curious quarter
of an hour passed madly in the whirlpool of his memory.

Here, on the contrary, in the silence of her eyes and
close to her charming face, he saw her as she really was.

Diane à la Houppe appeared too sensual. Philis too
lacking in tenderness. The one consumed, the other
played, but neither had in her glance that tiny flame
which calls and holds love the moment it appears.

He held Line's two hands, and she did not lower her
eyes, but left them half open as if always ready for a
kiss. She had the lips of a girl, still a child, high rather
than wide.

He did not speak. He would not have known what
to say. Vaguely, one by one, phrases which he had
repeated a hundred times came to his mind. To begin
with he rejected them, then with a smile, almost sad,
thought that spoken in a different tone, these phrases
would not be the same. He told himself that these
hyperboles, and the most unlikely ones, would suit this
situation better than any : that the little fibs of gallantry,
excusable in an adventure, would become quite touching
at the commencement of a real passion : lastly that he
could deceive his new little friend, blamelessly according
to ordinary methods, knowing that it would give her
pleasure and sensing how much was due to her.

" What is the matter ? " said Line.

" I love you, " he replied.

" I love you, too, Djilio. I love you with all my heart. I am quite happy to tell you so. "

" But I have loved you for a long time. You never knew, did you ? "

" For a long time ? " Line repeated. " You have loved me for a long time ? But yesterday morning I didn't know you. "

" I have loved you for three years, " said Giguelillot sighing.

" And you never told me ? "

" I didn't dare. I longed for you, but you were so exalted, so far from me. How could I believe that you would ever consent to listen to me. I loved you from a depth. I thought of you ceaselessly, but I never dared hope that a day would come, when, by some extraordinary piece of luck, I should be able to speak with you alone, hand in hand, eye to eye. "

Line looked at him tenderly.

He continued :

" Don't you believe me ? "

" Yes, of course. "

" I've written poetry to you. "

" Poetry ? You write poetry. Oh ! I am so fond of poetry. And you wrote some to me ? Really ? "

" Would you like to read it ? "

" Would I like to read it ? Of course. "

" Here it is. "

Giguelillot took from his pocket the first book of verse, and turned over the leaves. Agnes... Alberte... Alexandrine... Alfrède... Alice... Alix... Aline !

" Read, " he said simply.

Line took the thin volume and read greedily :

Appearing from out the cerulean blue
Lighting with love beams the darkening hue
Innately conceived by my yearning desire
Near to your soul, do you feel mine seize you
Enfolding your breasts with its heart-searing fire.

Line raised her big eyes.

" But how do I know that these verses are for me ? "

" It's an acrostic. You must know what an acrostic is. Surely you take in the *Journal de la Jeunesse* ? Read the first letter of each line. "

" A, L, I... Aline ! " she cried with a joyous smile. " Oh ! it's true. And how beautiful ! I have never read more beautiful lines. How clever you are ! "

" When I speak of you, Line... you alone inspire me. Do you understand. I dared not write your name in a book which all the world could read. I hid it in an acrostic... secretly... for you and me. No one knows besides you and me. "

Line threw herself into his arms. He clasped her passionately, and attempting nothing more direct on her little folded body, he pressed his lips to hers which were offered so tenderly, almost cautiously.

" What ! " said Line. " You know that too ? Mira- belle told me that she had invented it. "

" Some one taught it to her, " said Giguelillot.

" To you, too ? "

" Oh, I guessed it instinctively, the first day I saw you. "

" Then... she deceived me ? "

" She deceived you nicely. "

" It's all the same. She lied to me. I'll never forgive her as long as I live. Lies are wicked, aren't they ? "

" Nothing is worse, " said Giguelillot.

Line pondered with compressed lips.

" I love you more than my friend, " she said.

Here, Giglio could contain himself no longer. He took Line into his arms, carried her to the bed without taking his lips from hers, but she contrived to say :

" Yes, lie there, quite close... quite close. "

And an hour later, the fair Aline, lying in his arms, said emotionally :

" Mirabelle is a storyteller. I love you more than her, much more. I love you... as I have never loved anyone in the world. Oh ! don't go ! don't go ! "

" I must. "

" Why ? "

" The King is expecting me. Mirabelle will return. "

" I don't want to see her again. I love only you. Only you. Stay here... I want to touch you from your toes to your head and stay like this for ever, hand in hand, my lips on yours... I don't want you to go. Obey me. "

Giglio hastened matters.

" All is lost, if we stop here, " he said. " Mirabelle would claim you in an hour. She, herself, would be taken an hour later, and we could never, never, see each other again, for the King would imprison you once more in your rooms in the Palace. "

" Well, take me with you; let us go. Are there no other countries where we could live quietly without anyone tormenting us ? "

Giglio took pity on Pausole.

" You love your father, Line dear. You love him very much. Were you to go where he is not, you would very soon regret it. "

" Yes, I love Papa, but why does he shut me up ? If I go back to the palace, I shall never be able to see you again and I shall be as unhappy as before. I know now. I was very unhappy, but I never knew it. "

" There is a way of arranging it all. Do you remember the house I spoke of yesterday ? The house of those good old people who take in ill-treated children and look after them ? "

" Yes, 22, rue des Amandines. I even remember the address. "

" Exactly. Go there. Go at once. And when they have given you the room that suits you (ask for the girls' section), I will see to it that you leave it again with all your liberty. "

" For ever ? "

" For ever. "

X

WHEREIN WE REACH THE END

Διὸ δεῖ ἦχθαί πῶς εὐθὺς ἐκ νέων, ὡς ὁ
Πλάων φησίν, ὥστε χαίρειν τε καὶ λυπεῖσθαί
οἷς δῖε ἡ γὰρ ὀρθή παιδεία αὕτη ἐςτίν.

ARISTOTLE, *Ethics* II. 2.

IT was four o'clock the next day that Pausole and his
two ministers were received at the rue des Amandines, where the good King, good as he was, never
believed he would enter as a father.

Giguelillot, since morning, had zealously and patiently
first to persuade the King that this visit would be full of
charm, then secretly to instruct his hosts so that they
would speak to him in a suitable way.

The president of the Society led Pausole to a sofa,
bowed three times, and then spoke in a satisfied and
pointed way, the following words :

" Sire :

The Tryphemian Union for the Safety of Childhood
would not be compared to similar societies in neighbouring
countries, any more than the laws of Your Majesty would
stand comparison with those of rival nations.   Here we
gather together children who have been ill-treated either

physically or morally, but the moral danger we try to combat is by no means that which our foreign colleagues fear; they do not understand the welfare of children as we do. "

" I can well believe it, " said Pausole.

" We value, as you do, Sire, the fact that the young boy or girl soon acquires some rights of liberty. We recognise that in submitting youth to paternal authority during twenty one years of life, the old European laws retain in their breast numerous roots which have descended from the slavery of old. The rights of a father over his son, as those of a husband over his wife, are in the main, call it what you like, the heaviest distraint on the weakest shoulders, and they borrow from tyranny their boundless despotism at the same time as their pretext and their flag, protection. The motive which persuades a free citizen to shut his child up in those horrible gaols called boarding-schools is no different from that which urges them during the holidays to chastise the poor child with the hand or the ruler. Man, who no longer has any rights over the liberties of his fellows, and who can no longer imprison or whip a human slave with impunity, retains his power over the child and as of necessity he abuses all the powers given him, he abuses this one, to compensate for those he has lost. "

" Very well thought out, " said Giguelillot. " Is it not so, Sire ? "

" Excellently, " said Pausole.

" We class with abuse of paternal power, every attempt against free expression as against free exercise of the child's will, if these wishes concern him only. In this home of ours we offer a sanctuary to all unhappy children without asking them why they suffered in their family circle, but stating with a legitimate pride that they will be happy under our protection. We instil into them a spontaneous wish for study instead of forcing them to hate all kind of work by imprisoning them in a class room. Their emulation is by no means diminished, and we have noticed many a time that with a loved teacher the hope of reward is worth more than the fear of punishment. The two sexes are brought up together and learn to know each other and are thus less exposed to be cruelly deceived in after life. When they want to go and play they are free there as elsewhere. Nothing is forbidden them except quarrelling. They mingle as they wish, in the playground as in the dormitory. Respecting the laws of nature rather than those of man, we do not restrain the senses of our pupils by an artificial constraint from which they might wander with fatal results, causing the greatest harm to their fragile health. On the contrary, we favour the expansion of precocious youth, convinced that in restraining passion one only renders it more formidable, and that by making dreams supplant pleasure one is doing great harm. That is not education in the true sense of the word... "

Pausole interrupted the speech :

" And when the children ask advice ? "

" Sire, we deprecate intimate friendships, and we suggest multiple affection as a better outlet to their youthful tendencies. Love, exclusive love of an individual, love, in fact, as it is taught in the literature classes of the French and German schools, is a tragedy which generally results in the furious madness of Orestes, the sad end of Marguerite or the lamentable suicide of Romeo and Juliet. The great ' dailies ' are filled with similar catastrophes. Imbued with our duty and with the salutary influence we are able to exercise, we instruct our pupils about the dangers of a single passion : naturally, we employ the tact and discretion which such a subject demands, but we do not forget that on us depend the moral health and the entire future of our little orphans. "

" I approve with all my heart, " said Pausole. " Corrupt them, sir, corrupt them ! One only has to see what happens beyond our frontiers to receive a parallel of the two systems. On the one hand, in the upper classes, the claustration of the room, and the compulsory continence of youth against nature and commonsense, are multiplying a race which is emaciated, feeble, consumptive and anaemic and which is ruining the European aristocracy. On the other hand, whence come the strongest workmen, the wielders of hammers, the bread-winners ? From Charonne, and the East End of London, from Whitechapel and Menilmontant, from the extensive suburbs of Hamburg and the sewers of Marseilles, from all centres, in short, where children grow in freedom, mix and unite according to their instincts, without restraint or control... "

Pausole, fatigued from having spoken so much, lay back and asked :

" Do you achieve your aims ? "

" Not always, " replied the old man. " We are, nevertheless, satisfied, at least in comparison. A Society in a neighbouring country (a work of which however, I speak with the respect due *a priori* to a charitable institution) took as its mission only to liberate girls who were either virgins or married. One does not know why. But here are the figures : in thirteen years this Society collected nearly two thousand one hundred and fifty children... "

Giguelillot cried " That's a lot, said Candide "

The President continued :

" And of this enormous number of young marriageable girls, do you know how many it has married ?   Two ! "

Giguelillot muttered " That's a lot, said Martin. "

But the President remained serious.

" We, on the contrary, during seven years, out of eight hundred and forty six girls have debauched eight hundred and twelve.   I venture to say that taking the object of the two societies... "

" Oh ! Yours wins, " said Pausole. " There is no doubt about that. "

" Your Majesty deigns to recognise our efforts ? "

" Not only do I approve, but I will grant you a subsidy, " said Pausole. " I will set aside sixty thousand francs for you in my Budget.   If this sum is not sufficient for the good work you are carrying out, tell my ministers; it shall be augmented. "

The old man bowed deeply and, with a voice subtly altered, stammered :

" The kindly reception... which Your Majesty... I mean, the approbation so...flattering... with which our ideas have met... our trials... our attempts at realisation... encourages me to... "

" Speak. "

" Sire, the communication I have to make... is of

such a confidential nature... that I do not think I have the right to utter it at this moment... "

" Withdraw, my friends, " said Pausole to his counsellors. " And now, continue, sir. We are alone. "

" Last evening at seven o'clock... we received... an august visitor, Sire... Her Highness the Princess Aline. "

Pausole started.

" Here ? My daughter here ? In this place of ruin, this brothel ? "

" She asked for help, " murmured the old man feebly.

" And against whom ? "

" Her fate, Sire, against her fate. She accused no one. "

" Is she alone ? "

" Quite alone. "

" Then tell her I am waiting for her. She will throw herself in my arms. "

" Yes... but first of all... she asks that we shall assure her... of the liberties which you found so admirable just now, Sire, and which you declared should be given to the youth of both sexes. "

" Now, what does that matter ? Where is my daughter ? I insist on seeing her this very moment. "

She was sent for.

As if to assert, by an exterior sign, the liberties she had already taken, Line was clothed in the Tryphemian national costume : a coloured handkerchief on her head and slippers on her feet.

She took a few steps, very proud of her symbolic nudity, but a little timid.

Pausole took her in his arms.

" My little daughter ! My child ! Why did you go away ? "

" Because I met a good friend, papa, and because in your palace you forbid me to love anyone. "

" With whom did you go ? "

" With a girl who dances in the Opera. "

" With a girl ? Then it is of no importance. "

" Ah ! " said Line.

Pausole embraced her again.

" You will come back with me now ? You will kiss me ? "

" Yes, papa. I say ' Yes ' at once. I feel that I will follow you everywhere; but I feel also that you are going to whisper at once, as I did, something very nice. "

" That I love you ? "

" And that you let me do as I like. "

" But why ? "

" Because you love me so. "

Pausole, very moved, looked at his daughter. For a long time, he remained silent, as if a deep and painful struggle were taking place in his breast between the various counsels of his paternal affection. Then he said, rather sadly :

" Well, we shall see, my child. I love you enough to make you happier than I shall be. "

EPILOGUE

Sat prata biberunt, as said old Horace.
Le Temps, 20 th November, 1900.

HAVING returned to the palace that same night by a very tiring march which lasted nearly an hour and a quarter, King Pausole passed three days in silent meditation.

Tryphemia, after his departure, took up its accustomed life. The young girl, crowned by M. Lebirbe, continued each evening to set the creditable example which won her the palm. Mirabelle, torn with despair on learning that Pausole had recovered his daughter, went, all the same that night to the monument to Felicien Rops where she knew she would meet Galatée. That evening both gave themselves up to the limits of sensation in their union, and did not yet know the faithful and tender love to which this long tearful embrace bound the first memory.

Giguelillot raced over the return road with four strides of his little zebra, for he felt as incapable of hiding from the fair Aline the new feelings with which she inspired him, as of expressing to the beautiful Diane those with which she did not inspire him.

During the three days when the King, alone with his good conscience, pondered over questions of morality, Line and her friend the page met every night at the Mirror of the Nymphs, always full of moonlit water and dark foliage.

" It's very wicked, " said Line, thinking of Mirabelle.

" No, " said Giguelillot, " because she knows nothing of it. "

And he knew how to excuse all that was mean in this remark by all that was absolving and consoling in it.

At last Pausole, one sunny morning after Queen Alberte had received his courteous but slightly absent-minded favours, emerged from the palace, wearing his crown, and called for his mule, Macarie.

At the same time, he announced that all inhabitants of the royal residence, Queens, equerries, and ladies in waiting, ministers, pages and grooms, were to assemble before the cherry tree of justice to listen to such words as he might think fit to pronounce.

When he was seated in his red flowing robe with his golden orb and sceptre; he said.

" Ladies and gentlemen, it is hard to apply to oneself the principles which the wise spread abroad as benefits. I have long thought that I should be permitted to maintain the liberty of my beloved people without experiencing myself in certain difficult cases all that is painful in this liberty, at least for him who grants it. I thought that in a land possessing five hundred thousand hearths, I could, without detriment, except one, one only where a certain authority would still exist. It was quite natural

that that one hearth should be my own and that the giver
of independance should not be the first to suffer from
its possible excess. "

Here the King paused, plucked a delicious cherry, or
rather broke the thread which held it within the reach
of his fingers and, whilst sucking the juice of the warm
and succulent fruit, he followed with a slightly sad eye
the passionate excitement of the crowd listening to him.

" But, " he continued, " the King himself is his own
teacher. I have just made a secret journey during which
I have learnt a lot, as much of the human race as of my
duties towards it. I have seen free and happy crowds
whose happiness clung to liberty by roots so deep that
I cannot but doubt having sown this seed in the chosen
ground. It seemed to me that around me, people were
less happy because they were not so free and that was
enough to suggest a kind of abdication... "

Loud shouts prevented him from finishing.

" No ! Long live the King ! " they cried. " Abdi-
cate ? We don't wish it ! "

Pausole stretched out his hand.

" I will still be your leader, or, at least, the arbiter
chosen by general consent to ensure that your rights are
maintained, to which all are entitled; and for myself,
I will change none of the habits which I have found
necessary for the peace of my mind. But I will lift the
relative constraint which weighed on my entourage.
Taxis, my friend, return to France, whence you came to
us as a raven on the winds of winter. In future, my
wives and my daughter will follow their inclinations.
I set free their charming heads which yours rendered
even more charming by contrast of its hideousness. "

At these words there was perhaps less joy than tenderness in the crowd; and, like children who receive gorgeous presents without daring to touch them, the women pressed round him who was so good to them, and came with the fair Aline loyally to kiss his hands.

This completes the extraordinary adventure of King Pausole who, to recover his daughter went as far as to ride seven kilometres on muleback from his palace to his capital.

You will have read this story as it was meant to have been read, if you have been able, from page to page, to avoid mistaking Fantasy for Dreams, Tryphemia for Utopia, or King Pausole for the Perfect Being.

www.ingramcontent.com/pod-product-compliance
Lightning Source LLC
Chambersburg PA
CBHW011653010726
47499CB00010B/3245